THEN COMES LOVE

LINDSAY DETWILER

Then Comes Love © 2016 by Lindsay Detwiler

All rights reserved. No part of this book may be used or reproduced in any written, electronic, recorded, or photocopied format without the express permission from the author or publisher as allowed under the terms and conditions with which it was purchased or as strictly permitted by applicable copyright law. Any unauthorized distribution, circulation or use of this text may be a direct infringement of the author's rights, and those responsible may be liable in law accordingly. Thank you for respecting the work of this author.

Then Comes Love is a work of fiction. All names, characters, events and places found therein are either from the author's imagination or used fictitiously. Any similarity to persons alive or dead, actual events, locations, or organizations is entirely coincidental and not intended by the author.

For information, contact the publisher, Hot Tree Publishing.

www.hottreepublishing.com

Editing: Hot Tree Editing

Formatting: RMGraphX

Cover Designer: Claire Smith

ISBN (Paperback Edition): 978-1-925448-10-8

10 9 8 7 6 5 4 3 2 1

Dedication

In memory of Grandma Dorothy:
a cat-loving, bingo-playing lady,
who would have been best friends with Charlotte.

Chapter One

Charlotte
OCTOBER

It took exactly three weeks, a broken dish, and a game of bingo for Charlotte Noel to loathe Wildflower Meadows Nursing Home.

"Wildflower Meadows Assisted Living, Mom," her daughter, Annie, always corrected her when she referred to it as a nursing home. Either way you looked at it, though, it was a final rest stop. And if you asked Charlotte, the name was quite the oxymoron—there was nothing wild or beautiful about the place. In fact, it would be more adequately named Tumbleweed; the place was about as fruitful and exciting as a desert. Sure, there were activity days when overzealous women talked to them like they were five-year-olds about card making and Jenga tournaments. There were also rumors of after-hours secret activities like strip poker happening behind closed doors. Charlotte had almost vomited at this news, however, when a lady down the hall had winked and whispered loud enough for the entire place to hear about the event. Sure, she would like to pretend she was still the sassy, perky woman of her youth, but let's face it—at eighty, she avoided mirrors like the plague. You couldn't pay her enough money to look in a mirror at her own saggy, droopy, decrepit silhouette, so why would she try to win a glance at another equally repulsive body? Ugh.

Charlotte had gone into the place as a willing, albeit hesitant, person. She had tried, really tried, to have an open mind about it too. After all, she did agree with Annie; the house was too much with Charlie gone and her recent health scares. She couldn't handle it anymore. Something had to change. Plus, she felt terrible for the stress she was putting on Annie. The poor girl was having enough problems in her own life. She didn't need to be worrying about Charlotte, stopping to bring her dinner every day and doing her laundry. So Tumbleweed/ Wildflower Facility seemed like a reasonable option. Practical, however, didn't mean perfect or even likable.

Charlotte had dutifully masked the dread filling her chest when she had first taken the tour. She grinned at the "beautiful" dining facilities and the "efficient" layout of what would be her apartment, which was more like a dorm room. She nodded agreeably when the perky lady in charge, Cassie, explained to her and Annie about the fascinating activity hours and the daily dinner option.

So when Annie had nudged her and said, "What do you think, Mom? Do you think it's as lovely as I do?" she knew what she had to say. She couldn't admit to Annie she thought the place had a sour smell, like the inside of a trashcan on Thursday. She couldn't acknowledge she believed the residents looked more like hospital patients, who had no hope of getting better. She couldn't say to Annie the free lunch they were given reminded her of dog food or she considered her apartment sterile instead of homey. She wanted to say all this, she wanted to beg Annie to find her another option. But she couldn't. Because deep down, as much hurt and fear as she felt, she knew Annie was feeling one thing—relief. So Charlotte said something she didn't often say without a fight.

She simply said yes.

Within a few weeks of the fateful word, Charlotte found herself boxing up a lifetime of memories, taking a final glance at the faithful house where she had raised her only child, and moving into the cramped facilities where she would spend the rest of her days—alone.

***

There had been one sticking point, one element that had almost led Charlotte to reconsider. Actually, if she were being truthful, there were five elements—Peter, Arya, Alice, Gertrude, and Butternut.

"Mom, I'm sorry, I know this is hard, but you can't take them with you," Annie had argued when Charlotte had thrown a temper tantrum about the cats. With all the chaos that had happened, she hadn't been thinking about what would happen to her babies, and she was horrified to find out Wildflower had a no-pets policy.

"Annie, I will not have my babies end up in some

Humane Society or worse. How could you even suggest that? You know what they mean to me." There had been a long pause, a tense moment equivalent to a standoff.

"Well, Mom, what do you want me to do then?" Annie rolled her eyes like she was still the insipid teenager Charlotte remembered all too well.

Charlotte coolly stood her ground. "You keep them."

Annie's jaw instantly dropped, and she stared at Charlotte as if she had just turned into a large piece of fruit or had suggested Annie move to Mars. "Me? That's your solution?"

"Well, dear, to be honest, I think you could use some companionship in your life. They could help you. It's actually like I'm doing you a favor," Charlotte added in her matter-of-fact voice. She had to sell this to Annie. She had budged on moving and selling the house. She would not move on this.

"A favor? You think giving me five cats, one of which is named Butternut, would be a favor?"

"Your father and I named him. He's a very sweet cat who just so happened to like butternut squash as a kitten. So it is quite a perfect name."

Annie looked at Charlotte like she couldn't even think to respond. Because she couldn't. *You can't respond to a true statement,* Charlotte thought.

"Mom, I'm sorry, I just can't. Look, I'll work extra hard to find them great homes. I'll make sure they end up at a no-kill shelter. Please."

Charlotte had already given up on so many things,

and being passive just wasn't in her nature. In fact, Annie had been shocked when Charlotte had agreed to the move without a fight. Charlotte had backed down on the issue because she had to; she was not going to be labeled as a pushover, though. She was not going to curl up and die. Most of all, she was not going to give up her precious cats. No way.

So she did what she always did when she wanted to get her way—she gave Annie the silent treatment. She hobbled out of the room and grabbed her feather duster, which was from about 1970 and rather disgusting, she had to admit, and dusted furniture not yet moved. She ignored Annie's pleas to talk rationally about it. She slumped into her chair as her five babies gathered on her lap, coating her black sweater in a sea of hair. She stroked Butternut's chin and talked soothingly to Peter, her big black cat. She waited for Annie to come to her senses. After all, who could turn down these five amazing creatures?

It only took about five minutes.

"All right, Mom, listen. I'll make you a deal. I'll keep them *for now.* Just until we get things situated. And then we'll talk about finding them homes in a few months. No arguments."

As soon as the words exited Annie's pursed lips, Charlotte had sprung from her chair, tossing all five cats to the floor. "Oh, Annie. Great! Now listen, I'll give you the details you need to know. Do you have a piece of paper? Butternut's bath schedule is pretty particular and if you don't stick to it, he'll get a rash. And Arya can only eat two types of cat food, but Peter can't eat either of those..." Annie just stared as Charlotte gave her the details of the five cats' habits.

After she was certain Annie knew just what to do, she added, "Annie?"

"Yeah, Mom?"

"You're going to love them so much. You're welcome."

Annie grimaced and sighed audibly. "Oh, I just can't wait. I'll call and thank you every time I'm running the vacuum or dusting the shelves. Which will be what? Every six hours?"

Charlotte hugged Annie tightly. She was the best daughter in the world.

***

Charlotte readjusted her brooch, a gift from Charlie, as she shuffled into the dining area. It was Friday, which meant bingo after dinner. She inwardly groaned at the prospect. Friday was also fish night, Charlotte's least favorite meal. She had initially insisted she would never be caught dead in the community dining room. She had already given in, though, deciding gloppy fish she didn't have to cook was still better than the prospect of cooking for herself. What was the point when there was no one else to eat with? She might as well just take advantage of the benefits of this place.

"Hey, Charlotte, over here." Bridget beckoned her over from across the room. Wearing her bright red hat and orange floral-print dress, Bridget could pass for a bag lady on the street. In this place, though, she was a welcome sight. She was probably the sanest woman there, at least from her experience so far, and Charlotte was glad to be welcomed into her circle.

"Oh, my goodness, check out that brooch," Bridget proclaimed in a shaky yet exuberant voice, as Charlotte eased her creaking body into the chair. Bridget adjusted her glasses carefully on her nose so she could better eye up Charlotte's prized possession.

Charlotte gave Bridget a genuine smile. She might not love Wildflower Meadows just yet, but she certainly couldn't help but love Bridget's sweet personality.

"Thanks, honey." Charlotte cringed as soon as the words were out of her mouth. She was at the stage where she was calling everyone honey. *When did that happen?*

Cassie, strutting in high heels only a thirtysomething could sport, dashed to the front of the room where the crude excuse for a microphone sat. The room's dull roar hushed as people directed their attention to Cassie. It was like a celebrity was in the building instead of the activities director.

"Hi, everyone. Happy Friday," Cassie sang in her youthful voice. Charlotte tried not to roll her eyes. She had no problem with youth, but something about Cassie's cheerleader-like pep got under Charlotte's skin. *Maybe I'm just getting cranky in my old age,* she thought. *Or maybe it's just because I miss home.*

It had been almost three weeks since Wildflower

had become her home, but it certainly didn't feel like it. She was adjusting, it was true. She had been developing relationships with her inner circle/dinner group. She was growing fond of Bridget in her crazy hats, and Marla, who adored the color pink. But she missed her cats. She missed sitting on her antique sofa rubbing Butternut's belly in the evenings while she watched *Wheel of Fortune*. Now, Pat Sajak's voice just prompted her to reach for the cat who was no longer there with her. She missed her back porch where she would sip coffee and listen to the birds on misty summer mornings. She missed her neighbors, the weeping willow in her front yard, everything about her house back on Walnut Street. She missed the memories in the warmth of her own house, which had now been replaced by a stark loneliness haunting her days. In short, she missed her old life, every single ounce of it.

Cassie's announcement of, "Let's bow our heads for grace," echoed through the room at an earsplitting volume and snapped Charlotte out of her despondent reverie. She bowed her head, focusing on mumbling along with the short prayer. Marla's raspy voice, however, darted into her silent reflections.

"I don't have my card, Charlotte. Where is my card?" Marla screeched. Her hearing aid apparently needed to be turned up.

"Shh, honey, it's grace." Charlotte leaned close to whisper to Marla. Mistake number one.

"What? Did you say it's a race? Where? I thought

it was bingo night," Marla shouted as her eyebrows furrowed in confusion.

Charlotte was just about ready to explain what was happening when a nasally voice whined from across the room, "Honestly, Marla. Is it too much to ask for you to turn up your hearing aid? It's grace. Show some respect."

Charlotte had to admit she'd been thinking the same thing. But for some reason, this screeching voice annoyed her. How dare this person give Marla, her inner circle Marla, a hard time.

Charlotte turned to see who the voice had come from. She pinpointed it to a woman a few tables away. She wore a ruby-red floor-length dress and a fur coat, a fake bauble or a one-carat diamond ring perched on her finger. By the looks of the woman, the ring was probably real. In summation, she looked absolutely ridiculous for a Friday night fish fry at Wildflower or anything less classy than a ball at the White House or a trip to the Emmys. What did she think this was, the Titanic?

Charlotte shot the woman a look and then turned to Bridget to ask, "Who is that lady?" ignoring all social conventions for grace. Grace was pretty much ruined for tonight anyway.

"Oh, that's Catherine. She's sort of like a queen around here. She's in charge of the residents' council and the mission group. Haven't you met her yet?" Bridget asked. Awe radiated in her voice, circling the name Catherine as if it were the name of a deity.

"No, and I think I'll pass." Mission group or not,

this woman had no right to give Marla attitude. Charlotte could tell just by looking at her she wasn't going to like her.

Cassie continued chirping about delicious treats and the exciting prizes available during the bingo game tonight. The poor girl thought she was running a cruise ship instead of managing a community for the elderly. Someone should really tell her.

Charlotte stared blankly as she waited for her plate of fish to be delivered to her. She wasn't always like this. Wildflower was just making her so cynical. She needed to really work to make the best of it, to find some good things about it. It wasn't all that bad, right? There were good people here, and heck, maybe the activities wouldn't be so bad if she just let down her guard a little. She *had* to make the best of it, yes she did. She had to try, for Annie's sake and for her own.

So she smiled through the leathery texture of the cod and choked down the waxy, tasteless beans, even complimenting the dinner. She asked Bridget about what activities were the best, and she tried to have a conversation with Marla, although it pretty much just consisted of the words "what" and "huh." After the plates had been cleared, the true moment of excitement began—the weekly bingo ritual. Charlotte allowed herself to feel a little bit excited. In her day, she had been the bingo queen, often coming home with hundreds to show for her fire hall efforts. Maybe this bingo game was just what she needed to lift her spirits.

After chips were distributed and Marla was assured five times bingo was starting, Charlotte settled into the relaxing feel of the numbers being called. Cassie added some extra emphasis to each letter and number, but Charlotte didn't mind. The game lulled her into a calm state until Cassie called the one number Charlotte needed.

B6. It was hers. *The game was hers.* Things were turning around after all.

She leapt from her seat, yelling bingo like her life depended on it, her foot kicking against the chair leg with such force it tipped backward, threatening to fall over. As her hand waved in the air and she prepared for her victory walk to the prize table, an echo ricocheted through the room. Had she really yelled that loudly? Was Marla's hearing aid creating feedback?

No, she realized, her excitement waning. There had been another bingo.

Fur coat lady. Titanic lady. She also stood up, smiling at her victory. Cassie eyed them both up.

"Wow. Two bingos! Oh my, we have an exciting game here tonight, folks."

"I called it first, so I win," Catherine proclaimed snootily as she approached the prize table.

"Wait a second, we both yelled at the same time." Charlotte found herself retorting as she, too, stormed toward the front of the room.

"Sorry, chicky, but rules are rules. Around here, the first to yell bingo wins. So I win." Catherine enunciated each word as if she were talking to an invalid. Something about her tone of voice, her entire presence, made Charlotte rage. It was just a bingo game, she tried to tell herself. This woman was clearly a lunatic. But there was something about it that made Charlotte fight back. She could not let it go. Maybe it was because she had already given up so much. Maybe it was because she needed to hang on to something, even if it were just a bingo game victory.

"Sorry, *chicky*, but we both yelled it. If anything, I shouted it first." Charlotte shoved closer to the prizes as Cassie tried to guard the table, her bewildered face saying it all.

"Oh, really, new girl? You think you can just waltz in here like you own the place and cheat at bingo? Honestly." Catherine also inched toward the prize. Charlotte got there first, though. She picked up the wrapped package from the table as Cassie edged backward. She had apparently never been trained on how to deal with a bingo fight. She was about to get an education.

"I don't think so." Catherine grabbed for the prize. Her fingers latched on to the corner of the box, but Charlotte pulled right back. The crowd, those who were watching anyway, let out a collective gasp.

A ridiculous game of tug-of-war ensued. Both women pulled and grunted, trying to free the box. At first, the residents just stared in shocked silence, but then something in them snapped. They hadn't seen this much excitement since the hunger strike last May when residents refused to eat the dinners unless they started adding more spice.

"Go, Charlotte," Bridget shrieked, throwing her hands in the air. "Get it."

"Get her, Charlotte," Marla added, not needing to hear what was happening to figure it out. She may be hard of hearing, but she wasn't dense.

The wealthily clad women at Catherine's table followed suit, some jumping up from their table to cheer on the fight. Charlotte suddenly felt ridiculous, like she were in a high school cafeteria instead of a home for the elderly. But she couldn't give in now. She just couldn't. So she decided to do something a little preposterous... she slapped Catherine's hand. She slapped it hard.

Catherine shrieked, "Yow," as she pulled back, and Charlotte ran with her opportunity. She dashed her prize back to her table, her feet acting as wings to carry her away, as Bridget and Marla laughed and cheered in jubilant celebration.

Catherine wore a look of pure defeat and rage.

"This isn't over. But go ahead, have the prize. If you're so hard up for attention you need to win bingo, then go ahead. I'm okay with giving to a charity case." Catherine huffed, walking back to her table, straightening her fur as she went. Catherine's table glared at Charlotte's, but she didn't care. She had won.

Cassie tiptoed back to the microphone, tapping on it as if she needed to check its functionality. "Okay, everyone. Are we ready for the next game?" Cassie blew a strand of her hair out of her eyes, beads of sweat perceptible on her paling face. Her exuberant personality, however, wouldn't admit the bingo game had just become a total disaster.

As the next game started, Charlotte ripped open her prize. Inside, she found what she had fought a woman for in front of the whole group of residents. She found the prize she had started a war over, a prize she would probably pay for one way or another.

She found a box of delicious, buttery Cracker Jacks.

"My favorite," Marla yelled, eyeing up the box. "You got the best prize."

Charlotte handed the box over to Marla. It hadn't been about winning caramel corn. No, it had been about so much more. At that moment, Charlotte realized Catherine was the woman she had hated all her life, the woman who had tortured her in one form or another throughout her years.

And now it was time for her to pay.

***

Sometimes it takes a good night of sleep to find the clarity and perspective needed about a situation. Such was the case for Charlotte. She woke up on Saturday morning realizing how absolutely ridiculous she'd behaved the night before. Had she really had a trailer-trash-like fight over a box of Cracker Jacks? Had she jeopardized her reputation here at Wildflower over bingo? What in the heck was she becoming?

But something about the woman triggered her ludicrous reaction, set a fire to the anger bubbling in her.

It wasn't her fault. Yes, the more she thought about it, the more she couldn't stand Catherine. Yes, it wasn't fair. She didn't really know the lady, hadn't even officially met her. She was partially judging her based on her fur coat and her popularity.

However, Charlotte decided she did know Catherine. She was the woman she'd known her whole life. She was Melinda Jaspers of her junior high years, who flaunted her perfect blonde locks while criticizing Charlotte's mousey-brown ones. She was Janet Blour from eleventh grade, who'd told Charlotte she was fat and wore gross clothes. She was Johanna Malley of her twenties, who lived next door and touted her perfect wifely qualities for all to see, including Charlotte's husband.

Catherine was all of those women rolled into one. She was the picture of conceit, popularity, and condescension Charlotte was just plain tired of. So no, it wasn't about bingo. It was about the fact that Charlotte was already miserable and now she'd found out she was living in a place where she couldn't escape the social class issues of her youth. She was going to be living in a place run by a woman she hated, and she couldn't do anything about it.

But she was still embarrassed. People were probably gossiping about her. They were quite possibly calling her the bingo lunatic. Except Marla. She was just excited she got Cracker Jacks.

Charlotte ambled into her kitchenette to make a cup of coffee. She read her Post-it note Annie had written, explaining the Keurig coffeemaker steps. Why did everything have to be so complicated these days? She just wanted a darn cup of coffee without having to mess with this newfangled machine. She just wanted her life back with her coffee pot and her familiar home. She wanted her comfortable life, which was lonely but comfortable. She didn't want to be thrown into this stupid social mix that was half high school, half nursing home. She didn't want to deal with the Catherines or anyone else in this place. She didn't want to grin through fish dinners and pretend a card-making class really would change her life. The social complexities, the fake attitudes, the false pretenses exhausted her already. She had really vowed to herself to make it work. But now she just didn't know.

Sadness threatened to overpower Charlotte's normally perky mood. She hadn't always been in the doldrums of despair. In fact, most people described her as a happy-go-lucky, sweet lady. Where was that lady now? How did she find her again? What would Charlie think of this new Charlotte?

Charlotte sauntered over to the china cupboard as her coffee percolated. She looked up at the top, where her prized possession sat. The plate. It had been a gift from her mother-in-law, an antique, gorgeous plate passed through the family. The plate had sat in her china cupboard on proud display throughout all of Charlie and Charlotte's marriage. The yellow roses scrawled across the antique white china were as comfortable and familiar as her relationship had been with Charlie. It had been a cornerstone in her life, something that grounded her.

Now she just felt at loose ends, like her foundation

had been ripped from her. It had started with the loss of Charlie, but it had been finished with this newest development.

Charlotte reached up for the plate, needing to feel it in her hands to remember it was real. She wanted to run her fingers across the scratchy details of the design, to feel a connection to the Charlotte she was not so long ago, the sunshine-yellow Charlotte. The Charlotte who wouldn't have embarrassed herself by having a catfight over bingo. She ran her crooked fingers over the design for a few moments, basking in the feeling the plate evoked in her. A happy feeling, one of wonderful times passed. An odd mix of joy and loss whirling in her chest, she decided nostalgia had no place in her already broken-down psyche. Hands shaking from fatigue and sadness, Charlotte stretched to put the plate back, to resign it to the past that could never be again.

That's when it happened, the final nail in the coffin of her hate for Wildflower Meadows.

That's when the plate fell from her hand, shattering on the ceramic floor of her sterile apartment.

That's when she found herself drowning in tears, reaching for the phone to call Annie.

That's when she realized it was all Catherine's fault, that if it hadn't been for her highfalutin attitude, this wouldn't have happened.

When Annie got to her apartment an hour later to see what was the matter and expecting to find a true emergency, she met her mom's gaze with pure confusion.

Charlotte sat curled up against the china cupboard, shards of the plate all around her and tears pouring down her cheeks. Annie, the gracious daughter she was, slumped down beside Charlotte, putting her arm around her.

"It's going to be okay, Mom."

But Charlotte knew it wouldn't. It wouldn't be okay.

Charlotte knew her life, just like the plate, was in serious disarray. It would take a miracle to put the cracked relic of her past self and life, back together.

Chapter Two

Charlotte

"I'm sorry, honey. I don't know what got into me. It was just the plate, and I'm just tired," Charlotte said, wiping at her face as she moved her coffee from the Keurig.

She had spewed tears and words at Annie, both flowing uncontrollably for several minutes. When it was done, she felt foolish. It wasn't like her, and Annie had enough to deal with. She shouldn't have called her.

"Mom, it's okay. I know this has been hard on you. What can I do?" Annie asked after she had swept up the remnants of the plate, cautiously placing them in a sad little pile on the counter as discreetly as possible. Always empathetic. The poor thing had enough on her own cracked plate. She didn't need Charlotte behaving like an invalid.

"Really, baby, I'm fine. Just the stress of the move and then the plate happened. But I'm fine. I'm going to be fine. It's really nice here." Charlotte piled on the lies. White lies, she convinced herself. It would be fine.

"Mom, are you sure? Do you want to come home with me for a while, see the cats?"

If Charlotte said yes, Annie would certainly go through with the offer. Charlotte wanted nothing more than to see her five felines, to scratch Butternut. But that wouldn't help anyone. Annie had been working so hard; she deserved a weekend to herself. And Charlotte needed to acclimate to her new reality. Escaping to Annie's wouldn't solve anything. She needed to be self-disciplined, to make herself adjust.

"No, don't be silly, dear. I've got a lot going on here anyway. There's a new dance aerobics class happening I'm going to try out. Honestly. Tell Butternut and the others I said hi and give them a kiss from me. Thanks for stopping by. Now really, you scurry along." Charlotte tried to convince both herself and Annie she was truly stoic.

Annie paused, looking at Charlotte for a long time. "Okay, but you call if you change your mind, okay?"

"Don't be silly, dear. I just had a weak moment. Probably just needed my coffee. It'll be fine."

Annie still hesitated, but finally said, "Okay, Mom. I love you." She hugged Charlotte, who hugged her back, wanting nothing more than to hold on to her daughter forever. But she didn't. She let Annie go.

After Annie slipped out the door, Charlotte sank into her kitchen chair. She needed to pull it together. Yes, this was hard, but she could do this. She couldn't let this get her down. Charlie wouldn't want that. She had to stay strong. She had to do her best so she didn't cause Annie any more stress. She could do this.

Gosh darn it, stop feeling sorry for yourself, Charlotte scolded herself. Enough was enough.

She strolled straight back to her room and changed out of her floral nightie into a pair of turquoise slacks and a silky black shirt. She put in her best diamond earrings—an anniversary gift from Charlie—and brushed her hair. She dabbed on her lipstick and rouge, tossed her feet into some black sandals, and headed back to the Keurig. She fiddled with the directions again, pulling down a second mug, emblazoned with the words "cat lover," of course. When the coffee finished brewing, she armed herself with her two mugs and marched down the hall.

Her hands precariously balancing two full cups of coffee ready to spill over, she did a makeshift knock on the door with her elbow, concentrating on keeping the liquid in the cups.

Bridget came to the door in her lime-green nightie. "Charlotte, good morning! Great to see you. Do you want to come in? Is that for me?"

The lady was surely a morning person, despite her pajama status.

"Actually, I have an idea," Charlotte said, standing in the doorway. "At my house, I used to love going out on my porch and sipping coffee every morning. Yesterday, I noticed there's a beautiful bench out front by the door. I wanted to see if you would like to come and have a coffee with me."

Bridget's face lit up. "Lovely, dear. Just let me grab my key."

"Are you going to, um, put something more comfortable on?" Charlotte encouraged, trying not to sound obvious.

Bridget looked down at her outfit. "Oh, this is fine." She shrugged, edging toward the door with her walker. "Can you carry the coffee?"

"Of course." Charlotte smiled, feeling truly better. See, she just needed to take some initiative.

Charlotte and Bridget headed out the front door toward the targeted bench. Charlotte couldn't help but grin as the sun gently streamed across her face, the warmth heavenly on her skin. Birds chirped as the cloudless sky welcomed happy feelings and thoughts. It was the infuriatingly cheesy kind of day movies were made of.

Once Bridget and Charlotte were situated, Charlotte handed Bridget the cat mug of now-lukewarm liquid.

Bridget didn't seem to notice the less-than-perfect temperature of the coffee. "This is wonderful," she exclaimed as she closed her eyes, taking in the liquid and the sunshine. The two women sat in silence for a long moment, taking in the atmosphere, soaking in the positive feelings that can only come from being outside, even if it was outside a place like Wildflower.

That's when it happened. The van. The door opening. The cane flailing out. That's when Charlotte suddenly knew Wildflower Meadows might not be so bad.

Chapter Three

Charlotte

"Who is *that*?" Charlotte prodded Bridget to get her attention. A man in black pants and a light blue polo lumbered out of the van, leaning on a cane as a middle-aged man led him toward the door.

"I've never seen him before." Bridget raised the cup to her lips yet again.

Charlotte stared, curious about the guy and not even sure why. He was just an average-looking guy, no Adam Levine—her granddaughter, Amelia, was always talking about that rock guy. Although Charlotte wasn't huge on tattoos, she did have to admit there was something intriguing and mysterious about the singer. As far as older people went, though, this man was okay. Nice, respectable clothes. A handsome face if one looked beyond the somewhat saggy skin. As the guy inched closer, Charlotte also noticed the man's eyes were a gorgeous shade of blue. Just as she eyed up the man with the cane, the middle-aged man accompanying him halted near the ladies.

"Hi, how are you ladies doing this fine day? I'm Mike and this is my dad, Leonard. He's moving in today."

Charlotte recognized Mike's efforts. They were over-the-top and forced. They were the efforts of a man who wanted Wildflower Meadows to work out, if not just for his dad's sake, then for his own sense of relief to be validated. Charlotte smiled as Leonard looked into her eyes.

"I think I'm going to like it here," Leonard said, turning to his son.

Charlotte couldn't swear by it, but she thought he winked at her before he did. Heat rose in her cheeks, and then she tried to shrug it away. The sun was rather warm even though it was early. Or maybe she was just used to being cooped up in her apartment.

"Well, we better get going. We have a lot to get settled," the son said, as he and Leonard edged toward the entrance.

"Bye, now. See you later," Bridget said, as Charlotte sat in silence. She quickly brushed off the creeping feeling in her heart, an unfamiliar, distant notion now a stranger to her.

"He's cute," Bridget squealed once they were out of earshot. She sounded like a sixteen-year-old instead of the eighty-six-year-old she was.

"If you say so." Charlotte downplayed the encounter, her gaze now studying the final few drops of coffee in her cup.

"Did you see him look at you?" Bridget nudged

Charlotte painfully in the ribs.

"He was being polite."

"He *winked* at you."

"Bridget, stop. We aren't teenagers. This is a home for the elderly, not a frat house."

"Well, I don't know about you, but just because I'm old doesn't mean my heart is dead."

This struck Charlotte right to the core. Because up until this moment, she hadn't considered her heart could even still be alive. From the moment Charlie hit the floor, her heart had shattered into a thousand irreparable pieces, just like her floral china plate. She had never considered it would ever be glued back together into some semblance of a feeling element, not at her age.

But something about Leonard, something about his calm manner, the way he looked at her, those eyes... something about him, if she were being completely honest with herself, made her ask—why not?

Charlotte and Bridget spent the next hour on the bench, talking about husbands and children, QVC and cats; Bridget also had cats, but only two. They were living with her daughter as well. They talked like friends just getting to know each other, but they also talked like they'd known each other their entire lives. There was something to be said about friendship in your eighties. By this point in life, there could be a more pure type of friendship if one would let it, a friendship not built on status and hobbies, but on just getting to know someone, on companionship.

For the first time in twenty-two days, Charlotte started to feel like maybe Wildflower Meadows could someday feel like home, botched bingo game, cracked plate, and all.

Chapter Four

Charlotte

"Grandma? Hello? Are you up yet?"

Charlotte bolted up in her bed, a second of confusion stirring in her brain. Where was she? Oh yes, her new life. A month in a place wasn't enough to make it feel completely familiar, although it was getting easier. Was that Amelia? What was she doing there? What time was it? Questions swirled in her brain before she jumped into action. She threw back the covers and glanced in the mirror across from her bed. She almost screamed at the sight of her hair.

"Grandma?"

"I'm coming dear, I'm in my bedroom," she called. What was Amelia doing there so early on a Monday?

Just then, Amelia rounded the corner. The apartment wasn't much bigger than a shoebox, so it wasn't a surprise.

"Sorry, Grandma. I thought you'd be up already. Happy birthday," the black-haired girl proclaimed, as she handed Charlotte a bouquet of daisies, her favorite.

"Oh sweetie, they're beautiful." Charlotte crossed the room, reaching to hug her granddaughter and grasping the daisies only after she had held her for a moment. "You didn't have to do this." In reality, Charlotte had been taken aback by the word "birthday." She had completely forgotten.

"Sorry again I woke you. Aren't you usually up by now?"

Charlotte glanced at the clock. It was almost ten. Apparently last night's card playing tournament had been too much for her. Luckily, she had contained herself during the game, although Catherine had been excessively competitive, as usual.

"Oh, you know, we have some pretty rockin' parties here on Sundays, darling. We were up all night."

Amelia gave her the wistful look Charlotte had come to love so much. "Well, I thought we could go to breakfast to celebrate. Mom's planning a dinner for later tonight, but I have to work. So where do you want to go? Oh, I guess I should let you get ready first, huh?"

Amelia spewed out thoughts faster than Charlotte could process. That was her granddaughter, though. Always saying something, and doing something. Always on the go. Charlotte saw so much of her young self in Amelia. Okay, maybe not the spiky doodads on her bracelet or the ripped jeans part. But the vivacious, energetic part. The life loving, go with the flow girl. That's probably why Charlotte and Amelia had always been so close. They both saw something in each other they recognized in the mirror, despite the decades between them.

"Oh, wonderful. Did you already do your dog walking this morning?"

"Yeah. I just got Jojo a bit earlier today so I could be done in time to come here. The little fella actually walked the lap in less than an hour, surprisingly." Amelia turned to go back to the kitchenette/living room area.

"I'd love to see him again," Charlotte said before heading into the bathroom.

Charlotte did her best to make herself presentable, slapping on some moisturizer, her favorite rouge and lipstick. She combed her frazzled hair, eventually just writing it off for the day. She chose to wear a yellow top, her favorite color, and some gray dress slacks. Once she firmly attached the brooch to her shirt and looped some gold hoops into her earlobes, she was ready.

"You look so pretty, Grandma. But here, let me do your eyeshadow." Amelia was a whiz with cosmetics, so Charlotte agreed.

Once Amelia had perfected Charlotte's smoky eyes, which looked a bit too much like Cher for Charlotte's taste, they paraded out the door and off to breakfast.

"The usual?" Amelia asked as Charlotte stepped on trash in Amelia's passenger seat area. She gently tossed an empty Styrofoam cup off the seat and onto the floor. She tried to ignore the wet-dog smell. Amelia didn't have time for things like cleaning a car, but who would? The poor girl was probably exhausted from her ridiculous work schedule. Three jobs were just too many.

"Absolutely."

The two women headed to the usual, a tiny diner that hadn't progressed past the 1950s. Jimmie's was known for its massive waffles and fresh coffee. Charlotte loved it.

Once the two parked, sauntered in, and were seated, their conversation carried on. Neither needed to see a menu. The waitress, Flo, knew exactly what they would want.

"So how are you doing, Grandma? How's Wildflower? Are you adjusting?"

Annie always complained about Amelia when she asked too many questions at once, but Charlotte found it endearing. The girl had so much to ask, so much to know. So Charlotte never complained.

"It's getting better. I miss having my own house, but overall, it's going okay."

"I stopped at Mom's last night. Butternut is doing really well, and so are the others. Mom might not admit it, but I think she likes having all the company." Amelia smiled.

At the mention of Butternut, Charlotte couldn't help but light up. "Did you give Butternut a hug for me?"

"Absolutely. A belly rub, too." A slight lull crept into the conversation. Amelia looked wistful.

"How about you, honey? How's work? You look tired. I think three jobs is just too much. Can't you cut back?"

"Grandma, I'm fine. I love them all, and it's good money. If I were to give one up, it would have to be the dog walking stint, and I love my customers too much."

"Amelia, you've got so much talent. I hate to see you so... scattered. I do worry about you, working all of those hours."

"I know, Grandma. I just have to figure some things out first. But things with Neville are going well, so there's that," Amelia added, painting a smile on her face.

"That's great, I guess."

"Grandma, you're so transparent." Amelia grimaced.

"What?"

"I know you hate Neville."

"I don't hate him, dear. That's such a strong word. I just think he's downright dull. You're this gorgeous, shining woman who likes to live in the fast lane. And he's just... Neville. I mean, the name says it all, right?"

"Grandma, he can't help his name."

"You're right, but he *can* help acting like his name."

Amelia laughed as the waitress brought their food.

"Besides," Amelia added as she buttered her waffle, "maybe that's my problem. Maybe I'm living in the fast lane too much. Maybe if I slow down a bit, I could figure out my life."

Charlotte looked up from her plate, making eye contact with Amelia.

"Honey, no one ever figures out life. Ever. Let me tell you, I might not look like it now, but I was just like you once. I lived in the fast lane too. And slowing down, trying to settle in, isn't the answer. If you lose yourself, you won't ever find it again."

Amelia steadied herself, looking straight at Charlotte. "But you loved Grandpa, right?"

Charlotte sighed. She hadn't meant to sound offensive to Charlie's memory. "Of course I did, darling. We had a wonderful life. But that doesn't mean it was perfect. That doesn't mean there weren't times I wished some things were different. I just don't want to see you settle." Charlotte decided to leave it at that. "Now let's dig in, I'm starving, and I've got my dance aerobics class later." She poured syrup on her pancakes.

"Dance Aerobics? You?"

"What do you mean, me? Of course me. I've got to get my hips working." Charlotte winked.

"Grandma, I don't think you ever settled or slowed down. Trust me." Amelia shook her head as she plucked a piece of waffle from her plate and shoved it into her mouth.

"Maybe you're right." Charlotte shrugged, wondering if her granddaughter could see a distant fire in her she could no longer quite recognize herself.

Chapter Five

Annie

"Annie, dear, just so you know, this form goes in this pile, right here. See where I'm putting it? This pile, okay? Thanks, sweetie."

Sasha's too-tight black pencil skirt crept up her thighs as she overemphasized the placement of the form in the blue bin instead of the red. A smile worthy of a toothpaste commercial gleamed as her perfectly curled hair grazed her face. Annie just stood looking at Sasha with a look of death or, at the very least, malicious intent.

"Right, got it." Annie added, "Thanks, Sasha." She didn't even try to feign kindness, an obvious eye roll negating any hint of appreciation for the tip. She just couldn't manage it.

If Sasha detected Annie's sarcasm, though, she was either too stupid or too cheerful to note it. "Great, darling. And wow is your shirt just so cute. I could never wear something like that, though. It just would look too flowy on my body shape. It would make me look chubby.

So I'm envious you can wear something so loose." She smiled right through so it came off as genuine and sweet. Everyone else in the office might be buying Sasha's sweet-as-sugar routine, but Annie wasn't. For the past three years, Annie had always suspected Sasha was much bitchier than she let on.

In the past six months, Sasha's flaunting disguised as confidence, her over-the-top sweetness routine, and her calling Annie "dear" and "sweetie" had become unbearable. Annie feared if she didn't get away from her, she would claw her eyes out. Or stab the girl with her infuriatingly wobbly stiletto. What normal woman wore shoes of that height to an office?

But in an office of fifty people, it was hard to escape from anyone, let alone your direct co-worker in the customer service department. So the eye-clawing or shoe-stabbing incidents were becoming more likely every single day.

Annie had to admit Sasha was perfect for the job. She had mastered the art of faking enthusiasm and empathy. She had the perfect things to say, even when an irate customer complained about the amount of icing on her cupcake being less than the amount pictured on the box. Sasha also had the cutesy business professional look down, so much so that Annie's boss, Mr. Grison, absolutely adored her. Of course, it probably had something to do with the tight pencil skirt perfectly silhouetting Sasha's tightly shaped ass. Most days, Annie felt like she was the only one who noticed Sasha's obnoxious behaviors—which made the behaviors all the more intolerable to Annie, especially because she knew she wasn't just imagining them. Sasha just seemed to enhance the annoyingness whenever Annie was around.

Annie trudged back to her cubicle, her flowy shirt now making her self-conscious. She took a sip from her soda as she caught a glimpse of herself in the mirror hanging at her desk.

She looked old. She felt old. She noticed the roadmap of lines on her face and neck, the grays sprouting out of her mousey-brown hair. She saw the little crinkles on her eyelids—were they called crow's feet? Her skin, dull and gray, underscored her exhaustion. Her hair flittered about her head, a hot mess. Well, actually just a mess.

No wonder he left.

Pushing the thought out of her mind, she tried to refocus on the task. She had five more minutes of break until she was back on the headset dealing with angry customers. It was too much. She had never loved her job, not really, but she hadn't minded it either. Dealing with annoying people was much easier when it was only a part of your life, when you had a life to go home to.

Now dealing with whiny men, whom she imagined were over six hundred pounds, about cupcakes seemed so inconsequential. She wanted to tell them to get a life, who cared about icing on a cupcake? Who cared if the texture of the cake was too spongey or too dry or too crumbly?

But she couldn't. Because her job as a customer

service rep at Sandy's Sweets wasn't just a job anymore; it *was* now her entire livelihood, her entire life. This was now all she had.

She still had Amelia, of course. But Amelia was busy building her own life, so Annie was left to find her own life. And she was really sucking at it.

How do you just start over? How do you just say, "Oh, what, you're leaving me for a thirtysomething, who is the same age as your daughter? Okay, right on, I'll just pull a new life together, too, then." She felt trapped, she felt stuck, she felt frustrated—and she was tired.

Putting her headset back on, she picked up the first phone call. Perfectly armed and ready to paint on her cheery "the customer is always right" voice and mail some coupons for free boxes of expertly wrapped cupcakes, a familiar voice on the phone tossed her out of her routine.

"Annie, dear, I'm so sorry to bother you at work. I really am. But I'm having a bit of a problem, an emergency. Well, not quite an emergency, not one requiring immediate attention or anything, but an emergency nonetheless. I can't seem to find my pills. Do you know where they are? I'm sorry dear, really I am."

Annie took a deep breath. This was the fifth call like this from Charlotte this week. Annie slumped into her seat, feeling like the entire world was caving in on her.

"Mom, calm down, it's fine. Did you look in the cupboard above the stove? The tiny one?"

"Why, no. Is that where you put them?"

"Yes, Mom, remember? I told you yesterday when I stopped by?"

There was a pause and some shuffling of feet. A cupboard creaked open.

"Oh, my goodness, there they are. Silly me. I'm so sorry, honey. I guess I'm just tired. How's Butternut?"

"Mom, he's fine. Now listen, I have to go, okay."

"Right dear, I'm sorry. Bye." The phone clicked.

Annie knew her mom was just having a rough time. It had been over a month since her move to Wildflower, but a month didn't negate the sixty years she had spent in her house on Walnut Street. It didn't make up for the feeling of loss she was certainly going through. It also didn't make up for the fact her mom was getting older, that she was going to be experiencing the memory loss and forgetfulness typical of the age.

But it also didn't make it any easier.

Annie was physically and emotionally drained; the call simply reminded her of it. She was still working on selling her mom's house while trying to get Charlotte settled in Wildflower. She had been stopping at Wildflower at least four times a week to check on her mother, to keep her company, to get her acclimated. There was paperwork and the immense task of moving her mother. There was getting her mother settled into a routine while trying to keep her own routine going. Add to it the fact she was now alone, solely responsible for keeping her own house going, and Annie's mind was quickly fizzling out. She was losing her mind. As in completely losing it, gone for good, looney tunes gone.

And then there were the cats.

She knew the cats meant everything to her mom, especially Butternut. She knew this was just part of having an aging parent, having to make certain sacrifices. But five? Five furballs on top of her already chaotic life? It was too much. She felt simultaneously like she was living two lives, her own and Charlotte's life, while also not living any life at all. She felt stretched and worn out. She felt old and haggard. She felt like maybe she should check herself in at Wildflower Meadows Assisted Living.

Maybe she should broach the subject of a nurse or aide with Charlotte. Annie selected Wildflower Meadows because it gave Charlotte the option for freedom but also the option for help when needed. Charlotte insisted she was fine, she didn't need a nurse to stop every day to help with her medicines. She was smart. She knew what to do.

But this was the fifth call, the fifth time she'd started to worry Charlotte needed more help than she was letting on. She had fully recovered from the stroke, which was miraculous. She had a regular pill regimen down, she had various doctors' appointments, but she was good as new according to the doctors, as good as an eighty-one-year-old can be, after all. The Wildflower Meadows community reassured Annie to a degree. If Charlotte needed something or if there were a medical emergency, there were people to look out for her. Now, though, she started to wonder if it was enough. Other residents had nurses or aides stop in once a day, some twice, just to help with pills and check up on them. Maybe that was what Annie should set up, which would help ease her mind and take some of the pressure off.

Charlotte wouldn't like it, but maybe it was necessary.

That's what I'll do, Annie thought. *After work. I'm going to call Cassie and set up an aide, just to help Mom with her pills in the morning. That way, I'll know it's okay. And if I can't make it to see her a day, I'll know she'll get checked on.*

The overly pleasant voice Annie loathed pinged into her thoughts.

"Annie, dear? Is everything okay? I wasn't trying to eavesdrop, but you were talking pretty loudly, and I heard you say 'mom.' I figured something must be wrong if you were taking a personal call. Is everything okay?"

Annie wasn't stupid. She could read Sasha's hidden message, *Why are you being a terrible worker, taking personal phone calls? I would never do that.*

Annie decided today wasn't the day. Today wasn't the day she would get one up on the perfectly dressed thirty-year-old, who seemed to know everything. So she also stretched a smile on her face and said, "Yes, darling, everything is fine. Just a small issue with my mom. Oh, look, my phone line is lighting up. Back to work. Thanks for caring so much though, *dear.*" She let her almost-noticeable sarcasm drip on the last word. Sasha grinned, of course, and slinked back to her area.

She'll get hers. Sooner rather than later, Annie thought, as she clicked on the line, "Sandy's Sweets, this is Annie speaking, how can I help you better enjoy your delicious cupcakes today?"

Chapter Six

Annie

When five o'clock rolled around, Annie didn't waste any time sprinting to her SUV and peeling out of the parking lot. She'd had enough phone calls and Sasha for a lifetime.

Not wanting to cook dinner for herself, she decided to swing through the drive-through, a bad habit she had bought into lately. Her diet, if you could call it that, could wait. What was the point anyway?

She knew she should stop to see Charlotte, to check on her, but she just couldn't bring herself to do it. She loved her mom, she really did, but she just felt herself getting run-down. She needed a break. She needed to relax, to spend time on just herself.

Pulling into her driveway, she reached down for the crinkly paper sack and her purse. A cacophony of meows greeted her once she was in the door, along with a few hairs floating in the air. Despite her fatigue, she reached down to give Peter a scratch on the head. She didn't know what her mom saw in Butternut; if she were telling the truth, Peter was her personal favorite.

Not that she liked the cats. No way, not really. Any day now, she would start the search for homes for them. But that was something for another day, one when she wasn't so drained. Annie plopped herself onto the sofa, not even bothering to change into sweats just yet. Her stomach gurgled, reminding her she was famished, prompting her to dig into the paper sack now transparent with grease. With her free hand, she clasped the remote and flicked through to the channel she was seeking. She just wanted to pop on some *Young and the Restless* from the DVR, get lost in someone else's chaotic life for a change.

With five cats crowded around her, Annie unwrapped her chicken delight sandwich, oozing with mayonnaise. This would probably put another chunk of cellulite on her ass, but what did it matter? There wasn't anyone to see her ass anymore, other than Peter and the rest of the cats, and she didn't think they cared if she had a few more globs of fat on her. Silver linings were everywhere; she could now eat mayonnaise by the bucket and not even care. As she bit into her sandwich, mayonnaise squeezing out from under the bun, she realized how much better it tasted now that she didn't even care.

Amelia had been on her case lately, trying to convince her to get back out there, trying to convince her to take this time to live it up, play the field, reinvent herself.

"You're not too old, Mom. Let's get you a new outfit, a new hairstyle. Screw Dad," she had said just last week.

"Amelia, you shouldn't talk about your father that way. This has nothing to do with your relationship with him." In spite of everything, Annie automatically defended him. She knew this was the right thing to do, the motherly thing to do.

"Oh, Mom, please. You feel the same way. As you should. He's a dick for what he did to you. He deserves that hoity-toity slut. I don't really care if I ever talk to him again." Annie tried to look horrified, but inside, she felt the same thing. He *was* a dick for what he did, and although she would never expect her daughter to choose sides, it did feel sort of good to know Amelia was on hers.

Despite Amelia's pep talks, Annie hadn't been feeling like she "wasn't too old" these days. When she peered in the mirror, a corpse-like woman stared back, a faulty shadow of the person she used to be. Her skin had lost its elasticity despite her constant use of sunscreen. Her eyelids were sagging, and so was everything else. How was a fifty-year-old supposed to move on? She didn't even know where to begin. She didn't know who she was without Dave, without her marriage. She had no clue what she wanted for the rest of her life or even where to start.

And then there was the whole dating scene Amelia told her she should explore. Amelia made it seem vivacious and zesty, an adventure for Annie to partake in.

Annie, however, saw it as a disaster. How did one even maneuver the dating world? And how did one even find someone to maneuver the dating world with? The only man who had given her even a glance in the past few months was Ed, the produce restocker at Costco. And let's just say Ed wasn't much to look at, even though Annie wasn't shallow in the least. Plus, she had been getting a vibe from him women weren't exactly his thing.

It just seemed like too much work, work she was too exhausted to tackle. She wasn't sure she even wanted to move on. Dave had been it for her. For the past thirty-three years. She had spent the best years of her life with him, grown up with him really. From their marriage right after high school to Amelia's birth to everything that fell into place after it, they had been everything to each other for so long. They had built the proverbial American Dream together. They had been there through Amelia's goth/emo stages that had about sent both of them to the mental hospital with worry. They had been through Dave's job loss, through two houses and three dogs. They had been through endless vacations and family events, miscarriages, promotions, and holidays. They had built a solid core of a life together... or so she had thought. And now it was gone, ripped away by a tight ass, large breasts, and perfectly shiny hair. Ripped away by a woman who probably never touched a crinkly fast-food sack and, therefore, probably had a smooth ass—unlike Annie.

How could she ever even begin to trust again? If

it hadn't worked with Dave, who she was convinced was her soul mate, how could she even hope for any semblance of a working relationship with anyone else? All of those questions blurred together so much she didn't even notice whom the soap opera characters kissed or what schemes the hunk was muddled in. The characters' lives swirled together with images of Dave and the crumbs of her fast food.

The phone's shrill, piercing note caused her to jump, stirring Peter. Annie cringed, knowing it was someone from the real world calling. She would have to return to being the responsible, "I'm fine" Annie. The Annie who ran errands, helped Charlotte, and talked Amelia through her daily dilemmas. The Annie everyone else needed her to be.

"Hello?" Annie choked through the grease coating her trachea.

"Annie? Annie Amsley? This is Cassie from Wildflower Meadows," a perky voice announced. Annie's heart sank.

"Is everything okay?"

"Oh, yes, Charlotte's okay. Well, physically I mean. I was just wondering if you could possibly come to Wildflower to have a quick chat with me? There are some issues we need to discuss, if it would be convenient."

Issues? What the hell had happened? The way things were going, Annie didn't even want to imagine. She didn't want to deal with this; she wanted to say hell no, it's not convenient.

But she did what responsible Annie always did.

She hopped in her car, ignoring the French fries sitting in her bag to be eaten. She drove the five minutes to Wildflower in four and a half. She marched herself to Cassie's office, the worry lines on her forehead prominently displayed.

"Ms. Amsley, welcome. Have a seat." Cassie pointed to a padded chair.

Beside the chair where she was to sit, a man sat twisting his hands. He wore faded jeans and work boots, a Carhartt jacket over a flannel shirt. He also looked concerned.

"Ms. Amsley, this is Mr. Draden. I've asked him to join us."

Now Annie was just downright confused. This couldn't be good.

Cassie shut the door to give them privacy and, after both Annie and Mr. Draden declined a glass of ice-cold water, she began.

"So it seems there has been some tension building between your mothers, Charlotte and Catherine. I noticed it about a month ago during a bingo game, but I thought it was a onetime thing. However, things came to a head this afternoon."

Annie had questions popping up left and right. The bingo game situation? What did that mean? And who was Catherine? Charlotte never mentioned a Catherine. She wanted to spew questions at Cassie but opted for calm silence. She would let Cassie do the talking first.

"This afternoon was our dance aerobics class. Our instructor, Jamie, came to talk with me after the class and filled me in on the encounter."

Annie glanced at the man in the room for the first time, as if to say, "Do you know what's coming next? I have no idea."

"From what I've been told, a situation emerged during Pitbull's newest song. Apparently Catherine didn't think Charlotte was doing the routine correctly, so she tried to advise her of the correct steps. Charlotte, angry at being embarrassed in front of the class, apparently retorted with some not-so-nice words for Catherine."

"Oh dear," Annie said. Her mother was a good woman, one who paid close attention to social graces. But if you pushed her, if you got on her bad side... well, the woman could be a stubborn force to deal with.

"I'm afraid it gets worse," Cassie continued, her smile dampened. *This must be bad if Cassie isn't smiling,* Annie thought.

"Apparently it escalated into a physical encounter. Now the good news is no one was hurt. But there were a lot of expletives, and some scratching and clawing. Jamie had to pull Catherine off of Charlotte. It got pretty intense, and a lot of the other residents are talking about it."

Annie buried her face in her hands. Was this really happening?

Mr. Draden also seemed frustrated, his audible sighs the only sounds in the room.

"I'm sorry," Mr. Draden finally said, after all three had sat taking in the information for some time.

"Well, so am I," Cassie added. "Now look, I think Charlotte and Catherine are both lovely ladies. I don't really understand this conflict that has surfaced between them, but we cannot have this type of behavior at our activities. Both women have been banned from the class for at least the month. I have to warn you both, though, this has to stop. We at Wildflower pride ourselves on the sense of community and safety here for our residents. If your moms don't calm down, we are looking at possible eviction."

There it was. The word Annie anticipated.

"I'll talk to my mom. I'm sure she's just been under a lot of stress," Annie added.

"Same here, I'll talk to my mom," Mr. Draden promised.

Cassie's smile returned. "Excellent. I know if we work together, we can sort this all out and everyone can get along."

Is this girl from a Sesame Street commercial? Annie wondered, but she didn't have time to criticize the administrative team. She had bigger issues. Like getting her mom to stop fighting.

Cassie led the two out of her office with some more cheesy words. Annie decided to head outside and think for a few minutes before facing her mom.

What did you say to an eighty-one-year-old who had been accused of fighting at dance aerobics? Annie felt like she was the mother of a high school student all over again.

Annie strolled out to the patio, finding a bench to rest on as all of the complications of her life swirled around her. Weight pressed on the bench, and she turned to see the man from the office propped beside her yet again.

"Did you know about any of this?" he calmly asked, true befuddlement in his voice.

"No clue. Mom never mentioned Catherine, er, your mom to me. I don't know what's happening." Another sigh.

"It's so hard, you know. You want them to keep their independence, you don't want to insult them. They're your mom, you know. But then stuff like this happens and I just worry. Am I doing the right thing? Is this the best place? I know Mom puts on a good show, but she hasn't had the easiest time here. It's been so hard for her since Dad died."

Annie looked at him for a minute, taking in the soft flecks of gray in his dark hair, the light smell of car oil on him mixed with his oaky cologne.

"Same here. I've been trying my best to make this easy for my mom, to help her out. I know losing the house and her cats has been tough. But I thought she was doing well. This just makes me wonder."

"Well, I'm going to talk to my mom. Maybe I'll get through to her. I know eviction would kill her, even if she isn't completely thrilled about being here."

"Same here. I'll see if I can get through to her."

"Well, listen, let's work together. Do you want to give me your phone number, so we can keep each other posted?" the man asked, reaching into his pocket for his cell.

"Yes, sounds great, Mr. Draden," Annie added, warmth rising to her cheeks. She was suddenly aware of a furball from Peter on her black slacks. She plucked it off.

"You can call me Joe." He smiled, pulling his cellphone from his back pocket.

After giving Joe her number, she said, "I'm sorry for all this."

"For what? You didn't do anything. It was our moms who were having their catfight. Honestly, during a Pitbull song? Does it get any stranger than that?" He grinned now. The two exchanged a hearty laugh. "Guess I'll head up to give Mom a lecture I never thought I'd have to give." Joe stood from the bench.

"Good luck," Annie said, heading toward the facility as well.

"Trust me, I'll need it."

At least I'm not alone, Annie thought as she walked beside Joe. *At least I'm not completely alone in this.*

Chapter Seven

Amelia

"Okay, Brent, I'll see you tomorrow. And don't forget to restock the strawberries. Saturday evenings, they're our top sellers," Amelia shouted over her shoulder as she hung up her stiff blue apron for the night.

"Got it, boss. We'll be fine. Now get out of here," the teenage boy replied.

"You've got it." She clocked out in the office of Smoothie Q, which was little more than a closet with a few files in it. Heading to her Suzuki SX4, she took out her ponytail and ran her fingers through her semi-matted hair.

I won't have time to wash it before six, not unless Henry miraculously decides to love walking, she thought. *Oh well, messy is in these days.* She leapt into her car, started it, and accelerated off to her next task of the day.

Amelia had convinced herself this was what thirty-two was all about. Chaotic schedules, running all around, never sitting still. Sure, some women were settled down by now, had the whole Suzie Homemaker thing going on. But not her. She was young, she was full of life, and she wasn't ready to just sit down with some homemaking magazines and iced tea yet. Plus, she sort of needed the income from her three jobs to pay the bills. This living-on-your-own thing did come with a price.

Her mom constantly nagged her about it. "Amelia, you need to stop working so much," or "Amelia, don't you think it's time to start thinking about a family?" Of course, ever since Dad left, the whole family thing had taken a backseat in their conversations; apparently her mom had decided these past few months maybe family wasn't the answer to fulfillment.

But she still got her jabs in about Amelia running herself haggard.

Grandma had started putting in her thoughts here and there too, but it was always easier to take criticism from Grandma Charlotte. She had a sweetness to her that allowed her to say things that would be irritating or offensive coming from anyone else.

Amelia liked her life, she did. Yes, it was hectic. Yes, she sometimes felt like a wayward teenager working three odd jobs; it didn't help that almost all of her coworkers at Smoothie Q and at Book World were still in high school.

If she were being candid, this wasn't quite how she'd pictured her life in her thirties. There was a time long ago when she'd pictured herself in quite a different point of life. A career, one she didn't have to defend to old acquaintances and friends, was one thing in her vision.

A house, maybe even a husband by now. She pictured a life full of friends and vacations. She imagined a whole lot more exploration and smiling than smoothie making.

But somewhere between her midtwenties and now, she had decided life as a dog walker/smoothie manager/book restocker suited her, at least for now. So her business degree sat, a scroll that probably belonged in the Dead Sea, somewhere in storage, never to be touched. Amelia knew pretty much from her first business class that being an account executive or anything in corporate America probably wasn't for her. There was more to life than working just for a paycheck, right?

Of course, some would argue that was what she was doing now. She disagreed. Yes, she did her jobs for the money, but there were also things about each job she loved, truly loved. She loved animals, she loved managing people at a low-key setting, she loved strawberry smoothies, and she loved books. Plus, she loved how her jobs were pretty stress free, giving her time to pursue her one true passion in life, a passion few knew about.

Pulling up to the Stintson house, Amelia threw on her sunglasses as she headed to the hide-a-key location. Wiping her feet on the "wipe your paws" doormat and opening the door, she was engulfed by the familiar, homey smell of apple pie. She suspected it was just a plug-in, because even Mrs. Stintson couldn't be perfectly domestic, not every day.

"Henry," she yelled, waiting for the ogre of a client

to come to greet her.

He, of course, didn't, so she trudged toward the living room, knowing he would be in his usual spot.

Amelia didn't really know why the Stintsons thought Henry needed a daily dog walker. Not that she was complaining. They were one of her best-paying clients. But Henry would have been just as happy napping on the couch all day, his drooling lips oozing over the armrest as he snored away the hours. The bear of a dog hated moving from the couch, let alone walks. In fact, he passionately loathed walking, as evidenced by his emotive gaze stabbing into her as she approached him. Amelia had to drag all 227 pounds of him every inch. Three blocks took her an hour due to his methodically slow pace and stubborn resistance.

The Stintsons, though, insisted Henry adored Amelia and he would just be so down if she didn't come to walk him while they were at work. Perhaps they needed to feel less guilty about leaving him at home alone for so many hours, but truth be told, Amelia thought Henry would be feeling just fine with the house and especially the couch to himself.

While Amelia internally argued with herself, Henry finally got up from the couch and sauntered out to the kitchen, his seemingly dinner plate-sized paws plodding on the ceramic floor. He looked completely unamused and headed toward his bowl of food—which was arguably more like a feeding trough.

Amelia reached for his collar, hooking him up to

a leash. "Hey, buddy, listen. We need to work together on this one, okay? You see, I have a date in roughly 1.5 hours. And I would love to freshen up a bit, do something with this hair. So what do you say we make this quick?"

Henry responded with a dramatic yawn.

He managed to take two slow, tenuous steps with Amelia's encouragement, an audible groan underscoring his displeasure already. They exited the door side by side. Two minutes down, and they had officially commenced the walk. Now they just needed to finish it.

Amelia could certainly just say she walked him. She could take him outside the house for good measure. Sure, there were neighbors around, but with houses this size, few of them were probably at home. Most were probably working somewhere, or if they were home, they probably weren't worrying about what the dog walker was up to.

But Amelia couldn't do it.

Yes, it was stupid. Henry hated the walks, and she had places to be. But Amelia just couldn't lie to the people who put their trust in her. So come hell or high water, she would finish the allotted walking distance. Even if it meant Neville would have to see her like this, matted hair and all.

Once Henry got to the bottom of the driveway, things looked promising. With enough *good boys* to make her throat sore, Amelia kept coaxing the horse. Things were going to go smoothly, she just knew it.

And then the one thing happened that couldn't be reversed.

Henry sat down.

"Oh, no, come on, big guy, please, please, please," Amelia pleaded, getting down to eye level with the dog. Great, now she looked crazy. And desperate. A crazy, desperate, matted-hair girl walking with a huge dog. No, this wasn't ridiculous.

Amelia coaxed. She pulled. She begged. She pretended to run. She offered him treats. She skipped and sang Broadway show tunes.

Henry just kept sitting, looking thoroughly unamused by her antics.

"The only thing you have to know," Mr. Stintson had told her when he offered her the job, "is if you let him sit down, he isn't moving. And I don't know about you, but I sure can't lift him." Cue corny chuckles. Amelia had thought it to be ridiculous at the time. Really? This dog wasn't that stubborn, he couldn't be.

But after a year of Henry, Amelia could now appreciate the warning. It was true; once Henry was tired of walking, he sat. And once he sat, you weren't going anywhere with him until he was ready to continue. Which could take fifteen minutes. Or a half hour. Once, it had taken forty-five.

Just wonderful, Amelia thought. Things were finally going okay with a guy, she finally saw promise... and now she would have to cancel their date because of a dog?

"No way," Amelia decreed.

So she did what she never had done before, at least

not to a client.

She got behind him and started pushing. After minutes of grunting and shoving on the dog's rump, her feet kicking pointlessly with effort, after she started sweating profusely from the strain, it worked.

Henry got up. He took two steps, and Amelia tried to keep the momentum going. She chortled with glee, thrilled her tenaciousness had paid off. She was, in fact, the best damn dog walker in town. But before she could give herself a proverbial pat on the back, her ecstasy slipped down the storm drain.

After about three steps, exhaustion overpowered Henry's will to plod along. The leash ripped out of her hand as the elephantine creature decided not to sit, but to lie completely down. On his side in the middle of the road, tongue resting on the pavement, he looked like a huge pile of roadkill, and he had about the same energy as one.

"Unbelievable," Amelia announced.

But when you were a thirty-two-year-old dog walker/smoothie manager/book restocker who had seen so many situations and people, there really wasn't anything unbelievable.

***

"Neville, I'm so sorry," Amelia spouted, crazily dashing through her front door. It was open when she got there, so Neville had obviously let himself in.

Scampering toward the living room, she caught sight of Neville sitting on the sofa, playing on his phone.

He looked up, tried to mask his sheer horror at her appearance, and then stood.

"Honey, it's fine. What happened?" He took inventory of her outfit.

Amelia's holey jeans and tight black tank top were soaked. Sweat and rainwater plastered her hair to her head, and makeup smeared her face and neck.

She was a disaster. As usual.

"It was Henry. He refused to finish his walk. Again. And then it started to rain. I couldn't get him home. I'm so sorry. Oh, my God, I'm an hour late. I should have called. But I forgot my phone was in the car and I couldn't leave Henry and..." The words tumbled out and into one another, word-vomit style. She wanted to cry. Neville stood there in his perfect button-up shirt, his hair expertly spiked. And there she was, looking like a zombie bride from a third-rate horror film.

"Listen, it's fine. I figured you got held up. Why don't you just go get ready and then we'll go?"

"Did you make reservations?" Amelia implored, knowing he had. When Neville was involved, they *always* had reservations.

"Yeah, but we can change it up. No big deal. We'll be spontaneous." He leaned in to kiss her through her makeup meltdown.

"Neville, even the way you said the word spontaneous tells me everything. This is killing you, isn't it?"

He blushed. "You know me so well, don't you?"

Neville was a planner by nature, an obsessive plotter

by choice. His life was perfectly in order, from his job at a pharmaceutical company to his collection of exactly ten ties—one for each day of the week, one for formal presentations, one for funerals, and one for weddings. He was the definition of opposites attract for Amelia. In fact, her first thought when she'd seen him for the first time six months ago at Book World was, *Adorable, but I'm totally not his type. Too serious.*

Through a search for some Emerson and a marketing book, however, their conversation had struck them both at the core. There was an undeniable something, and it was more than just an appreciation for his awesome hair or her charmingly girl-next-door looks. There was palpable, insatiable chemistry, and eventually chemistry blossomed into something with a little more depth.

"I'll be right back," Amelia promised, leaning in to kiss him on the cheek one more time. He turned to her, catching her lips in his. Their kiss intensified, electrified, his hands grasping her hips and pulling her against him.

"We should go, I've already ruined our plans," she whispered against his lips, his hands now latching on to her shirt. "And I'm a sweaty mess."

Neville didn't seem to notice, didn't stop to acknowledge her words. He just kept kissing, and she kept kissing right back.

Before she could change her mind, before she could argue women with matted black hair didn't do this sort of thing, they were in her tiny bedroom—thank goodness it wasn't in its typical, apocalyptically messy state.

Somewhere between some more heavy kissing and the moment she actually ended up in the shower, Amelia thought to herself that at least one area of her life was going right, dog disasters, messy hair, and all.

***

"Water with lemon for me," Neville said as he peered over the menu.

Their spontaneous dinner date, once they got around to actually attending it, ended up being Darla's, a diner down the street from Amelia's apartment. Not quite the wild, spunky place she had hoped spontaneous would mean, but perfect just the same.

Her hair was still somewhat messy, but at least it was clean. She had tossed on a black-and-white dress, simple and chic; it made her feel like she was playing dress up. But she knew with a guy like Neville, she had to dress up just a bit more, had to trade in the holey jeans for more respectable wear once in a while.

"Iced tea," she said when Penny, the waitress, looked at her. She could be imagining it, but it felt like Penny could see Neville and Amelia's intimacy written on Amelia's face. Amelia glowed from their pre-date activity. And she also could be imagining the scowl on Penny's face, but Amelia didn't think she was. Amelia had grown accustomed to the looks over the past few months. Neville and Amelia just didn't look like your picture-perfect couple.

Not that Amelia was trashy or out of Neville's league. Not completely. She had grace, and beauty to her different than Neville's most accepted type. Her shiny black hair gave her a sense of mystery, a sense of darkness, maybe even a sense of punk because of the way she wore it, slightly disheveled and textured. Her raven-black eyeliner, a staple since junior high, only accentuated her edgy looks. And of course, the tattoo, bold and brazen, weaved its way down her arm and around her wrist.

She knew at thirty-two, she should probably try to "class it up" a bit.

"Amelia, you're never going to find the right man if you don't present yourself better. You look like you're trying to be in a rock band or worse," Annie had pleaded with her a few months ago.

"Wow, thanks Mom. I can only imagine what 'or worse' means. I won't even ask."

But Amelia liked her style, she liked who she was. She wasn't worried about attracting the right man. She knew he wouldn't care if she wore holey jeans instead of trouser jeans. He would deem her somewhat frizzy hair and intense eyeliner sexy, not emo.

She'd been right, because, miracle of miracles, Neville had seen something in her.

This didn't stop the stares though. Amelia certainly clashed with Neville's stoic, perfectly pressed shirts and ties. Not a hair was ever out of place. There certainly weren't any tattoos to speak of. He was perfectly professional in his looks and mannerisms. He was punctual, reliable, the kind of man a mother would trust leaving her two-year-old with for a second while she ran back to her car for her wallet. He just exuded responsibility and maturity.

Naturally, her mother loved him. "Amelia, he's amazing. How did you snag such a keeper?" she had asked after meeting him at dinner for the first time.

"Wow, Mom, so complimentary." Amelia smiled in spite of herself and her mom's verging-on-rude behavior.

Six months in, and things were still great. And not just physically. She could picture a life with Neville—a solid, calm, reliable life. A white-picket-fence, stainless-steel-dishwasher, linen-napkins, laundry-on-Sundays kind of life. Looking across the table now as Neville browsed the greasy choices, she smiled at him. He was responsible, respectful, and everything she could ask for in a man.

But deep down, churning well beyond the surface, hiding behind the afterglow of sex and her checklist of attributes, something stirred in Amelia. If she took the time to look beyond the physical attraction and the connection, if she looked deeper into her future life with Neville, she would see something particularly horrifying for a girl like her—she would see boredom.

At thirty-two, with her biological clock secretly ticking within her, though, she had fooled herself into thinking it was just what growing up was all about.

Chapter Eight

Amelia

"Oh my, Bridget, will you just look at this. Isn't my granddaughter talented? Honey, you should sell these. You really should."

Charlotte held a neon-yellow-and-turquoise necklace up to her shirt, admiring the beautiful beads and charms. It was a bit flashy compared to her typical taste, but she did really seem to like it.

"I knew you'd love it," Amelia added, truly happy to be making Charlotte's day.

"Honey, did you really make that yourself?" Bridget asked. They were all three sitting on the benches at the front of Wildflower, basking in the soft rays over cups of dark roast.

"Yeah, it's just something I like to do in my spare time. I can make you one too, if you'd like."

"Really? Can you make it hot pink? I have a gorgeous hot pink hat that would look lovely with a new necklace." Bridget's eyes lit up.

"You've got it."

"Well, I'm a bit toasty. Do you want to come in, Amelia? I have these delicious little scones Bridget's daughter bought for me. Plus, it's almost time for Owen to come."

"Who's Owen?"

"Didn't your mom tell you? She has this ridiculous notion I need a personal-care aide to check on me every day because I couldn't find my pills the other day." Charlotte waved her hand as if she were waving away a gnat.

Amelia grimaced to herself. She'd heard the pill story from her mom, had heard her question the need for someone to check on Charlotte. Amelia personally thought it was a bit over-the-top. Charlotte seemed fine, seemed perfectly with it. Hell, she was probably sharper than Annie or Amelia at times. But Annie was convinced Charlotte needed someone to monitor her more regularly. Amelia just didn't know someone had been officially secured.

"So has the aide been coming for a while now?"

"Just a few days. I think it's absurd. But, if I have to have someone check on me, Owen's not a bad choice. Wait until you meet him, Amelia. He's *fantastic*. And absolutely adorable, right, Bridget?" Charlotte winked.

"Yes. All the women have been eyeing him up. He sort of looks like Adam Ravine you girls all talk about."

"You mean Adam Levine?" Amelia asked, laughing at Charlotte and Bridget talking like high school girls.

"The cute tattooed guy with a tight behind? Adam Ravine, Adam Levine, whatever," Bridget replied, causing Amelia to laugh even more.

"Well, regardless of his behind, I would like to meet this guy. I want to check him out."

"Oh, you will be checking him out, I assure you."

"Grandma, not like that." Amelia cringed at her own stupid remark. "I want to make sure he isn't a creepo or something."

"Honey, at my age, I don't really worry too much about creepos. Besides, if he is one, I'm fine with it. He'd be a fine last sight before I got murdered by an axe." Charlotte rose from her seat.

"Grandma, you're ridiculous." Amelia headed to punch in the door code for Bridget and Charlotte to enter. The three ladies sauntered through Wildflower's entrance hallway and made a sharp left to head to the apartment.

"Do you want to come in for some scones, Bridget?" Charlotte asked when they arrived at her door.

"Why, I guess a few wouldn't hurt."

Amelia suspected she just wanted to eye up the man candy the women were obsessed with. Amelia had to admit, curiosity plagued her. After all, she wondered what looked like a gorgeous guy to someone in their eighties.

Not that she was interested. She was with Neville. This guy could *be* the real Adam Levine, and she wouldn't be interested.

The three sat around Charlotte's tiny kitchen table

as she served some scones and brewed more coffee. And then came the knock on the door.

"Coming," Charlotte sang, practically leaping out of her seat. Amelia laughed to herself as Charlotte fluffed her hair and smoothed out her blouse self-consciously. Some things never changed with age.

"Hey, Owen. How are you? My friend Bridget and I are just having some delicious scones. Come in, come in. There's someone I want you to meet."

Amelia glanced to the doorway as her grandma ushered in Owen.

The older women weren't kidding.

He was a dead ringer for her favorite singer—the hair, dark eyes, tattoos. And especially the tight body. Amelia's heart inadvertently fluttered, her chest suddenly twinging with the familiar dropping sensation. She just couldn't help it; there was something about a man with tattoos that spoke to her. She hoped she wasn't blushing but was pretty sure she was. Bridget kicked her under the table and then she raised her eyebrows as if to say, "See, we told you."

Amelia gave her a *play it cool* warning look and then smirked neutrally at Owen.

"Owen, meet Amelia, my gorgeous granddaughter. Look, she made me this necklace," Charlotte said. "And she has three jobs. Isn't she just lovely?" Charlotte's intentions were more than overt. Amelia would have to yell at her once Owen left for her ridiculous matchmaking attempts.

Owen looked at Amelia. No, that wasn't right. He didn't just look at Amelia, he drank her in, perusing her from across the room. He didn't flicker his eyes or avert them. He peered straight at her, straight into her. It almost made her feel uncomfortable. He was forward, direct, and purposeful with his gaze. The only thing softening it was his perfect light grin, which showcased the hint of stunningly placed dimples.

"Hi Amelia, I'm Owen." He reached for her hand.

When she shook it, she couldn't help but think of what perfect, manly hands he had. Slightly rough, bigger than hers, and strong. They were man's hands, which had probably worked on motorcycles and helped build things. Not the hands of a desk man. His hand gripped hers in a way that reminded her of strength. Her chest pulsed again. She was now certain she was blushing.

"Oh, did I mention she's available?" Charlotte winked, and Amelia gave her a look like she wanted to stab her.

"Grandma, that's not true. I'm dating someone. Not that you were considering… I mean, not that it matters...," she fumbled, looking from Charlotte to Owen. This was becoming weird.

"Well that's too bad," Owen muttered, a crooked smirk qualifying his appearance as boyish. "Now Charlotte, how about we take a look at those meds and you can tell me more about Amelia." He turned to the woman as if clients pimping their granddaughters were a normal thing.

"Right this way. And she *is* available. She just doesn't realize it. That Neville's a real bore," Charlotte whispered loudly enough for Amelia to hear as she led Owen toward her medications. Amelia couldn't help it, she rolled her eyes like a fourteen-year-old.

While Owen helped Charlotte verify her meds, Amelia raged to Bridget. "Can you believe her? This is absurd. Telling him I'm available when first of all, I doubt he cares, and second, I'm with Neville."

Bridget chuckled, reaching over to pat Amelia's leg. "Honey, when a man looks at you the way that man just did, trust me, he cares. I could feel the heat between you two from over here." She pretended to fan herself. Amelia was a little bit grossed out. "And second, Charlotte means well for you. She just worries about you. She worries Neville will end up boring you."

At the statement, Amelia recognized a word she had been trying to push down, trying to push away. The mere mention of it caused something to surface in her. It wasn't awareness. No, it was the thing that usually comes before self-recognition—fury.

She grew angry. Who were these women to tell her Neville was dull? They barely knew him. And why did Charlotte think this tattooed aide was for her? He was probably a creepo. Look at the way he looked at her. Look at him acting all unprofessional. Was he even working for a real agency? Who did he think he was, stomping in here, making eyes at her? It wasn't her mom's fault; Annie was just really overwhelmed with everything. So

Amelia would have to take charge, take the reins.

She stomped back toward Charlotte's bedroom where Owen helped her with her meds.

"Excuse me," Amelia demanded, arms crossed. "Can I talk to you, please?" She directed her words at Owen. Charlotte looked up, shocked but also grinning a bit.

"Well, absolutely," he said with a touch of egotism Amelia found infuriating. "What is it?"

"Well, where is your ID badge, Owen? How do we know you're legit?"

"Amelia, it's fine." Charlotte interrupted, exuding disappointment at Amelia. "Where are your manners?"

"Well, Grandma, you might be fooled by his charm, but I'm not going to let you get taken advantage of by some creepo. I want proof. If you're coming in here every day with my grandma, I need to know you're for real."

Owen grinned, his stance becoming more determined. "Did you just say creepo?" One eyebrow perked up slightly, and his dimples were again revealed.

"Yes, I did. Creepo. As in creeptastic, serial killer, or worse."

"Worse? What's worse than a serial killer?" He paused in sorting the pills. Charlotte actually had the nerve to laugh.

Amelia seethed, a tight feeling balling up in her chest. "I don't know who you think you are, but you're working for us. And I won't have this unprofessional behavior." She pointed violently like a teacher chiding a class of young children. It wasn't like her. Something about him got to her.

"Amelia, your mother contacted him. It's not like he showed up begging for work. Owen comes highly recommended. In fact, his own grandmother, Marla, lives down the hall. Why are you behaving like this? I know you're just looking out for me, but honestly, it's fine. He's a good guy. Really."

"Marla?" Amelia asked, now feeling sheepishly stupid.

"Yeah, Marla's my grandma. She actually got me this job because my boss saw how well I interacted with her and those at her dining table. Look, I get it, I'm sorry I teased you. I worry about my grandma, too. I would be suspicious if some stud showed up with tattoos and was supposed to be taking care of her. I get it."

"It's not the tattoos, obviously." Amelia motioned to her own visible tattoo.

"So is it because I'm a stud then?"

Amelia rolled her eyes. "You're incorrigible." She felt her mood lighten slightly.

"And you use words like incorrigible, too? How do you go from creepo to incorrigible?"

"What's that supposed to mean? Do I look unintelligent?"

"No, not at all. It's just I've never heard anyone under the age of sixty use 'incorrigible.'"

Charlotte stood back, silent, beaming from ear to ear

at their banter.

"Oh, young love," she murmured loudly enough for them to hear. Owen just grinned knowingly, and Amelia gasped.

"*Grandma!*"

"Deny it all you want, honey, but I knew from the second Owen came into my apartment a few days ago he belonged with you. You'll see it too, someday."

"Must you be so forward? We're both standing here!"

"At my age, I only have time to be forward. What's the point in poking around? Now let's finish these meds so we can get back to our scones." She acted as if she had commented on the weather instead of trying to convince the two they were in love. Owen glanced at Amelia, his eyes warm and inviting. He looked like he wanted to say something but just shrugged and went back to the medicine.

Amelia stomped out of the room shaking her head.

Bridget had downed two scones and now nibbled on the third, crumbs resting on her chin

"Oh, I'm so glad I came." She giggled through a mouthful of the delicious snack.

Amelia let out a huge breath of tension. There was no use trying. She grabbed a scone and shoved it in her mouth, all attempts at ladylike politeness overtaken by a vile rage burning in her chest.

"At this point, boredom looks delicious," she said to herself, crumbs falling onto the table.

"Oh, there's something delicious in here, all right, but it isn't boredom," Charlotte yelled. The woman might be old, but she still had good hearing. And a penchant for stirring things up.

Chapter Nine

Charlotte
December

It's true what they say about life speeding up as you age. Before Charlotte knew it, the leaves at Wildflower had blown away, replaced by snow. Christmas lights replaced scarecrows in the front entrance, and gone were the days of sitting on the bench drinking coffee. Instead, Bridget and Charlotte moved their morning sessions to the fireplace in the community room, where their friendship continued to blossom into one with depth.

Some things, though, didn't change. Charlotte continued to worry about Annie. The girl—she would always be a girl to Charlotte—looked run-down, and Charlotte couldn't help but feel guilty. She knew Charlotte's situation wasn't helping Annie at a difficult time in her life. The Dave fiasco wasn't easy; add to that Charlotte's ordeals and the flighty Amelia's wandering, and no wonder Annie looked shattered. Charlotte wished she would get out there, would find herself again. She wished Annie could see what she saw—fifty wasn't the end of one's life. She was still young.

Things with Catherine also stayed the same. The hoity woman continued to attack Charlotte every chance she got. There were the verbal jabs in the hallway, the constant complaining about Charlotte having her TV up too loud, the whining that Charlotte took too many cookies at the pre-Thanksgiving breakfast party. Charlotte knew she should rise above and ignore her, but it was just so dang hard. It didn't help that the people at Wildflower worshipped the ground Catherine strutted on with her bejeweled designer shoes. She was a goddess around there. A wise woman knew not to tick off the goddess of the kingdom, but Charlotte was too old to play by all the rules. She was sick of Catherine running the place and of her arrogance.

So Charlotte fought back.

There were small ways to undermine the mighty. Charlotte sweetened up the exercise instructor for starters, making homemade gluten-free, sugar-free—essentially chalk—cookies for the health-nut instructor. Suddenly, the instructor exulted Charlotte's impressive mambo in every class. Check one on the destroy-Catherine list.

Others were harder to sway, but sway she did. When Catherine was being witchy to Gilda, a woman at Catherine's inner-circle table, Charlotte stepped in.

"Here, dear, you can have my cookie. I don't need the calories anyway," Charlotte had offered with a sweet smile when Gilda got in trouble for eating two cookies instead of just one at the mission meeting.

The efforts made Charlotte feel better, and made Bridget smile, but they weren't quite enough. Something bigger had to be done, something to put the woman in her place.

She would not let Catherine become another Johanna in her life. No way.

***

"Ms. Noel, it's great to see you," the stiff-collared man offered as he reached to shake Charlotte's hand. Charlotte couldn't remember the last time she had given a handshake.

"Hello, Neville, great to see you. Amelia!" Charlotte swiped through the handshake to get to her granddaughter and give her a hug. "Don't you look beautiful in that." Amelia wore a hot-pink fitted dress complete with knee-high stiletto boots, her hair slicked into a tidy bun. Charlotte thought she looked a little librarian-esque, but she didn't want to say it. Amelia always looked beautiful to her. Today, she just looked a little less like Amelia.

"Thanks, Grandma. Do you have time for a visit? Sorry we didn't call first." Amelia pulled back from the hug and wandered in.

Charlotte waved her hand in an 'are you kidding me' gesture, ushered the couple to the table, and went to dig out her scones.

"Coffee, darling?" Charlotte motioned toward Neville.

"Do you have decaf?" His blue eyes sparkled as his

baby-smooth face formed into a perfectly symmetrical grin. He was cute. She could see what Amelia saw in him. But he was cute in an 'I always set my dinner table properly' and 'I only drink decaf' kind of way.

Amelia did not need a decaf man, Charlotte knew.

But Charlotte kept her mouth shut. Over the past few months, she'd tried her best to make magic happen between Amelia and Owen. She would invite Amelia over, timed perfectly for when Owen would be there. She would concoct a plan with Marla to make sure Owen was over when Amelia would be taking her to lunch. The four of them had enjoyed a few lunches and even a dinner at Wildflower together, but darn Amelia was too stubborn to see what was right in front of her.

Owen would be magic to Amelia's life. He would mesh with the spark she had, he would drift right along with her through her semi-chaotic, unorganized life. He had a wonderful sense of humor, was super respectful, and was just thrilling.

Charlotte could see the way Owen looked at Amelia, like he would take a bullet for her. Amelia, however, pretended not to notice. Once in a while during their encounters, Charlotte caught a wayward glance, a hint of color rising in Amelia's cheeks. But then the girl would turn the conversation to Neville and it was done.

Charlotte would have to let Amelia come to her realization on her own. It was plain as day—Amelia's body language said it all. Neville bored her. This guy would present her a life of dishes and laundry, of stuffy dinners and perfect pecks on the cheek. This guy would offer her a life of hot-pink dresses and pantyhose when all she really wanted was to walk in the park with a pair of cutoffs and a T-shirt. Charlotte knew Neville, knew him at the core. He was a good guy. He could give Amelia a comfortable life. There would even be love between them. But it wouldn't be the wildly enthralling love Amelia deserved, the love that awakened you to life in ways you didn't think possible. Charlotte knew all of that without even saying a word, without really talking to Neville one-on-one. She knew this because in her heart, she sensed a truth—Neville was just like her late husband, Charlie. The mannerisms, his career, his looks. He screamed Charlie at her.

And as much as Charlotte had loved, adored, Charlie, as much as she missed her life with him, she also knew another truth she had never admitted to herself, not in decades of marriage—Charlie's love was comfortable, but it sure as heck wasn't exciting.

She had a great life, it was true. She'd shared so many years of love with Charlie, and they had albums of memories. They had a beautiful home, a perfect daughter, and so many special moments. She couldn't complain about her life, couldn't regret the years they had together.

However, she also had to be honest in saying her life hadn't completely been the adventure her teenage self had imagined. It hadn't been the living on the edge, zesty ride she'd once craved. With time, those dreams had faded. As she settled into a traditional, predictable life with Charlie, she'd lost touch with the wiry, crazy girl she'd once been.

At eighty-one, she knew it was okay. It was too late for her to go back, to change things. Not that she'd want to anyway. She'd learned a long time ago that regrets and what ifs didn't change anything. All they did was taint your memories, ruin the good ones.

Her choices had been made, and she'd lived the life she was meant to.

But Amelia still had choices ahead of her, still had time to choose the life she would lead.

Charlotte just hoped she would make the right choice, one that would bring her the most out of life. The option that, when Amelia was eighty-one, would be a life worth remembering, a life to tell about from her rocking chair.

A life she would be proud to pass on.

Because now, at this age, Charlotte realized the life you live eventually becomes the story you tell, and she wanted Amelia to have a thrilling one.

***

After assuring Amelia next week would be fine for a shopping trip for Christmas gifts, Charlotte rose to refill coffee cups—digging for another decaf for square boy, as she mentally referred to him. The conversation was good. Calm. Polite. Proper.

Charlotte felt stifled. Worst of all, she could tell by the lines on Amelia's face she was stifled, too. And then it happened.

A doorbell. An escape.

"I'll get it," Amelia shouted, probably relieved to have an out, even if she wouldn't admit it to herself. As Charlotte continued pushing buttons on the coffeemaker, Amelia's voice wavered, almost undetectably.

"Oh, it's you," she said.

"What does that mean? Is that a good 'oh it's you' or a bad one?" a deep sexy voice responded.

Owen.

"Um, it's not time for... Do you want to come in?" Charlotte glanced away from the coffee to see Amelia's flushed face. She peered from Owen to Neville.

"Yeah, I just came to see if your grandma wanted to go to lunch with me and my grandma. We're going to Johnny D's today." Owen paused to take inventory of the table. His eyes landed on Neville, and something in his face fell a bit.

"Hi, you must be Neville?" He stood with his hands in his pockets. No handshake from Owen. Not his style.

"Yes, hello, and you are?" Neville stood, leaning forward with a hand outstretched. Charlotte couldn't be too harsh on him; it was probably a habit from his job as a sales rep.

"Owen. I'm Charlotte's personal-care aide." He awkwardly reached for Neville's hand. Charlotte couldn't help but notice the muscles rippling in his arm as he did, which made Neville pale in comparison—a short, scrawny fellow at best.

"Oh, Owen, you're more than that. This, Neville,

is a dear friend. His grandma and I are dinner pals," Charlotte added, wanting to see if she could stir things up a bit. If this Neville really liked Amelia as much as he claimed, she wanted to see if jealousy factored into the equation.

Neville nodded in acknowledgement of the statement, glancing at Amelia for confirmation. Amelia just smiled. She tapped her left foot unintentionally.

"I didn't realize you had company, Char. Sorry for interrupting," Owen tossed out as an afterthought.

"Don't be ridiculous. You know I love Johnny D's potato soup. Amelia? Neville? What do you say? Can you do lunch?"

"I would love to, but I have a meeting with a client in an hour. But Amelia, why don't you go?" Charlotte didn't detect any jealousy. Neville was apparently confident in himself, in his relationship. Or, at the very least, he didn't really see Owen as any sort of threat.

"Do you have to go? You have so many meetings." Amelia walked toward Neville and wrapped her arms around him casually. Owen turned away.

"I'm sorry, honey. It's an important client."

Amelia's disappointment was on her face. Neville certainly seemed to work a lot, but Charlotte couldn't hold that against him, too. At least not completely.

"Sorry, babe. Rain check?" Before Amelia could answer, Neville planted what was definitely not a platonic kiss on Amelia, and Amelia definitely kissed back. Okay, so maybe some chemistry bubbled between the two.

Or a lot.

Neville pulled away, and turned, arm still around Amelia, to Charlotte. "It was great seeing you. We'll have to come back again and do lunch." And then Neville did something shocking. He leaned in and hugged Charlotte. *Okay, he's playing it up a bit, asserting his manhood, asserting his ownership of Amelia and her family,* Charlotte thought as he squeezed her. *And maybe he isn't as scrawny as I initially determined.* He had a firm lock on her.

Neville turned back to Amelia. Another kiss on the cheek genuinely lit up Amelia's face. She did love Neville. She really did, decaf and all. Charlotte couldn't deny it, even if she wanted to.

Charlotte had been in her shoes before. She knew the pull of comfortable love over zany, zesty love. Heck, she had chosen it. It had worked for her. She had formed a beautiful life with Charlie.

But Charlotte knew as similar as she was to Amelia, as much as she could relate, there was even more spirit in the girl. This dog-walking, music-loving girl needed something more than a Cape Cod and a Labrador retriever. She needed thrill, she needed pizazz. And most of all, she needed the right guy to share it with.

As Charlotte and Amelia followed Owen down the hall to pick up Marla, Charlotte knew the answer to Amelia's life was right in front of her. A tattooed, rocking, gorgeous guy named Owen. A guy who understood Amelia without even fully knowing her. A guy who would create a sensational, enviable life with Amelia, but also give her the stability and loyalty she needed.

Charlotte was convinced all Amelia needed to do was to open those beautiful eyes of hers, dark eyeliner and all.

***

Charlotte didn't know if Marla was aware of the matchmaking conspiracy she was planning or not, but she played into the plot well. Like any proud grandma, Marla couldn't stop selling her grandson over Johnny D's soup, salad, and burgers—Owen and Amelia had the burgers. Their young stomachs could metabolize them.

"Owen, did you tell Amelia your exciting news?" Marla asked after blowing on her tomato soup.

Owen looked a little sheepish. "No, Grandma. It's not that exciting."

"Stop being modest. Owen's band is going to be playing a gig at Café Couture next month. Isn't that fabulous? I can't wait to get a latte and just listen to him rock it out." The words sounded odd coming from an older woman wearing a gummy-waisted, mint-green pantsuit.

"Are you part of a band?"

"Yeah, it's small. No Fallout Boy or anything. We've been kicking around songs for about five years now." He peered down at his meal and then back at her. Charlotte noticed the electrifying stare and smiled.

"Well, Amelia here has always wanted to be a songwriter, isn't that right?" Charlotte added in, not very smoothly. After the visit with Neville, she was overplaying it.

"Grandma, it's a pipe dream. Nothing I'm serious about."

"I'd love to see some things you've written."

"They're not very good."

"Let me be the judge of that. After all, I am a pretty big deal in the music world. Café Couture? Next stop the Grammys," Owen teased, and Amelia couldn't help but laugh.

Marla looked across the table at Charlotte and gave her a conspiratorial wink. So she had been thinking the same thing. Why did love become so crystal clear at their age but remained so murky at Amelia's? Was it just life experience that provided a doorway into the crazy dimensions of love? It was one of life's mysteries.

From that point on, a window opened between the two. Conversation flowed smoothly about musicians, their careers, and their histories. Owen opened up about how he ended up as a personal-care aide, revealing the dramatic details of his parents' deaths and how he had to care for his younger sister.

"So you put college on hold for Janie? That's so admirable." Amelia was obviously touched as he revealed the details of the boating accident that had happened his senior year of high school.

"Not admirable. Necessary. I couldn't let her life be shattered more than it was. I wanted her to live in the same house, to go to the same school. She had four years of high school left, and I knew what I had to do. I couldn't go away, not with all of that happening. So I pushed the music degree aside and took a job at a construction company."

"Did she go to college?" Charlotte chimed in.

"Yeah, she earned a full scholarship to Yale. She's in med school now."

Marla smiled. "Such a beautiful thing you did for her. If it hadn't been for you, she'd have never made it."

"So what about your degree? Didn't you decide to go back?" Amelia asked.

Owen shook his head, not looking regretful like one would think. "Nah, by the time I could have, I figured out a college degree doesn't equate to happiness or success. I decided to just keep at the workforce. I stayed with the construction business for a while, but I felt like I wasn't really doing anything. Grandma ended up coming here at the time, and I saw some terrible personal-care aides working their way through. I was always at Wildflower helping out, and I enjoyed working with the people. I liked feeling like I could bring something to their day. So one day, the boss of the personal-care aides was there. I got to talking with her, and that was that. Career change."

Amelia nodded, understanding on her face. She too had come to the conclusion college wasn't equivalent to success; for her, though, it had come after a degree, Charlotte knew.

"And we're so glad you made that choice. You're wonderful," Charlotte added, truly meaning it.

"Thanks. I love it. Plus, it gives me time to work with the band since I'm free in the evenings."

"I'd like to see you play sometime," Amelia added.

Yes, Charlotte thought. *Success.*

"Well, I think tickets might be sold out for Café Couture," Owen said.

"Really?" Marla asked, worried.

Owen grinned and shook his head. "Yeah, I mean, we're a big deal, I told you. But I think I may be able to get you ladies some VIP seats, if you want."

"Yes, please," Charlotte and Marla said in unison. Amelia also nodded.

"So what's your band's name?"

"The Truth."

"Really?" Amelia grimaced.

"What's wrong with it?"

"Nothing. It's... different." She smirked.

The two laughed, and Charlotte saw the start of something wonderful unfolding over some burgers, some potato soup, and some insights into this handsome and admirable man. By Amelia's body language, Charlotte thought Amelia was starting to see it too.

***

Later that evening, Charlotte decided to go down to the fireplace and have some tea. Bridget was already asleep, and lights were out at Wildflower. That was okay... she wanted some time to bask in the solitude.

It had been a successful day, with the lunch going well. She thought maybe Amelia was starting to have a revelation, but Charlotte knew it would take time. Amelia needed to discover things on her own. The two needed to get to know each other, take it slow. There would be plenty of time to live in the fast lane.

As she stirred in her thoughts and sipped her tea, a trusty *click clack* announced the arrival of another resident. Turning in the oversized chair she had plopped in, she looked up to see a familiar face.

Leonard.

They hadn't talked much since the first day. He lived on the second floor, which in Wildflower may as well have been across the nation. She didn't like to think of herself as old, but she could admit mobility was no one's strong suit at Wildflower. She saw Leonard at events and dinners, but just never got around to talking to him. She had noticed him from afar, but something kept her from pursuing a conversation. There had been trivial "hellos" and discussions about the weather, but she always felt herself pulling back. Something about him made her nervous, made her cling to an exit strategy when he was around. It wasn't because she didn't like him. No, in truth, it was because she liked him too much. There was something about him, something inviting that made Charlotte turn the other way. It made no sense, but then again, as Charlotte knew by now, few things did in life.

Now here he was. There was no exit strategy, and Charlotte was too relaxed to feign one. He came and sat beside her.

"Mind if I join you?" he asked, a quiet tone to his voice.

Charlotte smiled at him and shook her head, reaching for another sip of tea. They lounged in silence for several minutes, both relaxing before the flames in the serenity of the night.

"So you like it here?" Charlotte finally asked, breaking the silence. She couldn't help it; she was a talker by nature.

Leonard noncommittally shrugged. "It's nice. The people are great. But it's hard, you know? It's just not home yet, I guess." A sadness enveloped him, a sinking sadness swallowing him up from the core. Charlotte knew sadness firsthand. Sometimes it still crept in for her, too, behind her smile and sunshine yellow.

"I understand. My first few weeks here were terrible. I missed my house, my life, my independence. I missed Butternut and Peter and the others. I just felt sad, too, like this was it. The final chapter. And to be honest, it felt depressing that Wildflower would be my last adventure. I mean, it's nice and all, but it still feels like..."

"A nursing home." Leonard finished her sentence. "Or maybe even a coffin."

She gazed at him then, locking eyes and recognizing his understanding. She experienced a peace that came from knowing another human being felt as she did, could get where her mindset was. Her chest rose and fell with the intake of air she hadn't sensed in a long time. Her lungs felt refreshed, her heart felt at ease. Life seemed just a smidge brighter with the revelation she was honestly not alone.

Leonard continued the conversation. "Yeah, it's been hard ever since Lila passed. It just hasn't been the same. And then there was the sadness of the empty years. Walking the hallways where we had kissed and laughed. Sitting in the living room where we used to watch reruns on television. It was just all there. I thought that was the worst it could get. Little did I know," he added, his eyes drifting to another place, another time.

"When did your wife die?" Charlotte asked. She knew it was an okay question. She knew from her experience with Charlie it was worse to have people tiptoe around the death than to just come out and ask.

"Three years ago. But it still feels like I got the call yesterday." He paused. "Heart attack. A stupid heart attack took her, the love of my life."

Without knowing why, Charlotte instinctually reached across to grab his hand. He looked up at her, smiling. It was a warm gesture, one of friendship.

"That's what took my Charlie," Charlotte admitted. It felt strange to say his name out loud. It made Annie uncomfortable, so she tried not to talk about it.

"Was he your husband?"

She nodded. "Sixty-two years."

"Lila and I had forty-eight."

Another bout of silence punctuated the conversation before Leonard turned to her. "So if Charlie is your husband, who the heck is Peter? And Butternut?"

"Oh, my babies. Well, more like my cats. I have five. I *had* five. But now they're with my daughter. Which is okay. I mean, I miss them, but she needs them in her life."

Leonard raised an eyebrow. "Five? She needs five cats in her life?"

Charlotte grumbled, a playfully scolding look on her face, "And what is wrong with five? Don't tell me you're a cat hater, because if you are, I think this has to end."

Leonard's eyes glimmered. "And what is this?" he motioned between them. Charlotte felt heat in her cheeks. This was getting odd. She quickly shook it off.

"Um, you know, acquaintanceship?"

Leonard smirked. "Acquaintanceship? Can we at least bump it to friendship now? I mean, you did share with me about your hoard of cats and we talked about our spouses. That must count for something."

"Five cats is not a hoard. It's a family. You make it sound so ugly."

"If you say so. Did you say one's name is Butternut?"

"Yes. He's my favorite."

"How does one come to name a cat Butternut?" Leonard pushed.

"Well, he loved butternut squash. So obviously it was a perfect name," she added.

Leonard looked at her, probably waiting for her to start laughing. But when her face remained serious, he just shook his head and grinned.

"Okay. Makes sense, I guess." He shrugged. "Now let's talk about something that's not depressing and not cats. Not that I don't like cats. I just think maybe we can work on solidifying this friendship. Tell me about your life. Tell me something." He faced her now, the glow of the fire reflecting in his eyes. Charlotte let out a breath. And then she started talking.

Leonard and Charlotte spent the next two hours—minus a pee break—talking about kids, family, careers, the 1950s, and everything in between. They talked about memories, skydiving, and trips to Hawaii. They chatted about food, they spoke about pets and getting old. They talked as if there were nothing between them, no wall that typically constructed itself between people getting to know each other. Charlotte found once she started talking to Leonard, she couldn't stop. So, over a fire and a drained cup of tea, a friendship formed, one Charlotte hadn't expected.

Chapter Ten

The rest of the week passed quickly for Charlotte. There were Christmas carolers, a cookie-baking exchange, and a gift-wrapping night to pass the time. To her surprise, her nightly conversations with Leonard continued, sometimes with Bridget in tow. The three of them sipped their beverages, sat by the fire, and shared in laughter and discussion. Leonard was easy to talk to, an exuberant storyteller and listener. Charlotte imagined in his prime, he was a gorgeous man, whom the ladies swooned over. Even in his eighties, he had held up pretty well, she had to admit.

Leonard had been a bit of a wild child in his day, from what she gathered. Skydiving, a stint in the Navy for a few years, and even some bull riding were all parts of his early adult life. After getting out of the Navy, he had actually earned his pilot license and flown commercially. He and Lila had seen plenty of the world, had two sons, and eventually retired to a beach house on the Eastern coast.

It sounded like a life of excitement, Charlotte thought. A life quite different from the mundane, suburban life she had built with Charlie. Not that it was a bad thing, she scolded herself.

Leonard, though, was exhilarating. He had stories to tell, he had memories to share. Charlotte couldn't help but think her life had paled in comparison. But it was too late to fix it now, right? She had made her choices, lived out her life. And now, as things were waning, she had to be satisfied. No point in regretting anything.

On Friday, Cassie arranged a special treat for the residents of Wildflower. She had planned a field trip of sorts, a trip to the bowling alley.

"What, does she hope we all break our hips and end up in the nursing home?" Marla complained. A foot of snow coated the ground, and one risked falling even taking the trip from the door to the bus ramp.

"Oh, Marla, it will be fun," Charlotte screamed into her ear. The woman still just nodded nonchalantly as if she hadn't really heard her.

After settling Marla in, Charlotte took a seat. She beamed when Leonard got on the bus, his trusty cane leading him down the aisle toward her.

"So are you a bowling queen?" he asked, taking a seat next to her.

"I'm not bad, you?"

"Never was much for bowling, but when I did, I usually won."

"Well, well, aren't we full of ourselves." Charlotte grinned.

"Just telling it like it is." He winked at her.

"So, if you're such a pro, do you think you could humble yourself to have someone like me on your team? Or are you interviewing for teammate positions?"

"Well, you are up against pretty stiff competition, but I guess if you really want, since you're so pretty and all, I'll let you be on my team."

"Oh stop. I'm a bag of saggy skin and bones. If pretty is a qualification to be on your team, you better look around. I'm past those days."

He looked at her seriously now. "I disagree. I see a gorgeous woman sitting beside me." And with that, he turned to face the front as the bus edged forward, Charlotte unavoidably smirking a bit at his flirtatious comment—even if she didn't quite believe it.

Cassie animatedly attempted to get everyone's attention at the front of the bus, waving her arms like a preschool teacher would. Charlotte couldn't help but notice Catherine, wearing skintight leopard leggings and a shimmery silver shirt, perched in the front seat with one of her cronies.

Teacher's pet, Charlotte thought. *And who wears pants like those in her eighties?*

Catherine, of course.

"Hello, everyone. I'm so glad you all came on this wonderful trip," Cassie exulted, her mouth in such a painfully wide smile Charlotte grimaced.

Cassie continued talking right through her smile, her face unmoving as if she'd just had Botox. Charlotte knew better, though. The girl was high on life. She didn't need any enhancements to make her any peppier.

"When we get to the bowling alley, pick up your shoes and a ball. We will be playing in teams of four. To make things easier and make sure everyone has a team, dear Catherine agreed to help me out and make up team lists. I've got them right here. Once you get settled in, come check with me to find your team and the team you will be playing against. This is going to be so much fun. Aren't you all excited?"

No one made a peep despite Cassie's attempt at rallying the troops.

Charlotte glanced around to see if anyone else found Catherine's list making a bit dictator-like. Most of the people seemed to be glancing off into the distance, ignoring Cassie altogether. Charlotte huffed in outrage.

"Excuse me, Cassie, but can't we pick our own teams? We're not in high school, after all. I think we're all adults here," she inquired.

"Charlotte, honey, you're right, we are all adults. So I don't think we will mind being on a team with someone we don't talk to," Catherine interjected, painting on a sweet smile as she looked at Cassie with an *I've got your back* kind of look.

"She's right, Charlotte. And remember, we don't have any cliques here at Wildflower. We are all friends." Cassie beamed as if she were on one of those annoying commercials for friendship.

Charlotte sighed. "Right, we're all wonderful friends," she announced, turning to look out the window as she rolled her eyes. She hoped Cassie and Catherine detected her sarcasm.

Leonard chuckled. "Women," he muttered.

"And what is that supposed to mean?"

"You never stop. It's actually a bit entertaining."

"Well, I don't find it funny that she," she pointed wildly, "dictates every move that happens at this place. Cassie is like a dummy government put in place. Catherine is calling all the shots in her ridiculous animal-print pants and furs. I mean, really." Charlotte's words stirred her internal anger even more.

"Listen," Leonard whispered, putting his hand on Charlotte's knee. "You might be right about the dummy part, but I don't think things are so intense at Wildflower we need to use words like government and dictator. It's a quasi-nursing home, for God's sake. And second, you're right, her pants are ridiculous. But why do you let it get to you? She's the one who looks like a fool. She makes you look even more classy than you already are."

She was beginning to think she was right; he probably was a flirt in his day. Remnants of it still existed.

Charlotte sighed. "You're right, you're right. I shouldn't let her get to me. But I've dealt with so many women like her during my life. In high school, in college, even when I was married. We had this neighbor lady, sweet as pie, or at least that was the image she put on around Charlie. She would bring over casseroles, make small talk. And then one day, I overheard her talking to another mom. She was saying I was a terrible, mousey housewife and if she wanted, she could have Charlie in her bed in a heartbeat." Charlotte cringed and seethed, remembering the day she realized what Johanna was all about. "When I told Charlie about it, he laughed it off and said I must have heard her wrong, adding insult to injury."

Leonard looked like he had no clue what to say for a moment, but then chimed in. "Well, I don't care what this woman looked like. If Charlie even entertained the idea of anything with her, he was a fool."

Charlotte averted her eyes, not wanting Leonard to see the pain lingering there. She didn't know why she brought all of this up now. It was so long ago, and Leonard didn't want to hear about it, she was certain. "Well, I'd tell you to tell him that, but he isn't here." She grinned softly to ease the pain. "It's just women like that, they make me so angry. I feel like my whole life I've been just Charlotte, the woman who every other woman thinks she can walk all over. The nice housewife, the plain, mundane girl. Charlie's wife. That's it."

Leonard eased his hand toward hers, giving it a friendly squeeze.

"I'm sorry, I'm sorry." She waved a hand. "We're on our lovely trip and I'm bringing you down," she added.

"Never." He gave her hand another squeeze. "And there's nothing mundane or plain about you, Charlotte.

96

Nothing at all."

Before Charlotte could respond, the bus pulled up to the bowling alley, screeched to a halt, and they started the painstaking task of unloading themselves into the bitter wind.

***

"Another strike. Wow, you're amazing." Catherine swooned as she rubbed Leonard's shoulder. She gave Charlotte a glance. Charlotte swore she winked at her.

Marla turned to Charlotte. "Come on, Charlotte, we need to catch up. We can't let leopard print beat us." Of course, it wasn't a whisper, and the whole bowling alley seemed to turn and see what was happening.

"Don't worry, Marla, leopard print, er, Catherine won't win." She made eye contact with the infuriating woman as she said this, also loud enough for several other surrounding teams to hear.

When they'd arrived at the bowling alley, Charlotte wasn't really surprised to find Catherine had placed Charlotte and Leonard on separate teams. Charlotte had caught Catherine eyeing them up a few days earlier in the community room. Catherine had spies everywhere; she knew everything happening at Wildflower. And she seemed determined to make sure Charlotte wasn't happy. Now Miss Tight Pants flaunted herself as if she were sixteen and not eighty. Leonard, to his credit, focused purely on his game. And he was good. He hadn't lied on the bus.

Charlotte wasn't going to let Catherine win, though,

not this time. But it wasn't going to be easy. Besides Marla, Charlotte was with Ed, a mute man who stooped excessively due to his age, and Marcy, the oldest resident at Wildflower. Leonard and Catherine were with Joseph, who was previously on the Olympic Track team, and Martha, the youngest resident at Wildflower.

Needless to say, Charlotte's team wasn't doing so well.

She might not win the bowling game, but she could win the war. Women like Catherine were all the same, so it would be easy to bring her down.

"Oh Catherine, dear, do you need a break? I wouldn't want to exhaust you at your age and all," Charlotte sweetly asked.

Catherine smirked. "I'm fine if you are. I mean, you are about, what, ten years older than me?"

"Well, I don't know about that, but I know you're about fifty years too old for those pants."

Catherine seethed. Leonard laughed. Catherine seethed some more.

The game went on. Charlotte's team lost. Miserably.

As the last ball rolled down the lane, Catherine cheered. "We did it," she yelled, as if she had won the lottery. After a horrifying victory dance verging on raunchy, Catherine leaped into Leonard's arms, wrapping herself around him. "Celebratory nachos before the next game?" she asked him, pulling back.

Charlotte's heart sank a little. She admitted to herself she did feel threatened by Catherine. Okay, so the pants were too much. But she *was* tight in all the right places—probably surgically, but did it matter?—she had perfectly frosted hair, and she was essentially royalty at Wildflower. If this were high school, she would be head cheerleader and Charlotte would be last chair piccolo. Or tuba. She looked away from the scene, doubting herself for the first time in a long time.

And then she started to wonder why. Why did this matter? Maybe she was the one acting like a sixteen-year-old. She was in her eighties, for God's sake. What, was she really going to have a catfight over Leonard, a man who had lost his wife? Was she expecting an engagement ring out of this? They had only been talking for a few weeks.

But when Leonard pulled back from Catherine and said, "I'm going to go get a slushie instead," and walked over to Charlotte's team, she couldn't help but feel a bit lifted.

"Good game," he offered, reaching for Charlotte's hand. The warmth of it radiated through Charlotte's veins.

For the first time since Charlie had died, she felt something akin to companionship, to connection. Looking over at Catherine as Leonard led her to the snack bar, Charlotte actually felt something else surprising.

She felt sorry for Catherine. The woman gaped at her and Leonard as if she had been hit by a bus, shocked by the fact she wasn't first pick. The woman clearly suffered from insecurity and unhappiness. That should make

Charlotte happy. She had won, after all. Her tan pants and plain blue sweater had overcome Miss Hot Pants and shimmer. But it didn't make her happy. Because beneath the hatred for Catherine, the petty bantering, she felt something else for her.

Pity.

Charlotte turned and gave Catherine a sympathetic grin. "Do you want to come with us?" she offered, not a twinge of sarcasm in her voice. There, she had done the right thing. She had tried to be the bigger person, tried to put petty woman drama behind them. There was no reason they couldn't all get along.

But as she awaited the Kumbaya moment to come, the moment where the three of them skipped off toward the neon lights of the nacho bar, Catherine did something that almost shocked Charlotte right off her feet. Something that reminded Charlotte that being the bigger person didn't always lead to rosy, warm feelings of friendship. Something that proved to Charlotte she was right to wage war with Catherine, she was right to hate her.

Right in front of Charlotte's eyes, distinctly enough for there to be no doubt what she had done, Catherine flipped Charlotte the bird.

"Game on," she mouthed, in case the hand gesture wasn't enough. Charlotte's jaw clamped shut.

So much for putting the drama behind them. Although the bowling game was over, it looked like the real game had just begun.

Chapter Eleven

Annie

Annie felt as though she had melded right into the fabric of the couch, her dingy sweatpants and T-shirt covered in remnants of potato chips and French onion dip. She crinkled the chip bag as she mindlessly reached in for another to shove into her puffy face.

She only grabbed air, her fingers flailing around to find a crumb to satisfy her, her denial ignoring the fact she ate the whole bag.

When her fingers scraped a few worthless, grease-laden crumbs at the bottom, she admitted the harsh truth to herself. She'd devoured the whole thing in one sitting. Desperation creeping in, she turned over the bag to calculate how many calories she had consumed, but then decided it didn't matter. None of it mattered.

Peter, Arya, Alice, Gertrude, and Butternut sat around her, a blanket of fur, as she watched rerun after rerun of *Friends* on Netflix. Usually the cats provided a weird sense of solace she couldn't explain. Today, they just reminded her how sad her life was. She was now the mousey, jobless divorcée who owned five cats and couldn't pay her bills. She was the worn-out fifty-year-old who had eye wrinkles and now a couple of extra pounds on her ass. She was the fifty-year-old with no potential in her life, with no love life in the near or distant future, who was basically a crappy daughter and mother.

She was hopeless.

Her cell phone rang for the tenth time. She decided she may as well answer it, just for the purpose of telling whomever it was to go away and leave her to wallow in peace.

"Hello," she mumbled through snot, her voice cracking from lack of use.

"Mom. I've been so worried. I just got off work at Smoothie Q, and I'm heading over. Grandma told me the bad news, but I want to know what happened."

"No! Amelia, don't. I don't want any company."

"Too bad." She hung up.

So apparently the whole town had heard about the debacle already. Although that was the hazard of small-town life. Someone always knew someone else. There were no secrets. Someone would tell someone who would tell someone, and before you knew it, the whole town knew what a major disaster your life was. And now she would have to defend her actions to her daughter. For years, she'd been on Amelia's case to get it together, to settle down, to sort out her life. Now she guessed it was time to take her own advice. Except where did a fifty-year-old begin with the task when her life was such a royal catastrophe?

Annie pushed the chip crumbs off her along with some rogue clumps of cat hair. She told herself she wasn't going to cry again. She would show Amelia what it looked like to be a strong woman, one who could resurrect herself, who didn't need any man to pull it together.

But when the doorbell rang ten minutes later, Annie felt the tears start to flow again before she even got up off the couch.

Swiping her eyes and trying some deep-breathing techniques—which didn't work—Annie figured she couldn't ignore Amelia forever. She plodded from the couch to the door, tossed it open with reckless abandon, and stared at the floor as she ushered her daughter in.

After a long embrace during which Annie coated Amelia's hair in snot, the two women collapsed onto the couch as the cats scattered.

"Mom, I'm sorry. Tell me what happened." The pity in Amelia's eyes only made Annie feel more ashamed.

Annie sighed and began her woeful tale, shame the dominant emotion at first. As the story continued on, though, it became rage.

***

Annie was never late for work. Not a single day. No matter what happened in her life, her promptness was a constant. She set three alarms to make sure she didn't oversleep. She might have to run to work in barely clean clothes and frizzy hair, but she arrived on time.

Until that morning.

"How the...?" she exclaimed when she wearily opened her eyes and noticed sunlight stretching across the room at unfamiliar angles. She looked at the clock on the wall, her cognition taking a moment to kick in. When it did, she bolted upright.

She was already fifteen minutes late for work.

Scrambling from her bed as if the sheets were on fire, she tossed on some clothes from the floor. It was yesterday's outfit, actually, but who had time to be picky? Glancing at her alarm clocks to figure out what happened, she was surprised none of them were plugged in and one of the cords was actually chewed in half. Looking quizzically around to see if this was in fact an episode of *punk'd*, she saw Butternut, sitting by the cord, a guilty look on his face.

"All three? *Really?*" she screamed, and the cat ran away in fear. "Unbelievable." She knew she shouldn't be surprised. This was just her life, her luck. As she shook her head at the ridiculous cat and cursed at herself for not rehoming them all, she stepped in something slimy— cat barf. A big, warm pile oozed between her toes. Talk about being kicked when you're down.

She ran to the bathroom, finding a towel to wipe off her toes. She managed to rinse them in the shower quickly, figuring it was just cat food, so she didn't really need to sanitize. She would deal with the mess on the carpet later. She didn't even take a second to pee, deciding she'd have to manage until the morning break. She didn't peek in the mirror, figured it didn't matter. After all, the customers didn't see her, just heard her. With little alternative, she trudged to the car, telling herself it would be fine. No big deal. A few minutes late. Some cat barf. It happened to everyone. She would stroll in, apologize, and get right to work.

And then her car didn't start.

"Are you freaking kidding me?" She pounded on the steering wheel as the car refused to turn over. She kicked, she punched the dash, she pleaded.

Nothing.

After convincing herself it was actually happening, that she wasn't in some terrible reality show or a cheesy movie, she took a deep breath and did what any sensible adult would do.

She tried again. And again. She said a feeble prayer, asked God for a break. She crossed her fingers, crossed her barf-covered toes. And then... success! She actually laughed like an idiot at her luck. See, it would be fine. She wiped at the dash and got ready to peel out of the driveway, and that's when she remembered.

She'd forgotten to put gas in the car. She had planned on getting up five minutes early so she could swing by the gas station on the way to work. Glancing at the infuriating gas needle, she realized she didn't have a prayer of making it the ten miles to her office. Not a prayer.

It was 7:29. She had stepped in barf, was wearing

yesterday's outfit, and hadn't even peed or brushed her teeth. Now she had to stop at the gas station so she could have a hope of only being forty-five minutes late for work. Wonderful. She could call Mr. Grison and tell him about her dilemma, tell him she would be late, or even call in sick. But she had left her phone in the house. So she decided to get on with it. It was one day. One day late. It would be fine. He would understand.

She snapped off the radio, too stressed to hear happy tunes bellowing at her. She zoomed into the little gas station parking lot, thanking her lucky stars an open pump sat in plain view. *See, things would turn around,* she'd told herself. She had almost panicked, had a true breakdown, when she realized along with her phone, she'd left her wallet at home.

But no worries, she remembered. As the responsible adult she was, she'd left an emergency fund in the glove compartment. Creaking it open and coughing from the dust, she found her beloved ten-dollar bill crumpled underneath some fast-food napkins. Her saving grace.

She hobbled into the store carrying her money almost like a torch, blasting past everyone, forgetting other people might also have lives and be in a hurry. Nothing was as important as her need to get in, get out, and get to work. As she rushed toward the small line of customers, she actually took a breath. She would pay for her gas, pump it, and be off to work. Sure, the day hadn't started out great, but it was fine. It was okay. She was okay. As she waited for the man at the counter to dictate his ridiculous cigarette order, though, she turned to see the line behind her.

That's when she saw them. That's when all pretenses her terrible day could get better went straight down the toilet. That's when her fate was sealed.

Behind her, *he* stood, glowing at the woman beside him. She was dressed impeccably, the kind of woman a man was proud to stand by, the kind of woman a man walked into a convenience store with and said, "Look at this woman I'm with," with his eyes.

The kind of woman Annie wasn't.

They were locked in a longing look that probably seemed adorable to those around them. To Annie, it was disgusting. It was vile. Really? Couldn't anyone else see how gross it was? This fifty-year-old with a thirty-year-old who looked like she was twelve? She panicked then, wanting to escape but knowing she couldn't. In her fluster, she almost didn't notice, almost didn't see. When Melissa took one step back from Dave, though, Annie finally noticed the telltale sign. She should've identified it in the woman's glowing cheeks, in their sappy look. She should've sensed it somehow, in some way. Instead, it crept up on her like a ghoulish fiend, slapping her in the face with its truth.

Beneath a perfectly beautiful salmon sweater bulged the telltale bump, a bump that horrified Annie and made her want to vomit right along with Butternut. Dave's affair was no longer a lustful romp in the bed or a love-crazed moment. It wasn't some poor choice or an exercise of male independence. It wasn't something that would become a regret, which would have him begging for forgiveness—not that she would give it, of course.

It was love. It was long-term. It was forever.

He was going to be a father. Again. With Melissa.

As she prepared to make an exodus—screw the gas and work—his gaze found her, the woman of his past, the woman who used to be his one and only. The woman who used to make him glow when he looked at her.

"Annie, is that you?" he proclaimed, smiling like he was so excited. *What a ridiculous statement,* Annie thought. As if he could forget who she was in what, seven months? Did she look that bad?

"Hi, Dave," she solemnly replied. She wasn't going to even recognize the existence of that wench.

"How are you?"

"Fine, thanks. I see you two are glowing. Of course maybe that's the baby?" No point in trying to be polite or practicing social niceties now. What the hell.

Dave blushed, uncomfortable with the situation he had created. *Good,* she thought. *Let him squirm.*

"We're really excited," Melissa chimed, then seemed to choke realizing how inappropriate the statement was to make when you were a mistress speaking to your lover's ex-wife. Whom he cheated on with you. And you were having his baby.

"How fucking wonderful," Annie spewed before she could think. People around them gasped. She really wasn't the type of woman to use expletives freely, and she felt her stomach drop a bit after she said the word. People were probably thinking she was trashy now. Swearing at a pregnant lady in a convenience store? Who was she? Annie didn't even know. Dave and Melissa stood, stunned, Melissa's mouth actually popping open. Neither tried to say anything else, staring at Annie with a mixture of horror and pity. They stared as though she were wearing a straightjacket. Maybe she should be.

Annie slammed her ten on the counter, shouted a surly "pump two" and ran out the door into the gray day. She pumped gas, jumped in her car, and sped off toward work, determined to forget about Dave and his pregnant slut of a mistress.

She should have known better.

Annie flew through the office door and headed to her boss's office, huffing and disheveled. She wasn't winning any best-dressed awards for today. In fact, she'd probably be written up for being late and for her less-than-perfect hygiene. Top that with the scowl still painted on her face from her run-in with the ex, and she looked downright deranged.

"I'm so sorry, Mr. Grison. It's been a terrible morning, and I know it's no excuse, but the cat chewed the alarm clock and then I stepped in barf and then my car wouldn't start and I tried to get gas but my ex and his knocked-up mistress were in the convenience store. But I got here as fast as I could." Annie had spewed out the series of ridiculous events before she could think better. A simple sorry probably would have sufficed for the lanky Mr. Grison, who was going on his fortieth year with the company and wasn't a real stickler for working hard. He peered at her, eyes wide and taking inventory of her less-than-professional look.

"It's fine, Annie, I understand." He backed up in his wheelie chair as if to distance himself from her, the screeching wheels underscoring the awkward moment.

"Thanks, I'll get right to work." She ineffectually smoothed her hair. Her bangs were now plastered to her head. She tried to regain her composure, offered a weak smile, and then hurried to her desk to get to work. She vowed to forget about Dave and whatshername. She vowed to turn the day around. She got to her desk, sat down, and prepared to click on the probably millions of waiting calls.

And then Sasha came around the corner.

"Oh my, Annie. Are you okay? I was *so* worried about you. Look at you, you poor thing, you're such a wreck. I told Mr. Grison someone must have died or something even worse for you to be late to work. But it looks like it's even worse than I thought. Can I help you?"

Annie silently tried to remember some meditation techniques or some anger management systems. She told herself to belly breathe, to not let Sasha get to her. But really? The woman exuded ridiculousness. First, her thinly veiled concern was clearly an excuse to make Annie look bad. Second, what the hell was worse than a death? And third, who cared what she looked like? They were taking phone calls, not video chats. Of course, with Sasha, you never knew.

With gritted teeth, Annie articulated, "I'm fine, but thank you for your overwhelming concern. What would I do without you?" She added some bite to underscore her sarcasm, but Sasha was too self-absorbed to notice. She grinned like an idiotic puppet and sashayed back to her desk.

At least one thing is going right, Annie thought. Sasha went away. Annie went through a dozen calls, all mindless ones thankfully. Calls about expiration dates and faulty packaging. She seamlessly rotated through her "I'm so sorry" and "The coupon is going in the mail today." She should have been thankful for the easy morning, except the ease of her job gave her more time to think, to muse over Melissa, over the baby bump, over the way he'd looked at her.

And as she thought about it, she became more angry. And as her anger mounted, frustration threatened to boil over. Who the hell were these people, having time to call in and complain about a cupcake when her life was *actually* a disaster? Did they have an ex whom they had been married to for decades who left them for a younger, perkier woman? Did they have to face the pregnant mistress of the man they had loved for years? Anger seethed in her core, a tightness formed in her chest.

And then it simmered over, a dripping concoction of burning feelings melting her.

A twangy, nasally woman from Virginia blabbered

on and on about her cupcake not being the correct size while Annie was experiencing her full-fledged emotional explosion. Annie could feel the anger creeping into her voice, could hear herself getting short and choppy in her answers. And then, when the woman started talking about lawsuits over a cupcake—*a cupcake, for God's sake!*—she blew it.

"You know what, lady? Screw you and your too-small cupcake! I doubt your ass needs a full-size cupcake anyway!"

And she hung up.

A momentary silence, an indisputable lull haunted the moment. She should be horrified by what she had done, but it felt so good. It felt good to say the words on her mind, to stop pretending. It was such a relief to give in to confrontation when she had been letting everything brew inside. Sure, it hadn't been about the woman on the phone or the frustration over a cupcake. It was much more. But in some small way, Annie had claimed ownership of her sucky life, of her sucky situation. She had stopped someone from stomping on her like she was a cupcake crumb on the floor.

Then reality set in. The ever familiar, dreadful *clack-clack* announced her arrival.

Sasha came around her cubicle, mouth agape in sheer horror. "Oh, my God, Annie, what happened?" Sasha spaced the last two words like they were heavy in her mouth. She looked truly aghast at what Annie had done, as if Annie had committed the worst of crimes.

Sure, her response was taboo and unprofessional. But it wasn't like she had murdered a kitten. So she had told off one of the millions of Sandy's Sweets customers. Big deal. There were worse things.

Sasha was now the one apparently trying to buy into the meditative techniques. She stood in Annie's cubicle for a solid minute in silence, weighing the situation.

"Okay, Annie, now I know you're having a rough time and all, being a frumpy middle-aged woman who has lost her husband. But that doesn't mean you can take it out on customers. Now I'm going to talk to Mr. Grison about this and see if we can't work things out with the lady you screamed at. We can't have a complaint filed against our department, after all. How will that make us look? Don't you worry, I'll straighten this out."

Annie stared at the perfectly tanned specimen verging on a panic attack. Who did she think she was, calling Annie frumpy? Yeah, it was true, but you didn't march your tight ass around an office calling senior members frumpy and giving them lectures about customers. Annie had been working there before Sasha graduated from diapers. It was too much.

The power, the relief she got from telling off the customer, well, it was contagious.

"You know what, Sasha? You go ahead. You tell Mr. Grison I swore at a customer. You tell him how sorry you are, and how you'll make it up to him. You kiss his ass right to the top. Big deal, sweetheart. You'll be top dog at a cupcake office. Wow, that's amazing."

"Annie, you need to start taking your job more seriously. We are important." Sasha huffed, standing with an air of confidence befitting her tight-fitting outfit, but it was completely appalling to the already downtrodden Annie.

So Annie decided to practice her telling-it-like-it-is one more time, one final time. She might not be able to tell Melissa how she felt, at least not completely. She might not be able to change her life's sucky status. But she could make one thing right. She could stop being the dowdy, frumpy, mousey Annie everyone had come to expect, the Annie everyone clomped right over. She could be bold, she could have self-confidence. So without any more thought, she did the terrible, career-ending thing that would obliterate her job at Sandy's Sweets, would send her box of office stuff in hand to her empty house with five cats, and would result in her spending her day crying into a bag of potato chips.

At the time, it felt totally worth it. It felt like pure heaven as the words flowed right off her tongue.

Now, though, as she told Amelia those words she had shouted, not whispered, across the office at Sasha, she felt ashamed and foolish. She had thrown away her career, the last thing in her life that wasn't messed up, all so she could say two words to a pointless woman.

Because as Sasha stood there with her arrogant stance, chest out and condescending gaze stabbing into Annie, she found the words she had been wanting to tell Sasha for a long time.

"Fuck. You."

Sasha had burst into tears, the other workers had collectively gasped, and Mr. Grison had, moments later, told Annie to pack up her desk.

***

When the tale of Annie's terrible day was finished, she let out a ginormous breath.

"Wow, Mom. That's intense," was all Amelia could manage. To Amelia, Annie had always been a stoic, rule-following, dependable woman. She was a bit quiet in her approach and always about social graces. "Fuck you" was something Amelia had probably never imagined coming out of her mom's pale pink lips. Not in a million years.

"Intensely dumb," Annie murmured between snot bubbles. "What am I going to do now?"

Amelia hugged her again. "You'll figure it out, it's going to be okay."

The women sat in silence as one of the cats meowed from afar.

"You know what, though?"

"What?"

"I'm pretty proud of you. I mean, two 'fucks' in one day, and both to women who deserved it? That's kind of amazing. Especially Melissa. A baby? What the hell?"

"You didn't know?"

"Of course not. You think I'd keep that a secret from you?"

Annie shrugged. "He is your father, Amelia. Your

relationship shouldn't be affected by what happened between us."

"Are you kidding me? I don't care if I talk to that arrogant asshole ever again."

"Amelia, don't."

"Why not, Mom? He's an idiot. Melissa is younger than me. Do you know how disgusting that is?"

Annie sighed. "Yes. I do. But that doesn't mean it has to change things for you."

"They're already changed. It's my choice, Mom. Stop feeling guilty about it. You have enough to worry about."

"I know. Don't remind me."

Now that it was all off her chest though, she felt calmer about the situation. Maybe Amelia was right. Maybe she'd figure it all out. Maybe it was what she needed to start a new life, to start fresh.

Who knew a four-letter word, deemed explicit by most, could be so deliciously powerful?

Chapter Twelve

Annie

Within three days, Annie knew two things for sure—being off work was overrated, and her life really couldn't get much worse. A few days spent at home watching game shows with five cats was enough to make any fifty-year-old feel dead inside. She had to do something, find something, be something new.

She started with a lunch date with Amelia. She might be on the verge of poverty thanks to her joblessness, but she needed to get out of the house. She needed a reason to take a shower, to put on some deodorant, to rejoin the real world. She thought maybe talking with Amelia would put things into perspective. If nothing else, maybe Smoothie Q was hiring. She was good with a blender, and Amelia did say the discounts were great.

Over a plate of French fries and a sandwich, Amelia confirmed although Smoothie Q wasn't hiring, Book World was.

"I can get you an app, Mom, it will be fun. You've

always liked books. This could be a new start for you."

"Yeah, if I don't tell a customer to eff off," Annie muttered, feeling thankful Amelia was trying to help but not sure if Book World was where she saw her career going.

"Well, it'll be a start. It'll give you some experience until you figure out what you want to do."

"Amelia, I'm fifty. It's not like I'm twenty-five and have years of opportunity in front of me. I'm a used-up old woman. I can't change careers on a dime."

"Well, you have no choice. And you're not an old woman, Mom. There are plenty of options for you. It's exciting, if you ask me. You can reinvent yourself."

"I guess."

"It'll be great. Trust me. It's a new beginning for both of us. I can feel it. It's going to be a good year coming up."

"A new beginning for both of us? What's happening, Amelia? Do you have news?" Annie put down her French fry. She could use some good news, something to live for vicariously through Amelia.

"Well, not yet, but I think I might soon," Amelia said. She was obviously dying to share something. The poor girl had probably wanted to tell her days ago, but Annie had ruined it with the curse word escapade.

"Amelia?"

"I think Neville's going to propose. He's been acting all weird and saying he's planning something special for us. And Kristin, the girl I work with at Book World, said she saw him at Cliffman's Jewelers last week. Mom, I think he's going to ask me to marry him."

"Amelia! That's fantastic!" Annie exclaimed, and she meant it. It was great to see Amelia so excited. It was great to think her little girl was settling down, had found someone to make her happy.

She hoped things would be different for Amelia, that she wouldn't get her heart broken. Neville was a safe choice, a constant choice. From what she knew of him, he would be loyal, he would be trustworthy. He would give Amelia a simple, dependable life. He had a meekness, a humility in him Dave had never had.

"Mom, are you sure you're okay? I didn't want to tell you about this, you know, with everything going on."

"Don't be silly, I'm ecstatic. I am so happy you're happy. And you know what this means, don't you?"

"What?"

"First, I get to be in an amazing wedding. And second, babies are on the way soon," Annie shrieked. She loved babies, had been waiting for her chance to hold a grandbaby for way too long now.

"Mom, calm down. First of all, we don't even know if he's really proposing, it's just a guess."

"He is. I just know it."

"And second, babies are not in the near future for us, no way. I'm not ready for that yet."

"Oh, come on, babies are great."

"Yeah, okay," Amelia said, sarcasm dripping.

"Well, one step at a time, I guess. But seriously,

Amelia, I'm happy for you. I can't wait to see the ring. I knew Neville was a keeper." Annie reached across the table, carefully avoiding the ketchup on the French fry plate, to grab Amelia's hand. They had temporarily abandoned their meals in light of the conversation.

"Tell that to Grandma Charlotte."

"Oh, Grandma Charlotte will be thrilled," Annie said, letting go of Amelia's hand to reach for a fry, now somewhat soggy and cold.

"Yeah, if I were walking down the aisle with Owen instead of Neville."

"What?"

"You know, Owen, the personal-care aide."

"I know who Owen is, but why would Grandma want you with him?"

"She thinks Owen and I are perfect for each other." Amelia added a twinge of cool incredulity to her voice. But Annie caught a twinge of something else—something that told her maybe Amelia had feelings for this Owen character. She had to admit, he was easy on the eyes and he was hilarious. He was sweet with Charlotte, he was full of life, and he had a band. If she had to pick a man from a lineup who would suit her daughter, he would probably be a first choice.

But he wasn't Neville. He wasn't safe, reliable Neville, who would never dream of breaking Amelia's heart. Heck, the guy probably didn't step on an ant for fear of hurting it. He was gentle, he was mild. He wouldn't be like Dave.

Owen, on the other hand. That guy was a wildcard.

"Well, Grandma Charlotte is crazy. She is a fool for rockers. Neville is perfect for you. He adores you. He will treat you well. Trust me. I know a thing or two about warning signs in men. And Neville looks perfectly safe to me."

There was the word. Safe. Was that what life had come to for Annie? Was everything about safety? Who said relationships needed safety? After all, safety had gotten her to that point in her life, the point of being jobless and loveless. Purposeless.

Amelia sighed, shaking her head. "Yeah, Neville's great." She weakly smiled as she reached for her sandwich and resumed eating.

But that was the problem with being a mom. You knew when your daughter was faking it.

***

After lunch, Annie decided to go and check on Charlotte, see what she was up to. She fought against the blustery wind, her boots stomping through the freshly fallen snow. As her hands grew numb and her cheeks tightened in the cold air, she caught sight of him.

Joe. He was headed into the building too.

"Hey," she yelled, feeling her energy zoom.

"Hey," he yelled back, turning to face her and slowing to let her catch up. They burst through the door to Wildflower like two freed snowmen, kicking snow from their shoes in the entrance.

"God, it's cold," they both said at precisely the same

time. They laughed awkwardly.

"Is jinx still a thing?"

"Yeah. If it means you have to buy me a hot chocolate."

"Deal." He smiled, warmth exuding from him. "It's been too long. Although around here, it's sort of a good thing, right? Maybe it means our moms are both behaving?"

"Well, behaving enough in front of Cassie, at least. I don't think they're skipping down the hallways holding hands or anything. And from talking to Mom, I'm pretty sure the battle is still raging. It's become sort of a covert thing."

"Women." Joe shook his head.

"Watch it."

"Well, I've got to go check on my soldier—I mean my mom. I'm assuming you're here to check on yours?"

"Yep."

"Well, how about we do that and then meet back down here in, say, an hour?"

"For what?"

"Hot chocolate, obviously. I'm a man of my word. I figure we can head down to Tina's Café. It'll give us time to catch up on the latest details. I'm sure we're both getting quite different stories from our moms."

Annie blushed. Was it a date? *Don't be ridiculous,* she scolded herself. It was a man buying her a cup of hot chocolate and wanting to investigate the tenuous situation between their moms. Nothing more.

"Okay, deal."

"Deal? I'll say. You get free hot chocolate with a handsome guy," Joe joked as he adjusted the shoulders of his shirt in a gangster-like movement. Annie laughed.

"Clearly," she said and then headed down the hallway. She shook her head on the way. There was something loveable about the guy. Despite his crazy mother—according to Charlotte, anyway—there was something very intriguing.

Something safe, Annie realized as she knocked on her mom's door.

***

"Are you out of your mind? She's a psycho. I'm sure her son isn't any better!" Charlotte screamed when Annie mentioned Joe.

"Mom, it's just hot chocolate. And don't you think you're being a bit dramatic? Psycho? Really?"

Charlotte huffed. "Well, so much for family loyalty. And yes, she's a psycho. She's assaulted me and she makes it her personal mission to attack me in every way. I call that psychotic."

Annie rolled her eyes. "Isn't drama supposed to end in high school, Mom? Don't you think, I don't know, maybe you play a role in this whole debacle as well?"

Charlotte looked like she might explode. "I absolutely do not. She started this whole thing with her ridiculous behavior. And besides, I would think you would sympathize with me trying to take Catherine down. I may have had a few scratches with her, but I did not drop the f-bomb at her," Charlotte announced, stabbing back.

"Touché." Annie knew she had been beat. Charlotte did have a point. And if Catherine were an elderly version of Sasha, well, she could see Charlotte's perspective. "But Joe is not a psycho. He's really nice. And it's just hot chocolate."

"You're going to fall in love," Charlotte announced as she sipped her coffee.

"Mother! Don't be absurd. I barely know him."

"I'll tell you, I think you and your daughter are both blind. Am I wearing special love goggles or something around here? Am I the only one who can see things like this? Honestly."

"Well, Miss Love Goggles, I think you're wrong about Amelia. Word has it she's going to be engaged very soon."

"What?" Charlotte practically spit. "To the square?"

"Mother."

"Well, really. Do you mean to tell me this Neville fellow is right for our Amelia? Really? The boring guy who drinks decaf?"

"What's wrong with decaf?"

"Nothing, if you're a sleepy man named Neville. He will *never* make Amelia happy." True disdain emerged on her face as she choked out his name.

"He will make her happy. He's a good pick."

"He's safe."

"What's wrong with safe?"

Charlotte set her cup down and looked Annie in the eye. "Nothing, if you're okay with quiet nights eating baked chicken and watching reruns. Nothing, if you don't mind a predictable schedule and some humdrum routines."

"I like baked chicken and reruns."

"Yes. But I don't think Amelia does."

Annie sighed. She hated to admit it, but Charlotte did have a point. She had seen it on Amelia's face, behind her smile.

Doubt.

"Well, Amelia will figure all this out. You stay out of it, Miss Matchmaker." Annie rose from her seat to rinse her cup.

"Oh, you know me."

"Yes, I do. Now I've got to go," Annie shouted over her shoulder as she headed toward the door.

"Some steamy liquids calling your name?" Charlotte lingered on the word steamy.

"I don't know why, but the way you said it makes it sound... disturbing."

Charlotte cackled. "There are some perks to being old. You can say disturbing things without being judged."

"I'm judging you." Annie paused at the door, hand on the knob.

"And I'm judging you for going out with a psycho's son and falling in love with him."

"It's not love."

"Okay, then. Go have hot chocolate with your not-love interest. But wipe your silly smirk off first. You don't want him seeing love on your face. He might get the wrong idea."

"All right, Mom. I love you," Annie said seriously, returning to the table and leaning in for a hug.

"I love you too, dear. Have fun."

Annie was out the apartment, down the hallway, and off to a not-date date with a man she didn't love... but felt warm around. And safe. Baked chicken and rerun safe.

"Shit," she muttered to herself. She hated it when her mother was right.

***

"Refills?"

"Absolutely," Joe said just as Annie was about to say no. The waitress smiled, taking their mugs to refill them.

"I really shouldn't have another cup," Annie said, smiling.

"Come on. Live a little," Joe said, smiling right back.

"I don't know if hot chocolate is really living. Although it is the best hot chocolate I've ever had."

"Well, regardless, a second cup of hot cocoa means more time for me to get to know you. We've talked all about me. Tell me more about you."

"There's not much to tell." She shrugged, not really feeling awkward. Joe's gaze was warm and inviting. She felt like she was talking to an old friend and not someone she barely knew.

"What do you like to do?"

Annie opened her mouth, ready to say… to say what? The truth was, she didn't really know what she liked anymore.

In reality, she didn't know what she'd liked ever. From the time she graduated from high school, she'd been living the domestic life. Dave and Amelia had been her whole world. Now, with Amelia grown up and Dave gone, she was left to be anything she wanted, to do anything she wanted.

And she spent her nights watching soap operas with a blanket of cats.

She knew she could lie, could make up something. With Joe, though, she didn't feel the need. She simply said, "I have no idea."

He seemed to appraise her answer for a moment. The waitress came back with their hot chocolate refills—whipped cream and all. Annie knew she was never going to sleep tonight from all of the caffeine, but she didn't care. Joe was right. A second cup meant more time to talk, and, suddenly, going home to the silence of her home wasn't appealing. It felt good to sit at this table for two near the tiny fireplace and talk. It felt even better to have someone who really listened and wanted to hear about her. It felt great to have someone she wanted to learn about.

Joe took a sip of his drink, paused for a moment, and then spoke. "So how do you plan on figuring it out?"

"Figuring what out?" she asked, confused. She'd

already told him about Dave, about the breakup. What was there to figure out?

"What you like. Who you want to be. How are you going to figure it all out?"

"I don't know." She hadn't thought about it, hadn't really planned on doing any soul-searching.

"Well, what do you say I help you? I mean, if you want."

"So what do you propose?"

"Snow tubing."

She sputtered, a sip of hot chocolate in her mouth. "Snow tubing?"

"Yeah. Snow tubing. A buddy of mine has a cabin with the prime spot for snow tubing. It's a lot of fun."

"So you think the answer to my identity crisis and my divorce is flying down a hill on an inner tube?"

"Maybe. Maybe not. But give it a try. That's the thing. You can do whatever you want right now. Try everything. Go snow tubing. Take a synchronized swimming class. Go dancing and skiing and join a band if you want. You might hate it all, you might love it. But you've got to do something, because otherwise, what's the point? Look, I've been pretty much alone my whole adult life. Had a few flings here and there, but nothing serious. But you know what I've found during that time? You've got to figure out how to be happy with yourself. Figure out what moves you, what fulfills you. For the first time, Annie, you've got to put yourself first. Don't be Dave's Annie or Amelia's mom or Charlotte's daughter.

Just be Annie."

She felt her face soften with his words, with the logic behind them she hadn't really considered before. Here was a man in a flannel, sipping hot chocolate with her in a small café. He didn't know her favorite color or her favorite ice cream flavor. He didn't know the story of her first kiss or her first heartbreak. Hell, he probably didn't know her middle name.

Sitting there with him, though, she felt an ease she couldn't deny. He got her, understood what she was dealing with. He'd met her at this messed up stage of her life, this crossroads. He'd encountered her at a time most men would've probably gone running in the other direction. Here he was though, buying her hot chocolate and telling her just what she needed to hear.

She grinned, feeling excited for the first time since she'd heard those awful words come out of Dave's mouth months ago.

She shrugged her shoulders and said, "What the heck? Get my inner tube ready. Let's go flying down the hill and see what happens."

Chapter Thirteen

Amelia

Arms loaded with cosmetic bags, hairspray, curling irons, and bags from the pharmacy, Amelia weakly knocked on the door. She had a key, of course, to her childhood home, but she just didn't have the hand to root for it.

"Amelia?" Annie inquired when she came to the door. Annie was wearing her new uniform—sweatpants, a baggy T-shirt, and no makeup. That was exactly why Amelia was there. She burst through the front door, swept past her mother, and headed straight toward the kitchen table to drop all of her goodies.

"Amelia? What is this?" Annie looked horrified.

"This is an intervention." Amelia swiped her hands together.

"An intervention? Honey, I know my life sucks, but honestly, I can't even afford to buy alcohol let alone drink it."

"An appearance intervention. Remember how a few nights ago we talked about this being your second chance? Your chance to start over? Well, step one was to find a job." Amelia rustled in her bag. She handed Annie a piece of paper. "Check. Well… sort of. Here's an application for Book World. It's at least something to hold you over until you figure out what you want to do." Annie assessed the paper, her mind clearly whirling with Amelia's words.

"Second step—amp up your look. You need a change, mom. You're starting fresh, so your look needs to say it. I love you, I really do, but let's face some facts. You're covered in cat hair, you are dressed like a man, and you've had the same hairstyle since the 70s. It's time to let it go. You're beautiful, but you need to own it. Let's show Dad how much he messed up. Screw Melissa. She hasn't got anything on you." Amelia started pulling things out of her bags.

"Okay, whoa, slow down. What are you doing?"

"I'm helping you join the new century. I'm helping you reinvent yourself."

"But I like my hair, and what's wrong with sweatpants around the house?" Annie assessed her outfit and Amelia's reaction.

"Okay, your hair is fine, but you need a change. There's nothing wrong with sweatpants around the house, but I know for a fact that's all you've been wearing. And really, Mom? How many times have you talked to the cats today?"

"What?"

"Just answer the question. How many times?"

"A few, maybe, why?"

"My point exactly. You need to step it up. You need to get your confidence back so you can get back out there and have some fun."

Annie zoned out, a wistful look on her face. Amelia hadn't seen that look on her mom in forever, so she wasn't quite sure what to call it. Whatever it was, it had taken Annie to a different dimension.

"Hello? Mom?"

"Right, right. Okay, Amelia. Let's do it. You're right." Amelia had expected more of a fight, but something was going on with her mom. Maybe she just realized Amelia was right.

So Amelia got to work. She pulled out the hair dye and even some shears.

"Trust me, Mom, I cut my own hair all the time," she reassured Annie. In actuality, she had just watched a few YouTube videos before coming over, but how hard could it be? She worked on some makeup, blending eyeshadows and contouring lines until her arm ached. She had Annie try on a few outfits she had bought for her. She didn't let Annie see anything until she'd completed her transformation.

After a few hours of Annie begging to see what was happening and Amelia starting to doubt her abilities, the makeover was finished. If she were being honest, it hadn't all flowed together like she'd hoped. It wasn't the type of reveal worthy of *What Not to Wear*, but it was… different. It was edgy. It was a complete 180 from the mousey Annie everyone knew.

That was good enough, right?

***

"Oh, my God, Amelia! I love it!" Annie shrieked.

Okay, so that was just what Amelia had imagined.

In reality, Annie had screamed, "Oh, my God, Amelia! *What have you done?"* at a decibel loud and shrill enough for dogs across the block to start howling. Amelia's heart sank. It was not going well.

"Mom, it's fine. You look... edgy."

Edgy was mild. Amelia had imagined a modern, tough-ass chick vibe. A don't-mess-with-me in a soft, sexy way. What stood before them now was more like an edgy, I'm-going-to-kill-you kind of look. An "I don't care about society," anarchy-for-all kind of look.

Amelia had gone for a short, spiky hairstyle. She'd wanted to darken her mom's mousey hair, give it some depth. Annie ended up with a very short, very wild, finger in a light-socket hairstyle. The spikes were... well, spiky, sticking up every which way. She could not hide behind her hair now. She had a swoopy side bang that was not too bad, Amelia thought.

But the color. *Oh, the color.*

What was supposed to be chestnut brown was more like a purpley-black hue. Like the color Amelia's hair had been when she experimented with an emo phase in high school.

The clothes, well, they were okay. Perhaps a bit more revealing than she had imagined, with the neckline plunging down pretty low as the sheer fabric of the shirt revealed a lot more than it didn't. The leather pants were kind of snug, but they did make her mom look younger. And although Annie wobbled precariously in the heels, they made her ass look tight. The makeup was loud and noticeable, just like Amelia liked it. So other than the hair, she thought Annie was pretty smoking.

Annie did not think so, though.

"Amelia, I look like a biker chick mixed with a sixteen-year-old sad girl. With a much looser body." Tears were welling, and Annie was ready to lose her composure. It was not the makeover of Amelia or Annie's dreams.

"It's fine, Mom. Calm down. I'll fix it. I'll just..." She would just what? What could she possibly do to fix this? Amelia felt horrible and hopeless. "Look, I'll call Trudy from Smoothie Q. She's great with hair, she used to be a cosmetologist and stuff. We'll get the color fixed. That'll make it better," she promised, reaching for her phone.

But then the house phone rang. Frustrated, Annie ran away from the mirror, needing a distraction. "Hello?" Amelia heard her say. And then Annie's face went pale. "I'll be right there," she said, eyeing Amelia with concern.

"What's wrong? Is it Grandma?" Her heart stopped.

"Yeah, we have to go, now. Cassie said Grandma didn't come down for dinner like she usually does, and no one has seen her all afternoon. She called to see if she was with me. Cassie's going straight into her apartment right now just to make sure everything is okay, but I want to go over there in case something's wrong. It isn't like Mom to hide in her apartment all afternoon and evening," she said. Both women forgot about Annie's odd appearance. Suddenly the purple hair didn't matter.

Please be okay, please be okay, Amelia chanted to herself as she followed her mom to the car. *We can't take another disaster.*

***

"Oh, thank God," Annie proclaimed as they burst through Charlotte's apartment door. Cassie was already in there, chatting animatedly with Charlotte, who looked irritated.

"Yes, yes, it happens, Charlotte. We all nod off sometimes. It could be from your late-night caffeine habits. Maybe you're not getting as much sleep at night as you think," Cassie articulated. Charlotte jumped out of her chair as soon as she saw her escape route.

"Annie, Amelia, what a surprise. I'm sorry this, um, Cassie, worried you, but I just fell asleep in my chair. That's all. This is all a silly misunderstanding, right, Cassie? Cassie was just leaving." Charlotte didn't even try to conceal her annoyance.

"Thanks, Cassie. Sorry for the trouble." Amelia gave the woman a smile to save face and cover for Charlotte's verging-on-rude behavior.

"No trouble, not at all," Cassie sang. No wonder Charlotte got annoyed with the overly peppy woman. Cassie slipped out, her heels clicking as she wiggled her way to the door.

"Mom, you scared us," Annie proclaimed.

"Well, darling, I think you're the one doing the scaring. What happened to you?" Charlotte asked, eyeing up Annie.

"Oh, shit. I forgot. I was so worried about you I rushed out." Annie felt her hair tentatively, and tears started welling up. "Amelia decided I needed a makeover." Charlotte tried to hide a chuckle.

"Well, it's... different all right. In a Joan Jett meets Effie Trinket kind of way," Charlotte added. Amelia loved that her grandma was up on pop culture. Who had a grandma who referenced *Hunger Games*? Amelia did.

Annie's tears threatened to overflow, and Amelia gave her grandma a disapproving look. She wasn't helping. At all.

"Oh dear, it's not the end of the world. It's kind of badass if you ask me," Charlotte added, putting a loving arm around her daughter. "Look, the beautician is in tomorrow. I'm sure I could get her to help you out. Just stop back tomorrow afternoon. It'll be fine."

Annie looked at her through the tears that were now streaming, and nodded, seeming grateful for the help.

"And the outfit is really awesome. Good job, honey," Charlotte added, turning to Amelia.

Amelia gave Charlotte a grimace, saying, "I tried."

Charlotte insisted on making some tea after declining Amelia's offer to go to dinner. "I'm fine, darling, really. This old bird doesn't eat as much as she used to. Let's just have some scones." Charlotte was always looking for an excuse to eat scones.

After some scones, tea, more tears, and laughs, Amelia and Annie decided to get going. After all, Charlotte had a game of bridge to get to with Marla. "Owen's going to be having his concert soon," Charlotte said, as she leaned in to give Amelia a hug.

"Oh, great," Amelia said, trying to act casual.

"Yep. He looks like Adam and sings like him. What more could a girl want?"

Amelia shook her head. "Oh, Grandma," she said, not knowing how to finish the statement.

"Someday you'll realize how right I am. Then you won't be oh Grandma-ing me. Now try not to play beauty shop any more tonight, okay? I think Carla can work with that, but if you do anything else, we might be looking at wigs." Annie scowled, Amelia grimaced again, and Charlotte laughed.

Life was crazy sometimes.

***

Amelia dashed to keep up with Annie on the way out.

"Hurry up, I don't want anyone to see me like this," Annie whispered over her shoulder as she rushed out the door. She turned to see how far back Amelia was, and that's when the train wreck happened, so fast Amelia could only start to mouth the word "watch."

Before she could finish, Annie smacked into some guy in a flannel. The two were almost knocked senseless, and they wound up lying on the lobby floor at Wildflower, a tangled mess of arms and feet. Amelia skidded to a stop before she joined the odd game of Twister.

"Mom, are you okay?" she shouted, dropping to her knees to assist her mother.

When Annie sorted herself out, she laughed. "Hey again," she said.

The flannel-shirt man also grinned, saying, "What in the hell happened?"

"You ran into me."

"I'm pretty sure you were the one doing the running. I didn't even have time to blink because you were moving so fast. You almost killed me, woman. Is there a fire I should know about?"

Amelia stood, backing up to observe the weird encounter. Who was the guy? And why did Annie seem so comfortable with him?

"I was trying to get out of here before—" Recognition dawned on Annie's face. She turned bright red. "Oh, my God, my hair. Don't look." She tried to cover her head with her arms. It was pathetic.

Flannel man took in the sight, now reaching to move Annie's arms away. They were still entangled on the floor, which Amelia found odd. "Let me see," he said. Annie's face reddened, but she reluctantly moved her hands.

"I think it looks badass. Seriously, what's wrong with it?"

Annie didn't get angry, though, like she did at Charlotte. She didn't cry. She did something unexpected, something un-Annie like.

She started laughing. "Really? I look like a freak."

"No, really. It's not bad. I like it. It's unique." The man looked into Annie's eyes. They were practically nose-to-nose.

"If you like purple hair."

"Well, maybe I like purple hair. I've heard it's in," the man fired back, grinning. He was flirting with Annie. *Flirting with her.* But Amelia found something else shocking.

Her mom seemed to be enjoying it. It was definitely not the first time that man had flirted with her. It was not a run-in with an acquaintance. It was all over her mom's heavily painted face. The glistening in the eyes, the comfort in their interactions.

Her mom liked him. She liked the flannel-shirted guy named... What was his name?

"Hey, excuse me, hi, my mom's forgotten her manners. I'm Amelia," she interrupted, heading over and offering a hand.

The man took it, gave it a firm shake, and simply said, "Joe."

"So, you two know each other?"

At this, Annie blushed and hurried to her feet, trying to brush herself off. "Yeah, we met a few months ago. We're friends. This is Catherine's son."

"*The* Catherine?"

"If by the Catherine you mean the over-the-top woman who fights with your grandma, then yep, that's her. A real charmer, as I'm sure you've heard."

Amelia couldn't help but laugh. She liked the guy. A lot. There was something warm about him, something different from what her dad had. He seemed... genuine. Comfortable. Not out to impress anyone or to be impressed.

He seemed, she thought, like the man Annie needed.

Now if they could just fix that hair.

***

There were a lot of questions for Annie in the car on the way home that evening. Amelia wanted to know everything about Joe, how they'd met, how serious things were. Annie swore up and down, left and right he was just an acquaintance, but Amelia knew better.

Not that it was a bad thing. Amelia wanted her mom to find someone else, to forget about her scummy father. What her father had done to her mother was despicable, and it had taken a toll on Annie. Amelia wanted her mom to recover, to find herself again. Maybe the guy in the flannel was the answer, even if he was related to Catherine.

Holidays would get pretty awkward, though. Charlotte and Catherine breaking bread at the Christmas Eve feast? Now that was something Amelia was sure would go down in history.

***

Amelia was off from Smoothie Q and Book World the next day, so when Grandma Charlotte called to ask if she could come to Wildflower for lunch because she had a special surprise, Amelia agreed. She had finished her walk with Henry, which went surprisingly well. She figured the surprise probably had something to do with Annie's hair, which Annie was planning on getting fixed.

When she arrived at Charlotte's apartment at noon, she was, in fact, greeted by her mother, now a true brunette with some buttery highlights.

"Mom, it's great. See, aren't you glad I messed up?" Amelia offered, taking in Annie's new look. Annie beamed, something she hadn't done in a long time.

"So you admit you messed it up?"

"Well, you look awesome now, right, and that's all that matters," Amelia retorted, waiting for Grandma to bail her out and change the subject. "Good surprise, Grandma. Looks like Mom will be letting me live after all."

"Oh, that's not the surprise, dear." Grandma Charlotte twinkled. "There's more up these sleeves." She smiled as she pulled on the sleeves of her black cashmere sweater. She was up to something, which was never good.

"Oh, no. What is it now?" Amelia groaned.

"You'll see. We have a birthday party to get to, though." Charlotte led both women to the door. Behind Charlotte, Annie gave Amelia a baffled look.

"Whose birthday is it? And are you sure we're invited?" Amelia asked. Amelia's own birthday was months away, and so was Annie's. How did it have anything to do with her? Amelia suddenly worried that maybe Charlotte was losing her mind.

"Marla's. We've been planning a bash for her all

week. And of course you're invited. I was in charge of the planning." Charlotte grinned, leading them to the community room.

Amelia did some mental sorting. Marla. Owen's grandma. So that meant the surprise must be... As she prepared to verbally pounce on her Grandma and remind her she was in a serious relationship, one that would hopefully involve a ring soon, she entered the dining room and was taken back by the transformation.

The room was decorated in a slew of confetti, streamers, and balloons. A handmade banner that said "Happy 85th, Marla" hung at the front of the room. Workers were getting appetizers ready, and a huge yellow cake sat at the front. Grandma had outdone herself. They would probably give Marla a heart attack.

"You look beautiful," a voice whispered in her ear from behind, giving her chills. She knew the voice without even turning around.

Owen.

She turned but was taken off guard. There was no pretense of a personal-care aide today. He wore tight yet respectable jeans, a short-sleeved black shirt that showed off all his tattoos and grazed his pec muscles in a perfect way. He had on a black beanie, and he smelled like heaven. He looked the rocker part. The completely gorgeous, mysterious rocker part that clutched at Amelia's feelings. Her stomach involuntarily fell.

"I saved you a front-row seat. You should feel special. The women will be fighting over it once we get started."

He winked at her.

"A front-row seat?"

"To the concert."

Amelia left out a silent guffaw. "You're having a concert? Here?" She was stunned, but then gaped up front to see who must have been Owen's band members plugging in an amp.

"And what does that mean, young lady? Are you implying we're too old to rock out?" another familiar voice chimed in. It was Bridget.

"Owen happens to be the musician of choice here at Wildflower, so naturally I booked his band for the entertainment," Charlotte said, standing behind Bridget.

"I'm glad you're here," Owen murmured before looking into Amelia's eyes again and heading toward the front. Coming from anyone but Owen, it would have sounded platonic, a simple comment between two acquaintances. Coming from that gorgeous, confident man, though, it sounded...

Amelia stopped herself. So he was a rocker. A gorgeous one at that. Something she had always dreamed of. So he was funny at all the right points but sensitive toward Charlotte and Marla. He was adorable, exciting, and unpredictable. He was everything she had fantasized about.

But he wasn't Neville. And that was all that mattered right now.

"Something wrong, dear? You look a bit flushed," Charlotte asked sweetly, smiling.

"Was this the surprise? Really?"

Charlotte gave a noncommittal shrug, shared a grin with Bridget, and whisked Annie away to help set up party favors.

"If you ask me," Bridget leaned in to whisper to Amelia, still standing awkwardly by the door, "you better snag that one before someone else does. He's a good one." Amelia stared at the woman, who was wearing a royal-blue hat today. Bridget winked and then she too scurried off to help set the room up before Marla's arrival.

Amelia couldn't help it; all through the "surprise" yelling, the appetizers, and the cake cutting, she couldn't stop thinking about what Bridget had said.

More importantly, she couldn't take her eyes off the man up front, who seemed like he was made for her. *Maybe in another lifetime,* she thought as she took a bite of icing.

***

Amelia ended up staying after the party to help clean up. It had been a success, Marla at least feigning surprise. There had been laughter and presents. There had been stories about Marla and even tears from her.

And then there was the music.

Amelia didn't know what to expect, was afraid to get her hopes up. She had known some rockers from high school who had ragtag bands in their garages... and it was clear why they never made it to the big stage. Owen's band was different. They were good—really good. They were going somewhere, even if they didn't know it.

As Amelia peeled a plastic tablecloth off the appetizer table, someone shuffled behind her and a breath blew over her shoulder.

"So what'd you think? What's the verdict?" he half whispered. She turned to face him, suddenly feeling heat rising as she realized how close he was. He was near enough that a few centimeters would mean his lips were on hers. He was close enough that what were certainly rock-hard abs were only inches away. With just a step forward, her fingers would be close enough to feel those abs, to explore his perfectly solid body. She involuntarily shuddered at the thought, trying to push it back down.

"Owen, you guys are good. *Really good.* I mean it. You're going to be big," she said sincerely, looking into his eyes. She saw a smile form.

"I don't know about the big part. But thanks. I'm glad you liked it."

"I loved the originals you did. They were really beautiful. Who wrote the lyrics?" she asked, truly intrigued by the power of the words, especially given her own hobby.

"I did. They're okay, I guess." For the first time, she sensed a feeling of uncertainty in him, a lack of confidence. It was good to see him humble.

"They're more than okay. You're really talented."

"Your grandma tells me you are too."

Amelia blushed. Only Grandma Charlotte really believed in her song writing dreams. "Yeah, but it's just something I do for fun. I'm not good."

"I doubt it. All great writers say that. I would really love to work together some time. Maybe we can start with a cowritten song? What do you think?"

Amelia looked into his eyes, and she saw he was serious. For the first time, she didn't feel like her dream was stupid or ridiculous. He didn't think she was crazy; he got it. He took her dream seriously, and he even wanted to help her take it to the next level. She was stunned by this simple fact.

Amelia had never even told Neville about her deepest passion because she knew a man like Neville couldn't understand. He would think she was crazy to base her future career goals on something so unrealistic, something so risky. Who became a songwriter, anyway? She should have dreams of teaching or running a company, not writing angst-ridden songs in her room. True, it was unfair of her to make these judgments, to not even give Neville a chance to support her. But something in her soul told her he wouldn't get it, that he would crush this dream for her. And she wasn't ready for it to be crushed.

And now here they were, Amelia and Owen, two passionate people alone by leftover party appetizers, talking about music and dreams. Neither moved for a minute, neither breathed, recognizing that an important shift had happened. A shift Charlotte had predicted for months, a shift neither had thought would really happen. Looking into each other's eyes, they saw something familiar, a recognizable lust. Not simply a physical lust for each other, no, something deeper. A lust for life, a lust to live big, to live wild, to take risks.

So when Owen softly, gently leaned in, brushed Amelia's lips with his, she didn't pull back. She stayed, breathless, in the same spot, closing her eyes, basking in the taste of his lips, savoring the leftover taste of birthday cake, feeling a warmth radiate from inside out. She didn't protest as he moved his lips over hers, taking her into his arms. She let Owen kiss her with a fervor she had never thought possible.

By the leftover appetizers from Marla's eighty-fifth birthday party, Owen and Amelia kissed, felt their hearts open up to each other. They felt something inexplicable, indescribable building.

And so Amelia did what she knew she had to do.

She pushed Owen back, fearing what all of it could mean, fearing the wild choice over safety. She pushed him away, ran out the door, and ran toward the life she knew awaited her, a life of steadiness and certainty, one with Neville.

Chapter Fourteen

Amelia

Amelia spent the rest of the evening and even part of the following day replaying the kiss by the appetizers in her mind. It had rattled her, made her question everything about her life, about Neville, about what she wanted. And if she were being honest, it scared the hell out of her.

As she walked Joey, a tiny Yorkshire Terrier, in a soft morning drizzle, she thought about Owen. She thought about how good it felt to have his lips on hers, how good it felt to know their dreams aligned. But that was all she knew for sure about him. She had no idea where a life with Owen would take her. Would she become a roadie if he became famous, traveling from city to city? Would they have time to stop and settle down? What would life look like?

It looked scary. Sure, she was a bit of a rebel, a bit of a wild child herself. But she also sensed her biological clock ticking. As her mother constantly reminded her, baby-making days didn't last forever. Didn't she want that, a family, at least eventually? A life in suburbia with carpools and PTO meetings and handmade Mother's Day cards? Wasn't that what she was supposed to want?

The kiss with Owen suddenly made everything so confusing. Because as much as she thought she needed safety, wanted security and reliability, the kiss had shifted something in her. The scary part was she didn't know if she could quiet down the voice in her mind telling her Bridget was right, Owen was a good one. And she couldn't stop wondering if the electricity between them during their kiss was the tip of the iceberg.

***

"You didn't forget, did you?" Neville asked after telling Amelia he would pick her up at six.

She had forgotten. Forgotten it was the special Friday. The Friday he would probably propose. What kind of woman could just forget something like that?

"No, I didn't forget, honey. I get off at Smoothie Q at five, so I'll head straight home. Can't wait to see you."

"I love you, Amelia. I'm excited for tonight." She could hear some heaviness in his voice, some momentousness. She wasn't imagining it. As she hung up the phone and headed for her shift, she felt like such an idiot. *You're a fool, Amelia. You have this amazing man swooning over you. You finally found someone you can imagine settling down with, someone who will give you a dependable life. Someone you have chemistry with. Don't be an idiot and throw away your chance now,* she lectured herself.

But for some reason, she couldn't help but wonder what Grandma Charlotte would say in this situation. She would probably say Amelia was a fool for thinking about marrying a man after she had a knock-your-socks-off kiss with someone like Owen.

Life's complicated, she thought again as she pulled out her pink apron and prepared to whisk away her worries in the bottom of a blender.

***

Amelia had felt extra pressure getting ready. She had to play it cool in case she was totally off base, but in her mind she couldn't help but think this could be it, the night that changed her whole life. She didn't want to wear any old outfit for this occasion.

The blender had worked. With each smoothie, her fears and her confusion frothed away. She started to get excited. She loved Neville, she did. So what that she'd had an amazing kiss with Owen? One amazing kiss does not seal away a lifetime of happiness or promise anything. It was a single kiss. A really good kiss, yes, but she would have plenty more of those with Neville.

She swore off thoughts of Owen and his delectable tattoos, his sinewy arms. She told herself she would focus on Neville, on her future. Her solid, steady future.

As she slipped into a classy, yet sexy, black dress and put on some small diamond earrings, she mentally prepared herself. She glanced at herself in the mirror, deciding she looked elegant with a hint of edge that made her Amelia. She smiled, giving herself a pep talk. When the door creaked, she tried not to let the fluttering in her stomach or her sweaty palms become too obvious. *Be natural,* she told herself. This might not be happening, and even if it was, she wanted to look surprised.

There was the usual kissing to accompany Neville's arrival. Hungry kisses. Kisses that a few days ago had felt passionate, untouchable. Now she wondered if they were really all she thought they were.

Stop it, she scolded herself as their kiss continued.

Neville eyed her with curiosity. "Are you okay? You seem tense," he noted. She noticed he was also appearing a bit flighty, a bit sweaty.

She pulled on her best, toothiest smile. "I'm great. Now where are we going?"

He winked, leading her out the apartment door. The couple headed to Neville's SUV and off to a fancy, high-class, reservation only restaurant of course.

***

It was between the waiter's pouring of the wine she couldn't pronounce and the first course when it happened. Even though she was anticipating it, it still surprised her, caught her off guard.

At first, it sort of looked like Neville had fallen to the floor, and she let out an uncontrollable gasp. This only made things worse because now he looked totally embarrassed. Neville wasn't the kind of guy who liked attention on him, so this was probably painful, but he continued on, sweat beading. He steadied himself beneath Amelia, one knee propped up in the indisputable symbol.

Other glamorously clad patrons of the restaurant eyed up the situation with smiles and nudges, awaiting the show. Amelia felt herself redden, felt her hand instinctively go to her mouth in an "Oh, my God" pose. She suddenly felt like vomiting. Was one supposed to feel like that during a happy occasion as this? She had no clue. And then she, for the tenth time, scolded herself, told herself to pay attention.

"Amelia, from the first day I saw you in those holey jeans and Grateful Dead T-Shirt at Book World, I knew there was something about you. I went into that store that day looking for a marketing book, and I came out with a new sense of what life was all about. I fell in love with you that very moment. I knew I couldn't experience life without you by my side. You are my best friend. You bring such excitement to my life, with your dog-walking, smoothie-making, book-sorting penchants. I love everything about you. I'm crazy about you. Will you marry me?"

The words came out in a flurry. Neville was usually well-spoken, careful in his words. He sort of sounded like a rambling sixteen-year-old at the moment, but Amelia didn't care. There was something sweet about this moment, something that caused her voice to catch in her throat. He loved her. This sweet, rational, always-planning-ahead man loved her. She gazed intently at him as he knelt precariously with a ring in front of her, a gorgeous ring. She saw their future of babies and a Cape Cod, a Labrador retriever, mutual funds, and chicken dinners around a table every Sunday. She saw predictability, she saw comfort, and she saw warmth. She saw love.

So Amelia did what any wild, crazy-spirited woman in her position would do.

She said, "Yes."

Chapter Fifteen

Charlotte
February

"You've got to let this go," Leonard urged as he worked on cutting out the next stack of hearts.

Setting down the ribbon for a second, Charlotte shook her head. "It's not so easy. She's making such a mistake. This isn't right."

"That may be so, but she's gotta figure it out. Not you. She's gotta live her own life."

"So… what? I just have to sit back and watch her let the best thing for her slip away?"

Leonard reached for her hand and simply nodded.

Leonard and Charlotte had fallen into an easy relationship, one with evening walks and afternoon tea. They were growing closer and closer every day, and Charlotte was finding something magical at Wildflower, something she never thought she would find again— love.

Now, sitting over the red and pink hearts they were

making for the annual Valentine's Day dance, Charlotte looked over at the man who had creeped right into her soul, becoming a rock, a steady force in what she thought was a washed-up heart.

It had really happened without Charlotte even noticing, a blessing in disguise. If Charlotte had sensed it at first, if she had realized how Leonard was tiptoeing right into her heart, she would have resisted, and they probably would have never arrived to the point they were now.

It had been slow, an imperceptible move on Leonard's part. Some would argue he didn't even notice the bond forming. Both had lost so much, both had been through decades of love. Both had given up on the notion love was still possible or relevant or needed. Both felt like nothing could compare to their first loves, like it wasn't even a remote option.

Over the months, though, their conversations became longer and deeper. Their time together became essential. They started functioning as a single unit, doing everything together, going everywhere together. People started talking around Wildflower. There was talk of budding love, of a torrid romance, even of a wedding. Charlotte had heard the whispers but swore they were crazy.

"Mom, it's okay to admit it. Dad's gone. He would want you to be happy." Annie had broached the subject one day, sensing the truth behind the rumors. "Leonard is great, and I think it's good you have each other."

"Don't be ridiculous, Annie. Leonard is a good friend," Charlotte said, feeling herself blush. She hadn't known why, but the notion of falling in love again was frightening. It was preposterous, actually. It seemed disrespectful to Charlie, to their life.

"Okay, Mom. I won't push. But I want you to know I think it's okay to fall in love again. I don't think love is once in a lifetime. I think love is always a possibility."

Charlotte stopped. "And when did you become such a proponent of love? Before or after you told your ex's mistress, well, you know what you said."

Annie smiled. "Well, I'm less bitter these days. Love doesn't always work out. Sometimes death or circumstance can end it. But that doesn't mean you can't find it again."

Charlotte paused, the revelation hitting her. So the rumors about Annie and Joe sharing secret dates were true.

Now, a few months later, Charlotte had been considering what Annie said about love, about it happening again. Maybe her daughter was right. Maybe love wasn't once in a lifetime. Maybe it came in different forms at various points in life. And maybe that was okay. If her daughter could be scorned and hurt so badly by a man and still open her heart, well, then what was stopping Charlotte?

She snapped back to the present, a pile of hearts in front of her needing ribbon. "I guess you're right. I guess Amelia will have to figure it out on her own. Love is complicated, huh? I mean one kiss, one look and everything can change. And yet nothing can change. Mind-boggling, really." She mindlessly fed ribbon into the hole in the heart, not paying much attention to Leonard. She didn't realize he had put the scissors down, was looking at her intently.

"Yeah, it's complicated. But I think it's still worth it," he murmured. As Charlotte turned to ask him what he meant, she froze. Leonard had moved close, and now something truly complicated was happening. Before she could even set down her stack of hearts, Leonard's lips were on hers. She wanted to push him away at first, to say people their age didn't do this sort of thing.

But she couldn't. Because it felt so good and right. All of the sadness over the changes that had happened in her life melted away. No, it wasn't the lusty kiss of a twentysomething. It wasn't even the romantic kiss of a fortysomething. But it was special, it was inviting.

It was love.

Charlotte wanted time to revel in this moment, to revel in the fact her heart was capable of waking up again. She wanted to take in every second of the kiss, to plant it firmly in the depths of her memory, a moment never to be taken away. She wanted to revel in the bond that had been sealed between her heart and Leonard's, to radiate in the beauty of a love found.

But she didn't get to.

Because as she pulled away from Leonard, pulled away so she could look into his eyes, to see if he was feeling the same thing, something slapped across her face. Cheeks stinging and eyes watering, she turned with shock and horror to see what had halted her beautiful moment, had tainted the first kiss.

***

The air in Cassie's office was stale, smelled a bit like old Cheetos if Charlotte were to diagnose it. There was no mistaking the mood Cassie was trying to portray, however, for it was one of gravity.

"Ladies, I'm so disappointed we are having this conversation again," Cassie scolded as if she were talking to kindergartners.

"Well, me, too," Charlotte muttered as Annie gave her a silencing look.

The office hadn't been designed to house this many people, so it was even more uncomfortable than it would have been. Charlotte, Catherine, Leonard, Cassie, Joe, and Annie were all seated around Cassie's perfectly organized desk. Wildflower was, in many ways, like a high school—gossip traveled at the speed of sound. Within a few minutes of the "slap heard around the assisted living center," Cassie was confronting the women and trying to figure out what happened. Within a few minutes of the conversation, the two women and Leonard found themselves in Cassie's office, waiting for Joe and Annie to show up. Talk about role reversal. Charlotte felt like she was at the principal's office waiting for her mom to get there.

Annie had looked flustered when she showed up,

which Charlotte could understand. Things kept going from bad to worse for the poor girl. The last thing she needed was to come here and hash out some drama over Catherine. Charlotte hated the woman even more for causing Annie grief.

Despite the chaos, Charlotte felt a warmth in her heart. As Leonard sat beside her, hand in hers, she realized it didn't matter if the egotistical maniac had slapped her or if she were forced to attend this little mediation meeting. He had kissed her. She had found something special here at Wildflower. She could deal with fifty Catherines if it meant she could feel like that, find someone like Leonard. It would all be okay.

Catherine, on the other hand, didn't look so sure. She looked a bit embarrassed, but more than that, she looked prideful. She was not a woman to back down, not even if she was wrong. Charlotte knew she would fight to keep her pride and her "I'm right" attitude intact no matter what. Looking over at Leonard, though, Charlotte only thought one thing—bring it on.

"Now, I've talked to all of you about this little war going on and how it has to stop. I love both of you dearly but I cannot have this hostility going on at Wildflower. It's bad for the community. And now we've moved on to physical assault? I should be calling the police. This is too much."

"Well, I don't know why everyone is looking at me," Catherine snapped. "She started this the second she walked in the door. She's the one who's been maniacal and cunning. She's to blame." Catherine shouted louder with every word, a bent finger pointing wildly toward Charlotte. Charlotte felt the need to snap it like a broomstick but thought better of it. Rage brewed, however, at the woman's words.

"Unbelievable," Charlotte remarked, unable to help herself. The warm fuzzies had worn off.

"Ladies," Cassie ordered.

"Well, I do have to agree with my mother," Annie said, and Charlotte practically gasped. Here was her conflict-avoiding daughter leaping in to defend her. The new haircut had really done wonders for her confidence.

"This is unbelievable. I mean, she slaps my mother, *slaps her,* and you call us all in here like this is a mutual problem?"

Catherine glowered as Joe cleared his throat, clearly uncomfortable. "Well, yes, Annie, my mother was ridiculously out of line. But you know as well as I do this is a mutual thing going on. They're both guilty," Joe carefully stated.

Leonard let out a barely audible "Oh no," and everyone else held their breath. This was certainly going a different route than planned.

"Well, sure, my mom has been sassy, but that's only because *your* mother started this whole thing. Giving her attitude, walking around like a queen in those furs. Your mom has the personality disorder, not mine." Annie was getting riled up. Even Catherine sat silent as the show unfolded.

Joe stood. "Personality disorder? Really? You're not going to put any blame on your mother for this? You have no clue what you're talking about."

Annie stood too, arms crossed in front of her chest to further symbolize the antagonistic state of the discussion. Cassie then stood as well, trying to coach Annie and Joe to calm down and to sit back down. They ignored her as Catherine, Leonard, and Charlotte all looked at each other, wide-eyed and silenced.

"You're the one without a clue. Don't tell me where to put the blame. Screw you. Come on, Mom, we're done here," Annie shouted, looking at the stunned Charlotte.

"With all due respect, we aren't done here. We need to chat about a few things," Cassie meekly noted.

"Honey, why don't you go ahead and take a walk. I'm fine, really," Charlotte assured, grazing Annie's arm, sensing the pressure building.

Annie nodded, coming down from her angry emotional high and seeming a bit embarrassed by her outburst. She stomped out the office. Joe rushed to follow her, leaving only four behind.

"Well that was certainly unexpected," Cassie muttered under her breath, trying to paint back on her typical smile.

There was an awkward, pregnant pause before Cassie began.

"Okay, ladies. We need to figure this out. Now I know I said there would be eviction notices if this whole thing continued, but given the apparent stress of your families, I would hate to do that to them, right? So let's come to some sort of agreement here, an agreement of mutual respect maybe?"

Everyone stared at Cassie, not sure what to say. "Right, I'll take that as a yes. Why don't we try to sort this whole mess out, talk about what happened. Catherine, do you want to start?" Cassie took on a counseling role. Although this was certainly outside of her job parameters, Charlotte wasn't going to complain. Cassie was right about one thing—Annie was certainly under stress, and an eviction wouldn't do.

"Well, that sanctimonious, uptight weasel saw Leonard and I had a thing going on, and she stole him right out from under me," Catherine touted matter-of-factly. Charlotte gasped. Eviction notice or not, this was too much.

"Are you kidding me? Stole him from you? He hasn't given you the time of day, sweetheart. Wake up!" There were some angry glares and some increasing heat in the air again before Cassie stepped in.

"*Ladies!* Enough. Clearly this isn't helping. Leonard? Do you want to say anything to, I don't know, calm things down?" Cassie implored Leonard with her eyes, desperation leaking from her face, dripping in her voice. This was unchartered territory. For the first time, Charlotte actually felt a little bit bad. She glanced out the window, noticing Annie and Joe were continuing the heated argument of their own in front of Wildflower. Charlotte looked away, hoping Cassie didn't notice. This certainly wasn't good advertising for the establishment.

She turned back to Leonard, wondering where this was going to go as Catherine, too, sidled up to their apparently joint love interest.

"Well, Catherine, I'm really flattered by your attention. Despite everything that's happened, I think you're a sweet woman, and I'm truly honored you're interested in me, even if it is to get back at Charlotte." Leonard smiled, turning to wink at Catherine.

Charlotte's stomach dropped. Was this really happening? Men were unbelievable. Charlotte found her mouth opening to dispute these words, to say something to set things right, but had no idea where to begin. So she shut her mouth, waiting for everything to settle as it would while Catherine's face broke into a giant grin. Her chin was raised in defiance at Charlotte; she was on cloud nine. She reached for Leonard's hand, but he smoothly moved it out from under her.

"With that being said," Leonard carefully enunciated, "I'm sorry, but I don't feel the same way. I never have. Any connection you've felt has been purely imagined. Because ever since I got here, there was only one woman I had my eyes on. A beautiful woman who stole my heart without me even knowing it." Leonard turned his back quite literally on Catherine, shifting instead to face Charlotte as she grinned carelessly. Catherine frothed with envy as Cassie stared, seemingly awaiting the next figurative or literal punch in the situation.

"Charlotte, when my wife died, I thought my heart

had died, too. I thought it was over. I thought I would spend the rest of my life alone, dead to the world in every way that mattered. And then I came to Wildflower, against my will really. I didn't want to live in this cemetery, didn't want to waste my final days eating gloppy food and sitting around as people tried to convince me everything was great. Sorry, no offense," he said, turning to Cassie on the final words. She waved her hands dismissively and motioned him on.

"But then I saw you on the first day, sitting on the bench in the sunlight. You were talking with Bridget, and you were alight with energy and full of life. I saw you the first day, and I saw something more important—the future. I saw that life wasn't over, that maybe even love wasn't over. In the past few months, as we've grown close, I've come to realize how true that is. You make my life worth living, even now. You make me want to keep going, to live for decades so I can spend more time with you. You've awakened me to life's beauty and to the fact it isn't over. I love you, Charlotte, and our kiss sealed it." Charlotte blinked back tears. Suddenly, the slap, Catherine, none of it mattered. All that mattered was Leonard articulating exactly what her heart was feeling. She came to life as his words danced around the room, realizing her love hadn't died with Charlie. No, love didn't just die, didn't just leave. As long as a person was breathing, there was love to be felt.

"I love you, too," she whispered.

"So let's forget about all of this jealousy and

slapping and nonsense. Let's focus on what's important." He paused, letting everything sink in. Even Catherine, although she wouldn't admit to it later, seemed caught up in the emotion of Leonard's words.

Then Leonard uttered the words that would set everything right, at least for Charlotte.

"Charlotte, I know this is crazy, and I know we're not in our twenties. But I don't care. I want to spend the rest of my life with you, and I want everyone to know it. Charlotte, will you marry me?"

And before anyone could butt in or slap her again, she shouted, "Yes," leaning in for the second kiss with Leonard.

***

Things with Catherine weren't all patched up, and Cassie was still making threats about eviction notices if anything else happened, but Charlotte didn't care. She was floating away in a sea of happiness, wrapped up in the beauty of second love.

She had always thought second love was a joke. First love was where it was at. First love would always overshadow a second love, always proving to be more exciting, more genuine, deeper. Now, though, as much as she had loved Charlie, she admitted to herself she wasn't so sure if this analysis was accurate. Walking hand in hand with Leonard out of the office, she saw a whole future laid before her... and she couldn't wait.

"Let's find Annie," Charlotte practically sang, pulling Leonard toward the door to find her daughter, excited to tell her the news. "Let's make sure she didn't tie Joe up on the bench outside."

As they exited the building and headed around the side toward the garden area, though, Charlotte temporarily forgot about all of her good news, about telling Annie about the wedding coming up. She forgot about the warmth radiating in her core, the good feelings that had pushed aside any hostilities between her and Catherine. Annie hadn't tied Joe up, and there wasn't a violent fight that needed breaking up. It was the exact opposite.

Annie and Joe weren't even talking any more. Instead, they were locking lips quite passionately outside of Wildflower Meadows, wrapped up in each other.

Her daughter and Catherine's son. Her daughter with the son of a tyrannical, sneaky, violent woman. Charlotte tried hard to let it go, to tell herself her daughter deserved to be happy, but a piece of her couldn't shake the bad feeling she got from the sight.

"Well, look at that," Leonard chuckled. "Looks like they worked it all out."

"Yeah, I guess they did." Charlotte turned to Leonard. Looking in his eyes, she was able to let go of her fears for Annie, of her disappointment that of all the men she could choose, she chose the son of Charlotte's current archenemy.

"Let it go, Char," Leonard whispered before leaning in for another kiss.

And she did. She really did.

Chapter Sixteen

Charlotte

"I hear congratulations are in order," Owen said as soon as she opened the door the next day. He was coming for his daily visit to check up on her. Although he was still technically hired to be her aide, Charlotte really didn't think of it that way anymore. He was more like a family friend, or maybe even family.

"Word travels fast." She smiled, ushering the tattooed hunk in. She couldn't help but notice, though, there wasn't the same light in his eye, the same quirky comments. He wasn't fooling anyone; she knew exactly what was going on with him. She knew what had triggered the sadness because it coincided perfectly with another big proposal in the family.

"Yeah, well, everyone's excited. A Wildflower wedding. This hasn't happened around here... well, ever really. Your family's sure been busy falling in love, huh? Two weddings, that's crazy." He blushed as soon as he mentioned it. "Sorry, it's none of my business."

"Stop being ridiculous. Of course it's your business. Especially since one of the weddings should be involving you."

"Whoa, easy Char, I don't want Leonard coming after me." He finally gave her his beautiful grin.

She nudged him in the ribs. "You know exactly what I'm talking about. You're not giving up yet, are you?"

"I don't know what you're talking about." He led himself to a seat at the kitchen table, a custom they had begun several months ago. Charlotte retrieved the scones from the counter, passing them to Owen as she brewed him a fresh cup of coffee.

"Don't be silly. You two are perfect for each other. Even Amelia knows it. She's scared, that's all. She's seen what her mom's going through, with the divorce and all, and she's afraid. She's trying to play it safe. But Neville's not what she needs. She knows it. She just needs to be reminded."

"They're engaged. She's made up her mind. She loves Neville. Besides, what do I have to offer her? A life of terrible rock gigs? Apartment living? I can't compete." He dropped his head into his hands. This had clearly been the topic of his thoughts for weeks.

Charlotte abandoned the coffee project to walk over to Owen, gently putting a hand on his shoulder.

"She's engaged, but that doesn't mean she's in love. Not with Neville, anyway. I see the way she looks at you, and trust me, it's not in a platonic way. And I see the way you look at her. I see the unconditional love in your eyes, the spark between you. I see a whole lot you have to offer her. Excitement, passion, love. You get her, Owen. He doesn't. He just doesn't. You need to make her see it too, before it's too late."

There was a long pause as Owen took all of the advice in, looking into her face, appreciating her insight. But then he snapped back to reality.

"But they're getting married, Charlotte. And with all due respect, I don't think you can be in love with someone else when you're marrying another man. It's too late already."

"Owen, I've learned one thing over these past few months here at Wildflower. You see, before I came here, I thought I understood love. I'd been married for decades. I had a beautiful life with Charlie, and I thought I got it. I thought love was easy to categorize, that it made sense. But after seeing you and Amelia, after Annie's whole situation, after situations of my own, I've come to realize something. Love doesn't always happen in the way we want it to or in the way we think it should. Sometimes when we don't want love, when we've sworn off it, it happens anyway. Love isn't about rationality or doing what makes sense; it's about finding what makes you feel passion, what makes you feel alive. And the really spectacular thing? The love that comes along, well, it's not always with the one you're first married to. Amelia may be planning on marrying Neville, but she doesn't love him. Not the way she could love you, in my opinion."

Owen looked at her quizzically, trying to make sense of her words. "You really think she could fall for me?"

"I do."

Owen didn't argue, didn't give any sort of statement. He simply nodded, sighed, and stood up to check Charlotte's pills. Charlotte nodded in victory, an almost imperceptible movement of assurance. Things would be okay.

"So what's new, anyway?" she asked when he returned to share a cup of coffee with her.

"Actually, a lot. I've got another gig set up for next month, and I'm moving."

"Oh? Not far, I hope." Charlotte's heart momentarily jolted.

"No, no. Just across town. My landlord raised rent, so I figured it was time to find a new place. I'm moving next week to this new complex. It's called Junction Estates, although it's not quite estate like. Pretty basic, shoebox apartment, but it'll work for this bachelor, I suppose."

Charlotte's heart jolted again.

"Junction Estates?"

"Yeah, you know of it?"

Charlotte winked, leaving Owen with a confused look when she uttered one statement: "This is *grand*." She left it at that, scurrying to the counter to find more celebratory scones, a jaunty skip in her step and a song in her voice.

Chapter Seventeen

Annie

Slapping some hair product into her spikes and touching up an eyeliner smudge, Annie couldn't help but smile at the woman looking back at her. She hadn't lost it; she still had a radiance about her, an energy, a get up off the ground and try again resilience. Dave hadn't completely stomped her into the ground. He hadn't won completely.

She knew this wasn't about a haircut or some Urban Decay eye products, though. No, it was much more than that. It was about a flannel-shirt-loving man with soft, inviting eyes. It was about the man whose mother may or may not be her own mother's enemy. It was the man she had fought with last week about their mothers and some slapping. It was the man who revived her heart's capacity to feel by softly planting a kiss on her lips.

She'd been downright pissed at him that day when she'd stormed out of the office. She knew deep down Joe wasn't being unreasonable. The whole Charlotte-Catherine fight was mutual; her mother was anything but innocent. But something about the way he had defended Catherine felt wrong, it felt malicious. It felt like something Dave would say.

She only realized it later, realized that was why she had been so angry with him. At the time, emotion had simply overpowered her ability to reason. She was literally seeing red, unable to process anything he said when she stormed into the courtyard.

He had followed her, trying to calm her down.

"Annie, wait, calm down, listen."

"Get away from me, Joe. Go back and defend your mother."

"Annie, why are you so mad? I didn't mean to point the finger at your mom. I just… I thought we were on the same page in there. They're both guilty. They're both acting crazy."

She had turned to face her assailant. She softened a bit, looking into his eyes. But then she remembered how he had made her feel in the office, how his words had said everything.

He thought she was inferior.

"You know what? Just because your mother's rich, just because she has fur coats and Chanel perfume doesn't mean she can treat my mother like that," she'd spewed, pointing angrily at him as the words tumbled out.

Joe had sighed, looking at her, rustling his hair with his hands. He looked into her eyes, embarrassed.

"You're absolutely right. I shouldn't have said that. I know my mom is being ridiculous. I'm sorry. It's just been stressful." He had wrapped his arms around her.

At first, she'd tried to hold back, to not give in to his touch. She wanted to push him away, to not let him in.

She couldn't though.

The feel of his arms around her brought her back, made her realize how stupid she'd been. She was doing exactly what she didn't want. She was pushing him away.

Sure, she'd been mad about what he'd said about her mom. She was fed up with his mother. If she were being honest, though, her anger hadn't been about any of that.

It was about Annie being scared.

They'd spent the past few months getting to know each other. They'd gone inner tubing in the snow—which had been a blast. He'd taken her to a pottery class, to dinner, to the ice skating rink. They'd tried a ballet class—which had been an utter failure. He'd taken her paintballing. She'd felt herself unexpectedly falling hard for the country music loving landscaper, who'd brought excitement to her life again.

He was so different from what she thought was "her type," so different from Dave. He was a fix it yourself, mechanical, classic car loving kind of man. He drank beer instead of wine. Despite his mother's snooty, sophisticated attitude, Joe was down to earth, simple. He was everything she thought she'd never fall for.

Yet here she was.

She'd been telling herself it was strictly platonic. He was just a good man, a good friend. She didn't want to admit that their time together was really something more, something building between them. She'd hidden their adventures from everyone, feeling like a ridiculous teenager sneaking out of her parents' house when she went out with Joe, lying to Amelia about where she was and where she was going. She felt the urge to keep their growing relationship covert. Perhaps she'd been trying to hide the truth from herself.

That day, though, sitting in that office, hearing him talk, she'd come to two realizations. First, she realized without a doubt she was falling for him. The secret adventures, the way he made her feel when he walked into the room… there was no denying it.

Second, and perhaps more frightening to Annie, was the fact that in Cassie's office, she'd seen something in him she'd never recognized before.

She saw a hint of Dave.

The way he'd accused her of being blind to the truth, of how he talked about her mother. Of how he made her feel inferior in the office, like her ideas didn't matter.

Standing before Joe outside, though, leaning against his chest, she realized how stupid she'd been. He wasn't Dave. He was Joe, the kind-hearted man who'd bought her hot chocolate and surprised her with her favorite pizza on Friday nights. He was the man who was always full of spontaneous ideas and surprises.

He was the man who was going to claim her heart again. The truth was, she wasn't sure if she was ready for it.

It was no excuse, however, to be mad at Joe.

"God, I'm sorry." She looked at the ground while running her hands through her hair. "I don't know what came over me. It's been so stressful. I know that's no excuse. It's just, in there, I got this feeling. Maybe it was a flashback to how it was with Dave. He always acted so smug because his family was rich. He acted like my opinion was never as worthy as his. No matter what the situation was, he was never at fault, his family was never at fault. I was the inferior one. I guess I screwed up. I'm sorry. I'm an idiot." True regret stirred in her heart. Joe's already soft face softened even more, and she saw compassion in his eyes. She saw understanding.

"It's okay, I get it. And I wasn't defending my mom. If anyone is being an idiot, it's her."

Anger dissipated, and she saw him for what he was. It was ridiculous she had seen anything but humility and softness in him. He was nothing like Dave, which was a gift in itself. He was kind and gentle, patient and understanding. He was humble and easy, relatable. He was perfect in his own imperfect, nonchalant way.

He paused, as if wondering if he should take the chance given the situation. But then she leaned in, almost imperceptibly, questioning herself as she did it. She moved her head just enough to give him the confidence he needed. When he went in for the kiss, he was cautious, communicating a willingness to be careful with her through his slow movements. The kiss was soft, a whisper of a touch, peaceful and fulfilling. She didn't feel passion or a hunger needing to be quenched. She had just felt at home.

When he pulled away, he smiled, flicking a piece of her bangs out of her eye. He was grinning. "Not too bad for a guy in a flannel, right?"

They had ambled back into Wildflower, his arm around her. Everything had changed in a moment. In reality, everything had changed with her mother's kiss, with Catherine's slap, and with the realization Joe wasn't Dave in any way.

***

Now, Annie was preparing for their first official date since the kiss, the kiss that reminded her she shouldn't give up yet. Annie was excited for the prospect of a new relationship but scared, too. Was it too soon? Had she let herself be enveloped by the warmth of their chemistry without thinking about what a new relationship might mean? Could she really let go of the insecurities, the pain Dave had caused? Was she truly ready to move on?

Their fight had brought up some harsh realities for Annie. She wasn't completely over the hurt Dave had inflicted, hadn't completely let go of old resentments. Could she push those aside now, could she fight the fear in her heart to pursue things with Dave? Was she fooling herself?

She would have to let go for now, at least for tonight, because as she wondered, the doorbell rang. She fluffed her hair one last time before clicking down the hallway to the front door. She hobbled awkwardly in her high heels, which were usually reserved for special occasions, but she'd wanted to put extra effort in. Beauty was truly pain. She wore a simple black dress, A-line with a touch of lace at the hem. The dress was off-the-shoulder on one side, giving it a much sexier appeal than most of her clothes.

Where a few weeks ago she hadn't been nervous to go out with Joe, had felt comfortable, she now felt painfully anxious. It was crazy how the word "date" changed everything, how suddenly she felt like she was going somewhere with him for the first time. She felt the pressure, for sure.

When she got to the door, she found Joe dressed in jeans, work boots, and a flannel. She was clearly overdressed... or was he just underdressed?

"Um, hey, these are for you. God, you look great," he mumbled as he handed her a bunch of daisies. She took the flowers from him and carefully motioned him in as she went to look for a vase.

"So where are we going?"

"Um, well there's this little diner about a half hour out of town I thought we could go to, but you're dressed so nice and I don't want to waste your outfit going to this place. It's kind of a dive," he admitted sheepishly, looking at the ground.

"Don't be ridiculous. I'll change." She kicked off her heels.

"No, we'll go somewhere classier, really."

"Joe, it's fine, I hate wearing high heels anyway."

"Listen, can I be honest with you?" he asked, and her heart stopped. This was going to be bad. This was ending before it even began. She really should have known better than to get her hopes up.

"Look, I haven't done this for a while. This whole official dating thing. And the last time I did it, well, it didn't turn out so well. You should know by now I'm a pretty simple guy. I'm no good at all of the fancy stuff."

She laughed. "Oh, man, thank God. I'm so relieved. Because as I stuffed myself into this dress tonight, I was so stressed out. I was thinking the exact same thing. I have no idea how to date. It's been decades. I felt like a wreck, and I wanted to impress you, too. Things just felt so different since we called it a date. I was kind of freaking out." She grinned. She breathed out. She finally felt like she could relax, be herself.

"What, a flannel guy like me? You thought you had to impress me?" He laughed now, approaching her, taking her hands in his. "Annie, I like you just the way you are. T-shirt and jeans, whatever. I think you're beautiful and perfect. I like your zest for life, your personality. There's no need to impress. So how about we cut the pretenses and go out and have fun? Don't worry about ordering a salad so I don't think you like to eat, and I won't worry if I spill beer on my shirt. Let's forget about the conventional rules. What do you say?"

She answered him by planting a kiss on his lips before heading back to her room to change into some comfortable clothes. "Screw conventions," she shouted over her shoulder, laughing the whole way. She was liking Joe more and more by the second.

***

As she laughed about the hot sauce dripping off her hands, Joe handed her a napkin. "Good thing we cleared the air about impressing each other, because I'm pretty sure a normal date would go running right now."

"Normal? I could be offended by that."

So far, the conversation had been so light, so easy. Annie felt like she had known Joe her whole life, like he wasn't just some guy who'd stumbled into her at Wildflower. She felt at ease with him, like she had spent a lifetime with him instead of Dave. She felt a sense of warmth, a sense of self-realization she had never felt with her ex. She felt like she could see an easy life stretched out before her, Joe at the center of it. Hot-wing eating, work boots wearing, outdoor work for a living, man's man Joe. And she couldn't be more excited.

"So why didn't you ever get married?" Her beer was making her lips a little looser and her conversation a little braver.

"Well, now we're cutting the pretenses, huh? Just kidding, it's fine. It just never really happened for me."

"Never found the right girl?"

"Nope. It's really as simple as that."

She knew he was telling the truth. That's what she realized about him; there was never a question of his genuineness. Joe oozed honesty.

"How about you? Was Dave your only love?"

She tried to avoid getting a wistful look in her eye, but she supposed it was the hazard of a long-term marriage. One could never quite escape the clutches of it, no matter how much she wanted to. It was always stained in her heart, a mark on her face.

"The one and only," she murmured.

"Sorry. Too soon?"

She thought for a second, setting her wing down to look at him. "No, I suppose not. It's just... hard. I don't want it to be. I want to absolutely abhor him for what he did. I want to erase any memory I have with him in it. But then, that would be like wiping out my entire life, you know? Everything was centered around him. And now that he's gone, it's just been hard to figure out what life looks like without him. Especially since I still loved him."

Joe nodded. "I can't say I understand, because it would obviously be a lie. But I understand it must be hard. It must be something you don't really ever get over. You just have to do your best, I guess, to find a new future for yourself, find new meaning. It'll never be perfect because it'll never be what you had in mind. But then again, who knows, maybe you'll find it could be better."

For some reason, all of this struck a chord with her. It had been stirring in her mind for a while, but hearing Joe say it made it feel real. "Yeah, I think you're right. When I first found out about the affair, I thought everything was over. And obviously, it was. I hated him. But I loved him, too. I cringe to think about how desperate I was to get him back. I begged, I pleaded. I went through a few weeks where I tried to be a better wife, tried to be sexier, more exciting. I tried to convince him I could be her, if he would tell me what that was. It was pathetic."

"I think it was probably natural. And I think he was a freaking idiot to ever make you feel like you weren't good enough. He sounds like an ass to me, no offense."

"None taken. You're right. It was just that at the time, my life was so wrapped up in him, in what he was, in who I was with him, I couldn't see past it. I couldn't admit to myself the man I thought I knew had changed. Then again, maybe he didn't change at all. Maybe Dave was always the Dave who was looking for a better version, the Dave who abandoned me when things weren't perfect. Maybe he was always the Dave going for a girl like Melissa, perfect, money-making Melissa. I just didn't want to admit I had spent my life with a man like that."

He looked at her then, his eyes taking her in, every inch of her, good and bad. "I would never do that to you."

They hadn't known each other for long. There was still so much to discover. She didn't know his favorite type of car or his favorite breakfast food. She wasn't even sure if they would ever even become an official couple long-term or if she was ready for that. She didn't know his entire background, his goals. She shouldn't trust his word, shouldn't believe him on a whim.

But when Joe said those simple words, stoic and straightforward, she knew Joe would never be Dave. And that was perfectly beautiful to Annie.

Chapter Eighteen

Annie

After several dozen wings, a few beers, and loaded nachos for good measure, Joe drove Annie home. At her front door, they stood in silent wonder for a few moments, both basking in the glow of a wonderful night, both thinking it was too perfect to be true.

"I had a great night," Joe said quietly, as he leaned in to kiss her once more.

The kiss, though, was different. It wasn't the calm, warm kiss of a few days ago or even the surprise kiss from earlier that night. It was a kiss craving more, begging to be finished in other ways than just the parting of lips. Annie knew that type of kiss, had answered its call many nights with Dave. A passion simmered inside that hadn't been for a long time, at least not since the night Dave uttered those fateful words.

Annie wasn't the type to give it all away on date one. Okay, so Annie didn't really know if that was true because her last first date had been decades ago. Weren't the rules different for a fifty-year-old? Was the fear of being labeled a skank unrealistic at her age?

Plus, it wasn't like she was standing on a street corner with a sign—not that the tactic would attract many takers anyway. She knew Joe, she liked him. She felt safe with him. She needed to move on. Her craving for physical intimacy rivaled her craving for hot wings. She had quenched one craving; couldn't she quench the other? They had shared dinner, shared intimate details of their lives, for God's sake. It was okay, perfectly okay. So she led him inside. Deep down, she knew it was probably what she needed. Dave had shattered her self-confidence, had made her feel inferior as a woman and a partner. There was a man, a good man, who wanted her. It made her feel worthy again, made her feel like Dave was the problem, not her.

Once the door clicked behind Joe, there was an urgent flurry. They ignored the conventions of typical first-date sex—whatever those were—clawing at each other's clothes in a fever. He rustled his hands in her hair, pulling her mouth hard against his. Underneath the loose flannel, Annie was pleasantly surprised to find a shockingly hard body, a lean build with a noticeable amount of sculpting. His skin felt enflamed underneath her fingertips as she traced a pattern on his chest, savoring their heavy kisses, electricity sparking in her body. She felt like she had just boarded a roller coaster at the amusement park, her heart fluttering and her stomach dropping in those final few moments before the car propelled down the first slope.

She led him backwards to her bedroom, which was down the hall. They danced a graceful choreography of kissing and walking, the passion continuing to build. She put her hands on the hallway walls, guiding them toward her bedroom as she walked backward, his lips stretching to meet hers the entire time. Their effortless movements signified the power of their desires. They wanted to know each other in every way. They wanted to go beyond the social niceties at the diner, beyond the deep emotional connection. They wanted to confirm the chemistry that was palpable from across the room was, in fact, also palpable in closer quarters.

Once in the room, they pulled apart, Annie pausing to turn on the lamp while Joe maneuvered toward her bed, breathing heavily. Her lips stung from his kisses and she felt breathless. After tugging the cord, her hands slipped to the hem of her shirt, ready to peel back the layers between them, ready to climb between the sheets of the bed she'd once shared with Dave.

But the physical break from Joe, the sight of him standing near the bed, it was a snap back to reality Annie couldn't avoid even though she wanted to. The roller coaster had propelled forward… but now it had crashed right off the track, its passengers careening to earth in a fiery oblivion that would forever taint the ride.

Looking at Joe, who was oblivious to what Annie was currently thinking, she realized something. It wasn't just sex. It was a big step, an emotional one, away from Dave. It was admitting she was confident enough in herself to trust another man with her heart. Annie knew once she took this next step, once she slept with Joe Draden, there was no going back. She would be a goner, sacrificed to the mercy of love yet again.

How did she know for sure Joe was true to his word? Even if he had the best intentions, even if he didn't seem like the type to leave her for a better version like Dave had, who was to say he wouldn't change his mind in six months, a year, ten years even? When she had said "I do," with Dave all those years ago, hadn't she thought he was faithful, trustworthy? Hadn't she thought he was warm and safe? Who could predict where one's heart would go? And did she want to feel that pain again? Did she want a replay of the past few months?

Joe came toward her and she backed up, knowing despite the warmth she was feeling, despite the desire, she couldn't do it. She couldn't make love to another man in that bed, the bed where she had lain at night believing her marriage was perfect, her love with Dave was untouchable, and she would never be one of "those" women.

"You okay?" he whispered, a sultry quality still lilting his voice.

"I'm sorry, I can't." She slumped to the bed, her head buried in her hands. Tears formed at the thought he was going to tell her off and leave.

But he didn't. He let out a sigh, punctuated by disappointment. He ran his hands through his hair. And then he sat beside her, wrapping his arm around her.

"It's okay, I understand," he whispered into her hair, softly kissing her cheek.

"You do?" Tears brimmed over.

"Yeah, it's too much too fast. Here we are, still getting to know each other. And plus we're in your bedroom, which is probably really weird for you since, well, I'm assuming this was your room with Dave? It's too much. I'm sorry. I don't want to screw this up over one night. One night I want badly, don't get me wrong." He grinned sheepishly. "But there's no rush. Let's take this slow, okay?"

She leaned into him, loving him in that moment for saying what she couldn't. For being the kind of man she needed right then, and for not pushing to be the man in her life just yet.

They sat on her bed for a while, Joe holding her tightly. When he finally got up to leave, she walked him to the door. Before he left, he softly kissed her cheek and whispered, "We can take this slow. You don't have to be afraid, okay?" Then he left without any fanfare, without any guilt trips.

As she closed the door, she realized Joe knew what she didn't. It wasn't that she was hesitant about sharing her body or having sex in the bedroom she'd shared with Dave.

It was that she was afraid, truly afraid, to fall in love again. She was afraid of getting her heart stomped on again. She was afraid it was all too good to be true. Because as life had taught her, sometimes love was nothing but a fantasy.

Chapter Nineteen

Amelia

Glancing at the glittering diamond solitaire on her finger, Amelia jumped as Holly let out a loud bark. "Okay, okay, let's go," she said, putting her hand down to get a tighter grip on the leash. "Here we go." She switched her saunter into a jog, which was much more the white bull terrier's speed.

It had been months since she said the one word that changed everything, that had landed the beautiful gem on her hand. She caught herself ogling it everywhere—while making a smoothie, while stocking shelves, while walking her clients. She caught herself glancing at it while driving, which was dangerous, as she quickly found out when she almost rear-ended someone. She would lie in bed at night thinking about the fact she was getting married. She would be Neville's wife. She would be a Mrs.

There had been moments she thought that would never happen for her.

If Neville had it his way, she would already be married. Despite his planning nature, his careful, follow a logical sequence kind of personality, he was in a rush to make the wedding happen sooner rather than later. He was talking about a June wedding, asking her opinion on ceremonies and receptions. He didn't want to wait.

Amelia couldn't wait either. She loved Neville, she really did. She wanted to have the Mrs. title, to take the next step in life. She wanted to play housewife, even if everyone told her the novelty would wear off. A part of her craved the security of knowing her life had truly begun, that she was settled into adult life in the important ways. She felt like it would be a relief to know her life was starting to head in a steady direction.

But she also wanted to take her time in this phase of her life. She wanted to soak in the glory of the engagement. She wanted to get used to the idea of not being solo through life. She would now be joined with someone else, be responsible for making decisions affecting both of them. She was no longer carefree, unsettled Amelia. She was grown up; she was traditional. She was almost married.

Honestly, it unnerved her a bit. Neville was a wonderful man. But there were things that frightened her, too. There was certainly chemistry there, and she knew he was a good person. She admired his work ethic, his charm, his charisma. He was handsome and well put together. He had everything figured out, and he made her want to figure everything out as well.

But there was so much she didn't know about him yet and more he didn't know about her. She couldn't help but feel like they were falling in love with concepts of each other instead of the real deal. She felt like there were still so many things they were keeping tucked away, afraid to reveal their real selves to each other. Were they fooling themselves into a fantasy life? Were they really ready for this next step? Could she promise her heart away to a man who hadn't yet uncovered all of her own heart's passions and needs?

Holly barked again, this time gleefully, as they made their way up the hill. Amelia was huffing by then, but the crazy white dog seemed to have legs like wings. She effortlessly sailed up the hill as Amelia let unsettling thoughts churn in her tired body.

The diamond ring glistened as a ray of sunlight hit it, and Amelia laughed at the cheesiness. She laughed also at the prospect she, tattoos and black hair, would soon be walking down a lacy white aisle with perfectly coifed hair and soft pink nails.

***

After walking Holly, putting in a shift at Book World, and stopping to get some groceries to make it through the rest of the week, Amelia headed back to her apartment for some Ramen noodles and reruns. Neville was away for the rest of the week, typical for his job. Although she missed him, she was glad to have some time to herself to think and also to not have to deal with his pressure to plan the wedding. She wanted to slow down.

Heading to her apartment door, she balanced her bag of groceries on her hip as she fumbled in her purse to get her keys.

"Hey, Amelia," she heard from behind her, startling her to the point of jumping. She turned to see a familiar face down the hallway. Squinting, she realized her eyes weren't deceiving her. She smiled in spite of herself at his face, angular and stubbly.

"Owen? What are you doing here?" She realized it was really the first time she had seen him out of the context of Wildflower.

"Just moved into 402."

Amelia froze. "Did you say 402? Like two doors down?" Her gaze moved from him to the door right down from hers and then back again.

"That's it."

She blushed and she didn't even know why. While she was trying to figure out what to say next, she noticed him glancing at her diamond. He shrugged, motioning noncommittally toward her hand.

"I hear congratulations are in order."

"Thanks." She didn't know what else to say. She decided to change the subject. "Have any more gigs coming up?"

Grinning, he said, "Yeah. Next month actually. It's a small bar an hour away, but it's a gig. You know, this is kinda cool, you living so close. Maybe now we can actually work on the song we talked about."

"Yeah, maybe." She didn't know how Neville would

feel about it. He didn't even know she was a songwriter. And she was pretty sure he wouldn't be crazy about her hanging out with another man alone.

"Well, I'll let you get back to what you were doing." He was less confident than usual, less forward. Rings could do that to men. Of course, a woman awkwardly pushing you away after an amazing kiss could do that too.

Amelia smiled at him, trying to hide her conflicting emotions. "So I guess I'll be seeing you?" She felt like she was in some odd 1920's movie.

He flashed her those teeth she knew so well, and had missed, if she were being truthful.

"Yeah," he said as he turned to saunter down the hall.

Her heart fluttered in a way she hadn't felt since Marla's birthday party. She smiled to herself, opened her door, and went inside to eat Ramen noodles and think about how strange the universe was sometimes.

Chapter Twenty

Amelia

Over the next few days, Amelia saw Owen several times. Their conversations remained basic and even icy. A nervous anxiety hazed over her every time she entered or exited the apartment, always wondering if coincidence would have them meeting each other in the hallway. There was a palpable fear now in her every movement, an awkwardness of what to say or how to act around the man she had kissed beside appetizers. She tried to push the kiss away, blank it out of her mind, but she couldn't. And she figured Owen was going through the same thing.

Tonight, though, the nerves weren't about seeing Owen. As Amelia argued with herself over whether or not a headband was too much in her perfectly curled updo, she told herself to calm down. Neville's parents were probably great, sweet people. His mom would probably be the typical pie-baking woman from the 1950's sitcoms, calling her dear and asking her if she wanted tea. It wasn't like she had anything to hide or be ashamed of. Neville loved her, and she had it together. She didn't have to impress them.

Except she knew she did. These people were now going to be permanent fixtures in her life, or at least soon would be. She wanted their approval, wanted them to say Neville had made a wise choice. She wanted to show them she was worthy of Neville, even if she did have tattoos and some interesting career paths.

She put an extra spritz of hairspray in her hair as her hands shook. She hadn't been this nervous since... well, ever.

"Well if they don't like you, you tell them to shove it," had been Grandma Charlotte's advice that afternoon when she had mentioned her nerves over the formal dinner. "Probably only serve decaf coffee and asparagus. I can tell by looking at Neville his people are like that."

Amelia had just grimaced.

"What's wrong with asparagus?"

"You get what I'm saying," Charlotte waved her remark off. "Besides—" Amelia stopped her before she could finish her predictable end to the sentence.

"Grandma, I know what you're going to say. Please stop. Will I need to keep an eye on you at the wedding when they ask for objections?"

Charlotte answered the question with a shrug, a frown, and palms in the air. Amelia couldn't help but laugh.

Now, though, Amelia tried to cling to her grandma's words. Why *was* she so nervous? It was dinner. Even if his parents didn't like her, did it matter? She was marrying Neville, not his parents. He would defend her no matter what, right? He would tell them Amelia was the perfect woman for him. She had already won him. She didn't need to prove herself.

When Neville came, dressed in a suit and tie, she knew different. This wasn't going to be a chicken barbeque on foam plates with red Solo cups. This was probably going to be one of the five-fork dinners Amelia secretly loathed. Her stomach flip-flopped at the prospect there would be even more ways for her to mess up than she had even anticipated.

"Are you ready?" Neville asked, kissing her on the cheek.

"As I'll ever be," she said.

Neville looked down at her footwear choice before ushering her to the door. "Can you maybe change your shoes?"

Amelia looked down at her favorite pair of sparkly flip-flops. "What's wrong with these?" she asked.

"Nothing. It's just, well, my mom's not a huge fan of flip-flops. She calls them shower shoes."

Amelia felt her stomach drop. She sighed, kicking off her comfortable shoes, exchanging them for some ballet flats. She was a little irked by his appraisal of her shoes, but she was too nervous to argue. She needed all the chances she could get to impress his parents by the sound of it.

Neville nodded in approval as he led her out the

door. "They're going to love you," he reassured.

She let out a huff of air, hoping against all odds he knew what he was talking about.

***

"I am *so* sorry," Amelia enunciated as she stared in horror at the gorgeous white carpet now drenched with dark red wine. It was probably the cheesiest thing that had ever happened to her, straight out of a stupid romantic comedy. She sprang to her feet to... what should she do? How did you even clean up wine from a carpet?

Mrs. Sanson tried to politely wave her off. "It's okay," she muttered, but there was no reassurance in her voice, no foundation to her words. She was horrified. And dinner had literally just begun. Mr. Sanson let out an audible sigh as he scurried to find some towels, eyebrow furrowed probably in calculation of how much money the gorgeous carpet had cost. Neville reached over as Amelia stood dumbfounded, wanting to cry.

"What happened?" Neville gave her a judgmental look, putting a hand on her arm.

"Is it bad if I say I don't know? I guess I'm nervous and I didn't pay attention."

This is going great, she thought as she eyed the stain and the family nervously.

Amelia had arrived at the Sansons' to be greeted stiffly and formally. There were no hugs or smiles as Neville would be met with in her family. There was no laughter or buffet style here. Instead, the formal dining room table was set to the nines, including what seemed like seventy pieces of silverware Amelia had no idea how to use. She was constantly glancing around the table to see what fork she should be on. She told herself it was just how Neville's family was, it was what a real family looked like at dinnertime. Just because she was used to eating on foam plates with sporks didn't mean that was what every family was like. It was... nice... to have formality in life.

When the dinner came out, though, she had felt herself yearning for mac and cheese with hot dogs instead of whatever the stiff brown meat and oddly presented vegetables were. Mr. Sanson was talking to Neville about stocks or something. Amelia was totally tuning them out. Looking across the table, she had seen a stiffly painted smile on Mrs. Sanson's face, but the woman made no attempt to talk to Amelia or ask her questions. Amelia didn't think she was the type who would want to hear about her dog-walking adventures or talk about the latest eyeliner at Ulta. There was something unapproachable about her. Once everyone else started digging in— meaning they delicately nibbled miniscule morsels while trying not to drop a single crumb—Amelia did the same. It was when she was trying to delicately cut her meat that the glass incident had happened. Perhaps it was because of her shaky hands, or perhaps it was because the meat was a bit dry. Her intense cutting, regardless, had led to a clink against the glass, a fumble to grab it, and ultimately a huge wine spill.

With the dumping wine, all pretenses of Amelia

impressing the Sansons came to an abrupt end.

If nothing else, though, the Sansons were gracious. Mr. Sanson tried to sop up the wine as Amelia apologized fifty more times and offered to help, leaning down and bumping heads with her soon to be father-in-law—or at least she still hoped. This incited a string of more apologies and eventually a "Screw it," from Mr. Sanson, who insisted they return to dinner. So Amelia carefully sat down as Neville pushed her in.

There was some stiff silence, the dinner music—did people really play dinner music?—the only sound in the room. Finally, Neville broke the quiet atmosphere.

"So we haven't set a date yet, but we're going to soon. We'll probably have the reception at the club, right, Amelia?" He turned to smile at her. She smiled back with delight at the prospect he hadn't asked for the ring back yet despite her social clumsiness. However, she was also taken aback. The club? They hadn't even discussed it. She didn't really imagine her wedding day, wasn't one of those fanatical girls who had fifty boards on Pinterest for the reception. But the club? That wasn't what she would ever imagine.

Given her recent faux pas, though, she decided to graciously smile and nod. Now was not the time to talk about a carnival-style wedding or anything less than club standards. The Sansons didn't look like the backyard barbecue type, not for a wedding. She could humor the vision a little longer.

Mr. and Mrs. Sanson mustered up smiles, looking at

each other.

"Is there really a rush, Neville? I mean, is there a reason this needs to happen so quickly?"

Amelia paused for a moment before realization hit her. "Oh goodness, no, Mrs. Sanson. I'm not knocked up. Yet." She chuckled, thinking the last word was quite the joke.

Mrs. Sanson didn't laugh. She calmly nodded as if she were sizing the comment up.

"Yeah, no, Mom, no pregnancy. We just, well, we're in love. Why wait? We want to get married, get things moving on the house, and take it from there."

Amelia almost choked on her food. *House? What was he talking about?*

"What house?" she asked, confusion on her face as she turned to Neville.

"Why, your house, of course," Mrs. Sanson said as if Amelia were the dumbest person on the planet.

"Neville?" Amelia asked.

He shrugged. "My parents set aside a plot of land on the property for me to build a house when the time came. Obviously, we'll be using it." He looked at her with a look that matched his mother's.

Amelia squirmed, not sure if this was the most appropriate time to get into a discussion about houses and plots of land and how she might want to actually have a say in their life before he planned it all out for her.

She took a deep breath, reached for her water glass carefully, and took a long, slow sip. She silently counted to five, anger boiling.

She had always known Neville was a planner, a rational, logical, man. But planning their housing without even mentioning it? It was like she was just an accessory in his plan he had drafted with his parents. She suddenly saw a side of him she hadn't noticed before—a side that ignored her needs, her wishes, in favor of his own.

Mr. Sanson interrupted Amelia's internal battle. "Well, I just think you are rushing a bit. I mean, this is the first we're even meeting Amelia. You haven't really had a long relationship. Maybe a long engagement would suit you?"

Amelia felt the tension rising. It was clearly not the first time the Sansons had discussed the relationship, the engagement, or Amelia. She could tell there was an undercurrent of resentment, of disappointment in their son's decision. And she couldn't help but wonder if it was just they felt like he was rushing... or if it had more to do with his choice of bride.

No one seemed to know what to say, especially Amelia. She waited for Neville to jump in, to defend her, to confess his love. He simply poked at a piece of asparagus on his plate.

A few minutes later, Mrs. Sanson decided to speak up, to try to assuage the situation. "So, Amelia. Neville tells us you're a marketing analyst on the managerial track? Tell us about your work."

Confusion again overswept Amelia. She certainly valued her jobs, all three of them. But a marketing analyst? The managerial track? What the hell was this lady talking about?

She glanced to Neville, who seemed to fidget in his seat.

"Yes, Mom. I told you. Amelia's a pro with marketing, and she's already advancing up the managerial ladder. Before we know it, she'll be on her way to being a business owner."

"Really?" Amelia and Mrs. Sanson said at the same time. Amelia's response, though, was loaded with sarcasm.

"That's wonderful," Mr. Sanson said. "A woman with business smarts is a woman you keep around."

Amelia felt like she was going to hurl. She glared at Neville. Who was this man sitting beside her? She barely recognized him. Where was the sweet, considerate, reservation-only, decaf drinking Neville? And why was he lying about her jobs?

She had never really considered he was ashamed of her or her work. He always seemed okay with it, more than okay with it. Here, though, with his formal parents, it seemed like there was a different story.

Amelia didn't take her eyes off Neville as she responded, "Why yes, that does sound like the kind of woman Neville should keep around. A marketing analyst on the managerial track. What a catch, huh? I tell Neville he should consider himself lucky. I mean, some of my friends are working menial jobs at a smoothie shop. Can you imagine?"

Neville looked back at her, a touch of guilt in his eyes. Mr. and Mrs. Sanson politely laughed at Amelia's words, not understanding the true intent behind them.

"So what are your long-term goals? Do you want to start your own business or do a takeover some day?" Mr. Sanson asked, his inner lawyer becoming apparent. He was really good at the cross-examination thing, or whatever you called it.

Amelia turned her gaze to him, deciding to take somewhat of a stand, to let her pride shine through. "Actually, I really love songwriting, so I'd like to get into that and see where it goes. But right now I love my jobs."

She noticed Neville looked at her with raised eyebrows, obviously surprised by the confession, too. She'd never actually told him she loved songwriting, so he probably didn't know if she were serious or not. He jumped into the conversation. "Yeah, but I'm sure songwriting is just a hobby, right? I mean, it's not really your goal."

Amelia felt herself boil. She was suddenly aware and honest with herself about how uncomfortable she felt there, how stifling those people were. Where was the laughter, the welcoming atmosphere? Where was the coffee and scones, the heaping plates of food? Where was the polite conversation and the supportive atmosphere? Where was the love that would surround her for the rest of her days? Amelia wanted a life, a family... but was that the family she would be faced with? Were those the people who would create the family foundation of warmth for her children someday? She couldn't even imagine it. And most of all, where was Neville's support when she needed him? How dare he dash her dreams, tell her what her goals were. Maybe it wasn't just Neville's parents who didn't know her, didn't respect her.

"Actually, it *is* a goal, Neville. I just haven't figured it all out yet," she retorted, smugness in her voice. At the proper table, the response clearly prodded some discomfort because the topic was then dropped. Everyone went back to wordlessly clanging expensive silverware against the porcelain plates and scarfing down vegetables and dry meat.

After Amelia had cleared her plate—accidentally eating the garnish, she realized later—she took in the silence, the stiffness, and wondered—*is this going to be my life?* Once they said their perfunctory good-byes after dessert, Amelia realized, as her stomach growled, that if it was, she was going to be really, really hungry... and not only because of the lack of calories.

***

After an icy walk to the car and a fake wave to his parents, Amelia sat in the passenger seat, seething.

"Amelia, can we talk about it?"

"Save it, Neville," she spewed, sighing with rage.

"Amelia, it's not what you think."

"And what am I thinking, Neville? That you're ashamed of me? That you're embarrassed of my career so you lied to your parents?"

"Amelia, I'm not ashamed of you. It's just… my parents are… difficult. Intense. It was just easier to tell them what they wanted to hear. And I didn't technically lie."

"A marketing analyst?"

"You're good at marketing. And you're great at making the Book World displays."

"The managerial track?"

"You're manager."

"The point is you're ashamed of me. Your parents would be ashamed of me, and that bothers you."

Neville reached for her hand, but she snapped it away.

"Amelia, look at me. Seriously."

Tears started to well, but she fought them back.

"I'm sorry. You're right. I was a jerk. It's just… my parents are so particular. They don't understand a life different from their own. I know I shouldn't care. I know it was wrong. But I just want them to get to know you. I don't want them writing you off because of what you do. I want them to see what I see, the gorgeous, spunky, loving woman I want to marry. I'm sorry. What can I do to make this right?"

She wanted to tell him nothing. She wanted to stay angry.

But something in his voice, something in his words softened her.

Tonight had scared her, had made her realize there were sides of Neville she didn't completely know about.

There were so many good things though, too. So many qualities she loved. Could she really hold this one mistake against him? Could she really blame him?

"Let's not talk about this anymore. Let's just go home," she said. Neville sat for a long moment, probably debating if he should say anything else.

Then, he put the car in drive, pulled onto the road, and drove to her apartment in silence, while she contemplated all of the night's disasters.

***

After closing up Book World on her late shift two nights later, Amelia headed back to her car with regret and foolishness swirling in her head. Two nights, some harsh words, and a few awesome rounds in the bedroom with Neville had cleared up any doubts she was having after the less-than-perfect meeting with his parents.

There had been more heated words after the car ride home, more questions, some talk about pushing back the wedding indefinitely.

But eventually, she had come to her senses.

Why did the Sansons have to live up to her perfect expectation? Didn't everyone dislike their in-laws to an extent? It wasn't like Neville hit the in-law lottery. She had some family issues, certainly. And more than that, she was marrying Neville. His family had raised him to be a handsome, reliable, successful man. She should be grateful, even if they did make her feel out of her comfort zone or like she wasn't good enough. Plus, what had she expected Neville to do? Swear off his family? She was the one who'd sprung the surprise of the songwriting career on him. She was the one who was unsettled and confused and working a bunch of different jobs. What did she expect?

So that night, after some discussions and some apologies, they had fixed things in the only way Amelia knew—they had spent the next evening and the following morning between the sheets, working away their frustrations and reconnecting in every way that mattered.

Now she felt ridiculous about the whole situation. The Sansons were good people. So what if dinner had been fancy? Most women wouldn't complain about that. She should have been more impressive. *That's what love is,* she thought. *Love is sometimes about putting on a good face, about putting your best foot forward, about putting on a different pair of shoes than you would normally walk in just to make sure everything is good.*

True, her heart still panged with fears about the side of Neville she had seen at dinner. The somewhat controlling, somewhat condescending side of his personality had emerged, its ugliness shocking her. Then again, she certainly wasn't perfect either, was she? What right did she have to demand perfection from him? He'd apologized. That should be good enough for her. Sometimes love was about forgiveness. She loved Neville enough to overlook his imperfections—didn't she?

***

Amelia drove the few miles to her apartment complex,

ignoring her paranoia at getting out of her car in the pitch black. It was ten o'clock, later than usual for her to be getting home. She pushed down her fears, got out of her car, and headed inside and up to her apartment.

When she got there, though, she froze in the hallway, terror paralyzing her. Her apartment door wasn't shut. It was open just a crack, an almost imperceptible crack, but it was open nonetheless. And what was hiding behind the door only God could know.

She knew it couldn't be Neville's doing, since he was in Ohio on a sales pitch for the next three days. Her mother rarely was around anymore, spending most of her time with Joe. She barely came to Amelia's apartment, let alone at ten o'clock on a Friday. Fear gripped Amelia, pushing her into action. Except she didn't have her phone with her, and she didn't want to call 911. What if she'd just left the door open? She didn't want to wake up the neighborhood over her own idiotic mistake. But she also didn't want to go inside and find Leatherface.

So she did the next best thing. She found herself covering the twenty feet in the hallway to the closest refuge—Owen's door.

***

"What the…?" he queried when she burst through the door, slamming it behind her and locking it. Good thing she was right—he wasn't the type to lock his door.

"Shh," she whispered as he looked at her like she was crazy. Then she noticed he was wearing only boxers. *Focus, Amelia,* she thought. There could be a murderer a few doors over. It was no time to ogle.

"I know you find me irresistible, but you could at least call first." He grinned, walking toward her with his typical swagger. His ab muscles seemed permanently flexed, the gorgeous ridges begging to be stared at. She pulled her gaze away, meeting his eyes.

"There may or may not be a murderer in my apartment," she blurted out, cutting straight to the chase.

"What?"

"Neville's out of town. I came home, and my door is cracked open. I didn't know where else to go."

"Well, let's call the cops then."

"No."

He froze again, throwing his hands in the air. "And why not? Am I in some weird horror movie? Are you feeling okay?"

"No, I just... well, I can't quite remember shutting the door this morning. So what if we call the cops and wake up the neighborhood, and it was just stupid me who forgot to lock it?"

He took that in, mulling it over. "Okay, fine. I'm going over." He headed to his bedroom.

"No, wait, you can't." She followed him. Despite the circumstances, she couldn't help but look around, see the disordered chaos of his apartment. She should be horrified, but she wasn't. She liked it. It suited him.

"You are so confusing," he muttered, grinning. "It's either we call the cops or I go over there, end of story." He pulled his shirt over his head.

"What if you get killed? I'd feel terrible."

"So you do care about me."

Leave it to Owen to take that as a compliment.

"Well yes, I mean, no, I mean... I don't want you to get killed."

"Okay, I'm going over. If I get killed, well, paint me as a hero in the newspaper, okay?" He retreated back into his room, rifled through a closet, and came out bearing his weapon—a baseball bat.

"Really?"

"What? You want me to take a kitchen knife and hack him to death?"

She shrugged as if to say *why not*? He shook his head.

"Stay here," he ordered. "I'll be back. And if you hear screaming, call 911."

Before she could say anything, he was gone. Her heart sank and her regrets swirled. What if she'd just killed Owen?

***

Amelia paced around Owen's apartment for five stressful, unending minutes. She listened carefully, vowing to dial 911 if she heard as much as a groan or something drop. She heard nothing.

When the door flew open, Amelia jumped out of her skin, fear painted on her face.

"Are you okay? What happened?"

Owen wiped his brow, dropping the baseball bat to the floor.

"Well, he's dead. I beat him to death. But don't worry, there's not too much blood on your carpet." He pounded his chest in an "I am man" motion.

"What?"

He burst into laughter. "Really? Do you think I'd be this relaxed if I just killed a guy? I'm not really a creepo like you thought I was on the first day. Listen, I looked in every corner and cranny, all James Bond style. Nothing. You must have left it propped open."

"Are you sure? Did you check the closet?"

Owen gave her a condescending look. "The closet? You think a burglar broke into your apartment to steal some high heels?"

"No, but I think if he wanted to murder me, he'd probably hide in there first. Don't you watch horror movies?"

Owen sighed. "There's no one in the closet. I checked. Of course I watch horror movies. Where do you think I got my burglar killing confidence?"

"Sorry, I feel like an idiot. I owe you."

His grin widened.

"Well, I mean, it was a very harrowing experience. I did risk my life for you. So I think you do owe me."

She raised her eyebrow. "Harrowing? And you talk about my word choices. I'll get you a coupon for Smoothie Q tomorrow. Seriously, thank you."

"Really? You pay men with Smoothie Q?" His face was incredulous, but in a non-patronizing way.

"And what do you suggest I pay men with?"

"Well..." He smirked, rubbing his chin. "I do have quite the idea, since old Neville is out of town and all," he added.

"I'm not like that."

"Like what?"

"Like the kind of woman to sleep around."

"Whoa, easy, cowgirl. Your mind is dir-ty." He playfully punched her in the arm. "I know me in my boxers is quite the sight, but wow. Straight to the bedroom."

"I thought, I just... well, what were you talking about?" This was humiliating. Good thing Owen had a sense of humor.

"I was talking about pizza. As in, ordering a pizza and watching some Netflix. Thirtysomethings shouldn't be alone at ten o'clock on a Friday night, especially after a terrifying experience like that one. I thought maybe we could kick back, watch a movie, maybe even talk music. But I mean, if you have other forms of payment in mind, I'm not a picky guy." Amelia smiled in spite of herself and punched him in the arm.

"I'll call Tony's Pizza."

"I'll put the baseball bat away."

Amelia shook her head. She should be grateful to Owen. Most girls would be thrilled at not only having a stud hero down the hallway from them but one who wanted to eat pizza with them.

Amelia, though, was a different story. Because standing there thinking about Owen in his boxers, well, she wasn't 100 percent sure she'd been honest.

Maybe she *was* that kind of girl, after all. She shuddered at the mere thought.

***

An hour later and three slices each, Owen and Amelia found themselves propped on his faded couch, shoes kicked off as Netflix played in the background. They were watching a comedy special, Amelia laughing so hard a pepperoni flew across the room and splatted onto the coffee table.

"Gross," Owen shouted, laughing as tears ran down Amelia's face.

"Really? I doubt you'd even notice that around here." She motioned toward the trash and empty food containers stacked on the counter.

"Well, sorry my apartment doesn't meet your clean standards. But at least I shut the door."

"You got me."

His laughter slowed for a moment before he said, "Yeah, I think I do." She too stopped laughing, stowing her plate on an end table. They were looking at each other like they had so many times at Wildflower, but it was different. Two young people, both with similar interests, looking at each other as if they were seeing each other for the first time. She saw beyond the muscles and the confidence, saw a man who had passion, creativity, and a wildness she'd never experienced before. Sitting on the couch with an almost empty pizza box between them, she saw a life together of chaos, takeout, and laughter.

On Owen's couch, Amelia felt more comfortable, physically and emotionally, than she had ever felt with Neville.

But when Owen leaned over the bubbly cheese, planting a hand in the pizza box to steady himself and leaning toward her to meet her lips with a kiss, she pulled back.

"I can't do this," she said. She bolted from the pizza box, the comfort of the couch, and the tattooed man who was threatening to steal her heart.

Chapter Twenty-One

By spring, there were many changes for Charlotte. Her left hand, which still held her engagement ring from Charlie, now held a second ring on the momentous finger—a yellow diamond from Leonard. He had placed it there a few weeks after her official yes, getting help from Amelia to pick out the perfect choice.

She had also become more active at Wildflower than in the fall, allowing herself to join new clubs and try new things. She became head of the gardening club, spending several mornings a week outside planting and weeding, something she had never taken up during her youth. There was something soothing about having your hands in dirt, something refreshing about making the place look beautiful.

There were a lot of things, though, that had stayed the same. She still had morning coffee with Bridget and now Leonard too. She still had her visits from Owen every day. She had been glad when he returned to his normal, jovial self. She didn't ask, but she had a feeling his new apartment locale had something to do with it. She still had visits from Annie, had dinners every night with the same table at Wildflower. She still missed her cats, but visits to Annie's house from time to time helped ease things. As Charlotte had expected, Annie never held true to her word of rehoming the cats. Charlotte knew they were an integral part of her life now, which helped Charlotte feel better about the situation.

She had built a routine for herself at Wildflower, had finally come around to making it not just a house, but a home. She had found a place there, found herself there, understood it wasn't just a final stop on the way to the grave. It was a place for her to explore a new facet of life, for her to explore who she could still become. Where before she had seen a final, closing chapter, she now saw possibility and change. She saw comfort and warmth.

If she thought about it, though, it wasn't necessarily Wildflower that had done that for her. It was Leonard.

If someone had told her ten years ago there would be another love in her life, she would have said they were crazy. First loves are the most powerful, everyone says. First love could never be overshadowed by second or third love, especially not at her age. So what was the point? She'd convinced herself there wasn't one, that she didn't need love again.

But then came Leonard. Then came love.

Leonard had opened up her eyes to the joys of living. As ridiculous as it sounded, it was true. Before

Leonard, she had seen herself fading into the twilight of life, waiting for an abrupt end to cut off her story. She hadn't really pictured it as life after Charlie, and she surely didn't picture there would be another person to claim her heart.

Leonard had taken that theory, though, and obliterated it. He proved to her that second love didn't have to overshadow first love—they coexisted. Second love, as Charlotte learned, was its own special kind of magic. Leonard could never replace Charlie in her heart, but then again, Charlie could never be Leonard. It was, in fact, possible for the heart to stretch, for it to accommodate two different types of emotion for two very different people.

Resting in bed—alone, of course; she might be old, but she still had principles—Charlotte thought about how much Leonard's love had changed her, how it made her want to be better. Suddenly, getting up in the morning wasn't a chore. She *wanted* to get up, get moving, see what each day could hold. That was because of Leonard, because of love.

She had noticed over the past few months a change not just in herself, but in Annie too. She knew what the cause of the change was, everyone did. Annie wasn't fooling anyone with her insistent claims things weren't serious with Joe or that they were just having fun. She could see it in the glow in Annie's cheeks, could sense it from the stories Amelia told. Annie had changed over the past few months too, and it was certainly for the better.

Sure, Charlotte still wasn't crazy about the fact Joe was Catherine's son. She still worried there was something untrustworthy about him, given his genes, but she was willing to let it go. She liked this new Annie, this happier Annie. She couldn't begrudge her daughter that, even if it meant extending an olive branch to Joe.

Love was like that sometimes. It made you change, made you want to be different while still hanging on to who you were. It was, Charlotte thought as she drifted off to sleep, one of life's best beauties. It was hard, it was complicated, and sometimes it was gray, but it was still worth it.

It was all worth it.

Chapter Twenty-Two

Charlotte

"You look like a woman on a mission," Leonard said after the customary kiss before coffee the next morning. Charlotte was tapping her feet impatiently, sucking down her cup of hot liquid like she had places to be.

"Sorry, dear. I've just got a few things I want to tackle today."

"Not Catherine, I hope." Leonard grinned.

"Actually, yes, but not in the way you're thinking."

Leonard groaned. "What are you up to now?"

"I'm going to extend the olive branch."

Bridget, who was also on the bench, almost spit out her coffee. "Are you joking?"

Charlotte shook her head. "I know, I know. It's crazy. But look, I think things with Annie and Joe are heating up and, well, it won't do for us to be so hostile if we could be family."

"So wait, you're going to be friends with her?" Bridget gasped, her mouth open to punctuate her disbelief.

"Now let's not get crazy. I still think she's a snooty psychopath who wears way too tight pants. I'm just saying, well, I'm going to try to be a little bit more... civil."

Leonard chuckled.

"And why is this so funny?" She scowled at him, eyebrows scrunched together as she leaned away from him to glare.

"I'll believe it when I see it. I love you, dear, I do. But you've got quite the stubborn streak." He leaned in to kiss her cheek, trying to soften the blow of his words.

"Well, I'll show you," she scoffed. She carefully creeped up from the bench, handed her coffee cup to Leonard, and headed inside, leaving Bridget and Leonard looking at each other questioningly.

"I give it ten minutes," Bridget said, winking conspiratorially.

"You're generous. I was going to say five. That one's a firecracker. Catherine picked the wrong woman to mess with." He shook his head as he worked on his own coffee.

****

When Charlotte went inside, she found Catherine by the mailboxes, dressed impeccably of course. Charlotte pushed aside a sassy remark about Catherine's cocktail dress. Things had to change.

"Catherine, can we please talk?" Charlotte mustered up her sweetest voice.

Catherine continued looking at her mail, acting

like the Publishers Clearing House envelope was life or death.

"Catherine?" she asked again, shoving the anger encroaching aside.

Catherine looked over at Charlotte, her nose slightly raised. "And why would I want to say anything to you?"

Charlotte sighed, fighting an eye roll. "You don't have to say anything. Just listen."

Catherine huffed, tapping her foot like it was the biggest inconvenience since WWII rationing. "Go on." She refused to make eye contact.

"This whole thing between us, it's just ridiculous. I mean, there's no reason we can't at least be civil. How did we get to this point? A bingo game isn't important in the scheme of things, right?"

Catherine turned to her now, facing her head-on, clearly demonstrating she was ready to play offense. "Well, I think it goes beyond bingo and you know it, Charlotte. Don't come to me all patronizing trying to act like I'm being juvenile. From the minute you walked into this place, you thought you could take over. Trying to make everyone like you, trying to weasel your way to the top. I've been here longer, I'm in charge. I'm the one running the mission group, I'm the organizer of the Labor Day picnic. I'm the favorite." She punctuated the final words, her voice growing in intensity with each syllable.

Charlotte stood, shocked. Why hadn't she seen it before? This war wasn't about Catherine being overly confident. It was about Catherine *lacking* confidence. She saw Charlotte as a threat, something Charlotte would have never dreamed of. It all made perfect sense now.

"You think I'm trying to take over? What are you talking about? Everyone knows you're queen bee. Heck, I wouldn't want to be the queen bee. So this whole thing is ludicrous," Charlotte retorted, a nervous grin on her face.

"Oh really, is it? You're telling me you didn't come in here jockeying to be top dog? You didn't swipe Leonard right out from under me like a jealous schoolgirl?"

At the mention of Leonard, Charlotte lost her resolve for civility. "You're joking, right? Get over yourself, lady. Leonard wasn't interested in you. He liked me, always has. I didn't steal anyone from you. He was never yours to begin with. You are unbelievable." She felt herself tighten in anger. This was not going as planned, but who could blame her? At least she tried.

"You disgusting excuse for a woman! How dare you?" Catherine had dropped the mail. Her hands were in tight fists, and she looked like she was ready to pounce. The cocktail dress coupled with her age only made the situation much more ridiculous and frightening.

Both women huffed, giving each other the stare of death women of all ages know too well. Finally, Charlotte broke the silence.

"Look. I came here to see if we could wave the white flag, agree to disagree, stop this war. Apparently that is asking a lot. But listen, my Annie can't deal with any more stress. She cannot deal with me getting evicted. And I know you care about Joe and don't want him to deal with this drama. So no matter how much we hate each other, no matter how much we wish the other could get evicted, let's at least agree to play nice for our children's sake. No plots, no schemes, no fights. When we pass each other in the hallway, we'll pretend we don't exist. We'll ignore each other's circle of friends, stay out of it. Agreed?" Charlotte reluctantly put out a hand.

Catherine snarled, but eventually her face revealed she'd been beaten. "You're right. Joe can't handle any more stress, especially since I've heard he's getting pretty serious with your wreck of a daughter," she said, rolling her eyes. Charlotte opened her mouth to put the woman in her place for badmouthing Annie, but decided against it. She bit her tongue, kept her hand outstretched.

Catherine looked at it, snubbed her, and slinked away saying, "Deal."

Charlotte let out a sigh of both frustration and relief. At least they had made some progress.

She still hated Catherine, and she hated the idea that her daughter was getting serious with any relative of the maniacal fiend. She shuddered to think about the familial proximity she would have with Catherine if Joe and Annie continued to get serious. But it was out of her hands now. She'd done her part, she'd made the effort. She'd done the right thing.

Charlotte headed down the hallway in the opposite direction of Catherine. One big task was complete, but she still had another stop to make, another big conversation to have. Hopefully, it would end in a friendly handshake instead of an icy snubbing.

***

Although her bladder already felt like it was going to burst from her partial cup of coffee, Charlotte graciously accepted Gina's offer of a cup of tea. Gina was a southern belle, a stickler for tradition, and just who Charlotte needed to talk to.

She had never been really close to Gina other than a quick hello in the hallway or a formal wave. Young people pictured the interactions of the aged as warm, but really it was no different than a high school setting. People liked each other, or didn't like each other, or they formed cliques. Gina had just never entered into Charlotte's inner circle.

But now, she was treading into Gina's circle with one mission in mind—to get Annie a job.

Gina's family owned a small event-planning business that was quickly on the rise. Gina's daughter, Macy, was sort of a one-woman band at this point, running the marketing, scheduling, accounting, and catering elements of Elegant Events, Inc. Charlotte had overheard Gina talking the other day about how much Macy needed help, how the business was growing faster than she could keep up with.

So the wheels had started turning. Annie had worked in the customer service department, so she was great at dealing with people. Annie was friendly, highly dependable, the kind of person Macy could rely on. Sure, Annie didn't really have experience in the event-planning industry. Heck, she didn't even know if Annie would be interested. Charlotte could see this turning into something wonderful, though, something to get Annie back on track and focused on her life again.

After some small talk about the weather and last week's card-making class, Charlotte jumped right in. "Listen, Gina, I'm going to cut straight to the point. I know your daughter is running the event planning company all by herself. The thing is, my daughter, Annie, is kind of in a bind. She's unemployed, just got a divorce, and really needs something to pour her energies into. She's a great worker and she's so reliable. I know all moms say that, but I mean it. I think this would be great for her, and I think Macy would benefit too." There, she'd said it, put it all on the table.

Gina sipped her tea, eyeing up Charlotte curiously before speaking. "I wondered what was up with the impromptu visit. But thanks for cutting straight to the punch," she said seriously. "Macy does need someone. I'll tell you what; you give me Annie's contact information, and I'll get it to Macy. Maybe we could work out a trial period or something. I've seen your daughter Annie. A real sweet girl. I think maybe you're on to something."

Charlotte stayed for a while, talking about Gina's grandchildren and other mindless gossip about Wildflower. She felt successful. It wasn't even 10:00 a.m., but she'd already somewhat smoothed things over with her archenemy, at least to a reasonable state, and had found Annie a job. Today was a hard day for her, a date that would always cling to her soul. It was the day that had changed the course of her life, had closed the chapter on her love story with Charlie. But this year, she had done something about it. She hadn't let the day creep into her like it usually did, hadn't let the moroseness of her loss overpower her. She had taken a tragic day and turned it into something positive. She knew this was what Charlie would've wanted; he would've wanted her to keep going with her life, keep making something of it. The conversation with Catherine was at least a push in the right direction, and it looked like the contact with Gina was successful.

Heading back outside to round up Leonard, she stopped for a second to look out the window facing the courtyard, thinking about how much her life had changed. There had been a lot of loss in the past few years; a lot of things had threatened to harden her into a woman she didn't want to be, but here she was, still standing, still moving forward, still accomplishing. Things weren't perfect, for sure, but they seemed to be moving in a good direction. Smiling to herself as the sun beamed through a cloud in a heavenly apparition, Charlotte couldn't help but feel peaceful in spite of the day's significance.

Sometimes things didn't work out, but then again, sometimes they just did.

Chapter Twenty-Three

Annie

Things were all coming together for Annie, yet it still felt like they were crumbling around her. Her career was certainly on the rise, thanks to her mother. She had been mortified at first, angry even that Charlotte had basically got her a pity interview.

"It's not like that and you know it. This was just me helping you out. You have to know someone to get a job. So I happened to know someone who was hiring," Charlotte argued when Annie had flat out accused her of begging for a job.

"I don't even know the first thing about event planning." Despite the truth behind this fact, Annie knew she really wasn't in a boat to be picky. It wasn't like hundreds of career opportunities were floating her way. Or even one. So she got her résumé together, tried to explain her recent exit from her job without divulging the whole ugly story, and got out her suit. She paraded into Macy's home office not expecting much, and not expecting to even like her.

She was wrong.

From the second the interview began, something clicked between Annie and Macy. Although Macy was twenty years younger, there was a common ground, a common personality between the two. There was the familiar, friendly ease found between two people who simultaneously uncovered the potential for friendship between them.

But when Macy offered her the job on the spot, Annie declined.

"I know my mother put your mother up to this. You don't have to hire me. I just appreciate the interview."

"Do you not want the job?" Macy inquired.

"The job sounds lovely, and I think I would really like working for you, but—"

Macy cut her off. "Then you start tomorrow. Listen, Annie, this is not a favor or a pity hire. Trust me, I don't have time for that. This is me desperately needing someone reliable, and you being a great hire. Say thank you, go home, and get ready for tomorrow. We have the Johanson wedding this weekend, so we have a lot to get ready." Macy offered her a huge smile. "Welcome to the team, Annie. I can't wait to work with you."

It was probably the easiest, warmest interview Annie had ever been to. And the best part? There was no woman named Sasha in the new business.

So gone were the days of Annie wallowing in cheese curls and cats on the couch, feeling like she would be forever unemployed. She had been at Elegant Events for two weeks, and she was absolutely loving it. She found she liked working face-to-face with customers instead of over a headset. There was a personal connection that couldn't be achieved on a phone. She liked organizing the chaos, she enjoyed pulling many pieces together to make someone's special day beautiful. She liked working with Macy, feeling like she had found a true friend.

Her love life, well, that was actually coming together too. Joe was nothing short of phenomenal. He was warm and funny, honest and hardworking. He was everything she wanted in a man and nothing she didn't. He treated her with respect, like a queen really. He would surprise her with coffee and doughnuts on a random morning before work, leave flowers at her door when she had a long day. They spent pretty much every moment they could together. They had gone to drive-in movies, ice-skating, even walks around the neighborhood. She didn't even think about Dave anymore, didn't wonder about his new baby. Suddenly, that part of her life felt like another woman, another time. She didn't even remember the Annie who was married to Dave. She only knew the woman she had become, vibrant and alive, with Joe.

She should be floating, should be dancing around the living room. She had found love again, a real love, a love she could trust in. She knew Joe would never do what Dave did, knew it in her core. She thought her trust, her heart had been shattered by Dave, but Joe had found the pieces and glued them back together. Trusting him was easy.

Still, there was a piece of her, a piece of her shattered heart perhaps that stabbed into her once in a while. It was a small twinge that told her it *could* all be too good to be true. She knew Joe was a good man, but what if *she* wasn't enough? There was clearly something about her, something that had pushed Dave away, had forced him to find comfort in another woman. She knew rationally it wasn't her fault; it was something wrong with Dave and not her. But her heart couldn't stop squelching the good vibes, squealing at her to slow down, to be careful. As much as she wanted to dive right in with Joe, she was scared.

It had been obvious on that passionate night when she had put the brakes on. Joe was understanding, never pushing her after that night, agreeing to take things at her pace. She loved him for it.

A part of her wondered, worried she would never be completely ready to move forward. What if she never stopped feeling the sheer terror, the daunting uneasiness about their relationship? She trusted Joe, she did, but she didn't know if she could let go of her own insecurities, her own feelings of not being good enough to fully succumb to him.

Dave had done that to her, and put a crinkle in her heart. Even though Joe had patched it back together, it wasn't the smooth, silky surface it had once been. The edges still needed buffing out. Annie didn't know how long it would take.

***

"A dance club?" Annie guessed as Joe drove down the highway.

He laughed. "Are we twenty?"

"Are you saying we're old?"

"No. But I'm saying I don't think I fit in at a dance club."

"I thought we were pushing ourselves to try new things."

"Yeah, but let's not get crazy here," Joe said, turning to smile at her.

He'd surprised her tonight, showing up at her house unannounced to tell her they were going somewhere special. Not that she minded. Any surprise appearance by Joe was a welcome surprise to her. Despite her hesitancy and her tendency to overanalyze what had developed between them, when she was with him, the worries seemed to fade away. He had a way of easing her into a state of peace, happiness, and excitement.

The truck drove on, 80's rock music playing on the radio. Joe mindlessly tapped out the drum part to a song by a singer she'd forgotten about. He was wearing his red flannel, his favorite, but this gave her no clue as to the location of their date. He always wore his flannel.

He took the next exit, and she felt her heart flutter. She'd experienced so many firsts with Joe over the past few months. The first snow tubing adventure, the first ballroom dancing class, the first time to see the town's local rock band. What was coming next?

As they turned onto a secluded road and she saw the

sign, she smiled. Joe had pulled her out of her slump, had helped her rediscover who she was.

She realized with relief Joe had been able to make her care about what was coming next.

Right now, that was all that mattered.

***

"Wine and painting? Doesn't that seem like a dangerous mix?"

"Come on, it'll be fun. Everyone is always talking about this place."

Annie grinned as she walked into the studio, three other couples already at their stations.

"Hi, I'm Clarissa! Welcome to Sip n' Paint. Is this your first time here?"

"Yes. And I'm quite sorry, but I'm not really an artist," Annie apologized as Clarissa handed her a glass of wine. This was exciting and fun… but she also felt out of her comfort zone a little bit. She couldn't handle the Mod Podge craft she'd tried from Pinterest a few months ago. Now she was supposed to paint a masterpiece? While drinking? This was probably going to be a disaster.

She loved Joe for trying, though.

"Stop right there. No apologies allowed in my studio. Art isn't right or wrong, so you just sit your adorable self down over here with your handsome date, and get ready to make a masterpiece."

She must've already been hitting up the wine bottle before class, Annie thought as she glanced at the redheaded art instructor. Joe gave her a knowing look and they grinned. He was thinking the same thing, she knew.

They took their seats on their stools in front of their canvas as Clarissa headed to the front of the room, paint already splattered on her palette.

"Welcome, lovebirds. Thanks for coming to our monthly couples painting session. I'm so excited to make a masterpiece with you. Today we're going to be working together to make this beautiful lake and tree scene. Who's ready to get their paint on?"

"Do you think she put something else in her wine? She's a little too happy, even for a zany artist," Joe whispered, and Annie giggled, almost spitting out a sip of her wine.

"Look how excited these two are over here. Aren't they precious?"

The rest of the room turned to look at Annie and Joe. Annie felt her cheeks redden.

"Let's begin."

With that, Annie and Joe picked up their paintbrushes and started following the instructions to make their first painting together.

All was going well, and Annie was amazed that their canvas wasn't looking too bad. They worked together to paint the skyline and put in the water, trying to mimic Clarissa's brush strokes.

"Okay, now let's etch in the outline for the bench by the water. See? Just like this."

"Go ahead, Annie. You've got this," Joe encouraged,

setting his brush down.

Annie leaned forward on her stool, trying to copy Clarissa's exact brush placement. Glancing back and forth between her canvas and Clarissa's, she was in full concentration. She could do this. So she wasn't an artist. That was okay. With Joe, she could do anything. Together, they were a great team, and…

Her own thoughts were interrupted as she felt herself falling, the brush still on the canvas. Everything felt like it was in slow motion. There was the off-kilter feeling of gravity pulling her body forward. Then, it seemed like everything returned to full speed as she struggled to break her fall. She failed epically, landing on her side under the canvas, the stool toppling onto her.

The next thing she knew, Joe was scrambling to her side, a panicked look on his face.

"Are you okay?" he asked, as she looked up at him.

She took a minute, rubbed her head, and assessed the damage to her body. Other than a bit of a throbbing on her left side, Annie thought she was okay. So, looking at him as she started to sit up, she did the only natural thing you could do when you toppled off a stool in an art studio in front of everyone.

She started to laugh at her disastrous self.

She heard footsteps rushing toward her. It was Clarissa now, peering over her as Joe helped Annie to her feet.

"Oh, dear. Are you okay? It's been a while since someone took a spill off a stool."

"I'm fine. I'm so sorry," Annie said, embarrassed now by the spectacle her clumsiness had made.

She carefully placed herself directly in the center of the stool, telling herself no more leaning, and tried to play off the incident. Refocusing on the art project at hand, she picked up her brush and looked back at the canvas.

That's when she saw it.

"Shit," she said as she eyed the large brown streak all through the center of the canvas. Her fall had happened mid bench painting. In other words, her fall had ruined the painting.

She looked expectantly at Clarissa, waiting for the woman to say there were no mistakes in art, no right or wrong.

"Oh, dear. Looks like that's ruined," the bubbly girl said, frowning as she peered over Annie's shoulder to assess the canvas. Annie felt heat rising in her cheeks.

"I'm so sorry, Joe. I'm a disaster. I messed it all up."

A smile grew on his face as Clarissa headed to the front of the class to get the other couples back on track. He looked at their canvas and then back at Annie.

"Annie, things don't have to be perfect you know. Stop putting so much pressure on yourself."

Pushing her wine glass to the side—falling off the stool once during a class was probably enough—she looked back at Joe, really seeing him. She realized he wasn't just talking about the botched painting. He was talking about so much more.

And he was right.

She didn't want to ruin the moment, didn't gush about her feelings for him. Instead, she simply nodded her head, leaning in against his shoulder as the rest of the couples finished their perfect lake scenes. Joe and Annie were perfectly content looking at their botched masterpiece, Joe deciding they'd just call it abstract.

They finished their wine, thanked Clarissa after class, and went off into the darkness with their abstract painting and a better sense of who they were together.

Chapter Twenty-Four

Annie tiptoed into the entrance of Amelia's apartment, not wanting to wake the girl if she was still asleep. She hadn't bothered knocking, using her key to let herself in. After all, it was only nine in the morning, and she didn't want to wake Amelia if she wasn't up yet. Amelia's Smoothie Q shift didn't start for another hour or so, and today's dog walking clients only got walked in the evening. She didn't want to intrude on Amelia's sleep schedule or pressure the girl. She'd just leave the fabric swatches for Amelia to glance at and call her later for a decision.

Annie was so excited for the wedding, even more so now that she was planning it. Once she got the job at Elegant Events, Neville and Amelia insisted they plan the wedding with them. Unlike other brides Annie worked with, though, Amelia wasn't quite sure what she wanted out of the wedding. Traditional or modern? Fancy foods or finger foods? Band or DJ? Amelia had no clue. Annie wasn't really surprised; Amelia always had trouble pinning down a decision.

Annie strolled into the kitchenette beside the entranceway, taking in the mess that was all Amelia. Shirts strewn everywhere, half-empty coffee cups collecting dust on the counter. Did Neville really know what he was getting himself into? Annie smiled.

She set down the linen samples on the kitchen counter, finding a small swatch of empty space. She had been telling Amelia for weeks now she needed to make a decision but hadn't heard anything. Annie was going to have to push this girl through every decision in the wedding or nothing would get done. They only had three months left to get things together. Amelia felt like it was an eternity, but Annie knew better.

Annie strolled around the corner toward the living room. She paused for a second, swearing she heard movement or murmurings coming from the direction of the living room. She felt herself blush, fearing she was about to walk in on something, but then she remembered Amelia saying Neville was going to be gone all this week for his job. *Thank goodness.* Annie mentally made a note to call next time. It certainly would be awkward if—

As she headed down the hallway toward the small living room, her gaze landed on the couch. She instantly noticed two people on the tan sofa, intensely lip locked. Shock slammed into her. She let out an uncontrollable gasp, backed herself against the wall. The kiss stopped, and the two stared at her in shock as well. They'd been so entranced by each other they must not have heard her walk in.

Mouth open for a long moment before recognition sank in, Amelia finally broke the silence. "Shit," she said as she scurried to get off the couch.

Definitely call next time, Annie scolded herself as she tried to recover. But it wasn't the sight of her daughter lip locked with a man, it wasn't the sheer awkwardness of it that left Annie speechless.

It was the fact that the lips Amelia had been kissing didn't belong to Neville. The shock, the involuntary gasp, had all come after she realized the man kissing her daughter had a familiar sleeve of tattoos and some spiky hair.

***

"What the hell, Mom? Don't you knock? What are you doing here?" Amelia spewed at her as she stomped toward her, dressed in some holey jeans and a baggy T-shirt. Owen slowly stood behind her, a hand rustling his hair in apparent nervousness.

"I thought you were sleeping. I knew Neville was out of town, so I wasn't expecting"—she motioned toward Owen—"all of this. What the hell are you doing? You're engaged!" Annie was furious. Embarrassment and shock fueled her. Amelia loved Neville, but she was throwing it all away, and for what? A gorgeous tattooed man who couldn't promise her what he was doing next week, let alone for the rest of a lifetime?

Amelia reddened. "It's not what it looks like."

Annie guffawed. "Really? You're making out with him on your couch while Neville's gone, and it's not what it looks like? I didn't think you were like this, Amelia. Honestly."

Owen exhaled loudly, eyeing the door, clearly not sure what his role was in the conversation.

"It's just… I don't know. It's complicated." Tears now forming, Amelia eyed Owen, hoping to get some backup. He just stared back. No one really knew how to approach the situation.

"So you're telling me you're walking around town wearing Neville's ring, planning this wedding to him, and while he's away, you're kissing another man?"

Amelia winced. "Mom, please, let's not go there. This isn't your business." Rage started to creep into her voice. "Just stay out of it."

"Stay out of it? For God's sake, I'm here with fabric samples for your wedding. I'm supposed to stay out of it? Pretend I have no idea you're two-timing Neville? He loves you, Amelia. This is so not fair."

"I know, Mom. I have to figure all of this out," she whispered, obviously upset. Annie wanted nothing more than to take Amelia in her arms, tell her it would be okay.

But she couldn't. Not after what she'd done. Not when she did the one thing Annie found unforgivable.

"I can't believe you would do this, Amelia. After what your father did to me?"

Amelia looked up now, tears turning to a searing, blazing wrath. "Well, Mom, this isn't about you. How dare you compare this?"

Annie sighed, wondering how things could, in fact, get so complicated. Wondering why anyone even bothered with love in the first place when it was such a huge mess.

"You're right. It's not about me. This is about you, your life. Neville loves you. And here you are, kissing another man behind his back. It's wrong, Amelia, and you know it. How could you do this to him? I will not be an accessory to your lies. I love you, and you're my daughter so I will no matter what. But I will not plan a wedding for you to a man you're lying to. So you sort this out, and sort it out quickly." She turned to leave.

"Mom, I'm sorry," Amelia offered, causing Annie to turn around.

"I'm sorry, too, Amelia. I'm sorry things are such a mess right now." Annie strolled out of the apartment, wanting so badly to forget what she'd seen but not able to. She didn't know why, but the whole scene, the whole conversation had brought tears bubbling, stinging in her eyes. She swiped them away as she marched down the apartment complex steps, ready to head into the unknown of the outside world. Ready to forget, to move on, but not sure she could.

Chapter Twenty-Five

Amelia

That night, Amelia tossed and turned in her bed, replaying the awful incident over and over. To have your mother walk in on you passionately lip locked was a huge level of weird in itself. To have your mother walk in on you with the man you were secretly kissing behind your fiancé's back—that was insurmountable.

Amelia hadn't planned to become one of those women. She hadn't wanted to be a two-timer, hadn't planned on letting things with Owen go so far. But when she was around him, all logic, all morality subsided to the electricity jolting between them. From the pizza date on his sofa the first night, she knew deep within her heart there was something about him, something that wouldn't let her forget about whatever was developing between them. If she really thought about it, it had hit her even before that. The first moment she saw him walk through Grandma Charlotte's door, something had hit her, something intense. Then, of course, there was the kiss at Marla's birthday party. There had been something brewing between them for a long time, something that scared her because it was so powerful. It was more than chemistry. It was a knowing, deep in her heart, Owen could complete her. She just hadn't admitted it to herself. As much as she tried to resist, to pour her soul into the wedding planning, she knew something was off. Neville was wonderful, safe, dependable… but the more time she spent with Owen, with his zest for life and his exuberance, she knew one fatal fact—Neville would never be Owen.

He would never light her up the way Owen did, make her feel like her songwriting dreams were more than just dreams. She would never laugh with Neville like she did with Owen. She would never feel the passion for love and for life as she did with him. She wouldn't feel free to help choose her life path, to see where things would take her.

For the first time, she admitted to herself the harsh truth. She saw her future with Neville as an endless string of feeling inferior, of feeling like she had to live up to both his and his parents' expectations. She saw a future as a marketing analyst instead of a worker at Book World. She saw herself as a bride at a wedding in the club with proper table settings and sophisticated toasts. She saw herself in a house planned by Neville without her consideration.

With Owen, she saw a lot of question marks, a whole heap of uncertainty. She saw a future of craziness, of chaos, of laughter.

But the important thing was that she saw a whole lot of herself. She saw a chance to just be herself.

As the weeks had rolled on, she found herself craving the days Neville was away so she could bask in the ease of her time with Owen. They spent many evenings on his couch, ordering takeout, watching movies, playing zombie video games. She told herself they were friends, told Owen they were friends, but even she knew the façade was crumbling.

She felt sick with guilt, felt like a total bitch. How could she do this? She loved Neville, a piece of her did at least. She thought of the way she felt with him, the way he looked at her. A reel of their moments and memories flashed through her mind. She was happy with him. She did love him. In spite of everything, she had so many beautiful moments with him. She knew he could give her a beautiful life, a happy life. They did share something special, a passion, a chemistry. He was good for her in so many ways.

So how could she do this to him? How could she hurt him like this?

She knew she was wrong, knew she was being unfaithful, knew she should tell Neville the truth, but she couldn't. Every time she thought about it, she thought about Neville, the sweet man who had claimed her heart, who made her believe settling down wasn't a bad thing. She was torn between the life of passion she saw with Owen and the life of stability she saw with Neville. She knew it wasn't fair, but she couldn't make the jump. She couldn't make the final leap, not yet.

On the morning her mother had walked in, she hadn't planned on kissing Owen again, on crossing the line that couldn't be crossed back over. It had started as a friendly knock on her door, Owen with two coffees in his hand. It had continued on her couch, two friends in her living room chatting before her shift at Smoothie Q. She'd told herself there was nothing wrong about two friends having a cup of coffee together, talking about songs and music. As they sat together, though, laughing about Owen's retelling of a joke from a comedian they both loved, he'd looked over at her with those eyes. She'd wanted to look away, to put the thoughts creeping into her heart aside. She'd wanted to convince herself they could be just friends, and that her heart wasn't actually accelerating at the mere thought of him kissing her. She told herself that kiss by the appetizers had been a mistake that wouldn't happen again.

And then he leaned toward her, the telltale lean of a man about to kiss a woman. She'd seen it coming, she'd told herself she should lean away. She'd told herself she couldn't kiss him again, that to do so would be foolish, would be ruination for her reputation, her relationship with Neville. She told herself if she kissed him again, there would be no going back.

Yet, when she found his lips on hers, she didn't pull away.

As much as she didn't want to be that woman, to be

the woman who broke Neville's heart, she'd let that kiss progress.

Now, she would have to pay the consequences.

Sleep didn't come easily that night. On her side, she spent most of the night flashing between pangs of guilt and the realization she liked the way Owen's lips had felt on hers.

***

The next evening, she was sitting on the couch thinking about how she would tell Neville about what happened when the doorbell rang, jolting her out of the jungle of her own mind. She knew who was at the door before she even answered it.

"Can I come in?" he asked when she opened the door. She hesitated, feeling like it was a bad idea. She already felt awful about the kiss, about everything. She knew this was going to rip Neville up inside, and she hated that she would be the one to do it.

But she also knew that kiss had changed everything.

Their first kiss, well, she could chock that up to temporary insanity. The kiss yesterday, however, had been different. It hadn't been a simple accident or mistake or heat of the moment sort of thing. It had been a deliberate choice on her part. More importantly, yesterday's kiss had made her realize she couldn't just forget about Owen.

She was falling for him. Hard. And it wasn't fair to stay with Neville when she felt like this about someone else. The façade was over. The truth had to come out.

So she let Owen in, holding the door open for the man who had closed the door in her heart for Neville.

She shut the door, plagued suddenly by an awkwardness she hadn't expected.

Owen stood, eyeing her. "So, I'm sorry things were weird yesterday. I hate that I put you in a strange position with your mom."

She shrugged. "It's not your fault. It takes two, right?"

He took a few steps toward her. She stood perfectly still. "Amelia, I know you're engaged. And I know kissing you was wrong in so many ways. The thing is, though, I can't stop thinking about you. From that kiss at the appetizer table, I haven't been able to stop thinking about you. It might be wrong, but I just can't make myself care. I'm falling in love with you."

Her heart felt like it was going to beat out of her chest; her feet felt glued to the floor. She looked at him, the man who had consumed her heart from the inside out without warning, without reason.

They stood for a long moment, staring, waiting to see who would make the next move, who would solidify their decision.

"I'm falling for you too," she whispered, taking a step closer to him. She closed her eyes and took a deep breath, knowing this was what she wanted, but also knowing it wasn't an easy choice.

Walking away from Neville was the right thing, but it still was going to hurt like hell.

There was no kiss. Both knew there would be time for that. Amelia didn't want to add to this shitty feeling of guilt and confusion.

The next time they kissed, she wanted it to be a kiss free and clear, one where the only feeling was love.

Neville would be home tomorrow night. She would tell him then, break it softly. Give back the ring, give back the life he'd promised her. As much as she was torn by the two vying dreams, she had to make a decision. Last night had forced her hand. It was time to own up to her actions. It was time to let Neville go because she knew he wasn't it for her, not anymore. In a different life, in a life where that spiky-haired, tattooed man didn't walk through Grandma Charlotte's door, Neville could have been enough. But not now. In the life where Owen existed, where Owen's lips sought hers, Neville could never fulfill her any longer. So tomorrow night, she would throw caution to the wind, banish the dreams of solidity and settling down, and go running into the storm with Owen, wherever it might lead her.

***

"So you're going to tell him tomorrow?" Owen asked, reaching to stroke her hand as he twirled linguine on his fork. It was an oddly sweet gesture.

Amelia nodded, not able to completely mask the forlorn look in her eyes. "Yeah, I've got to."

Owen put his fork down. "Are you sure about this? I mean, I want this more than anything, I'm crazy about you. But I don't want you to feel like you have to do

this. I want you to do this because it's what you want."
Owen's gaze pierced her, causing her stomach to leap.

"So you're crazy about me?"

He grinned. "Really? Hasn't it been obvious? I've been crazy about you since the day I met you."

"Even though I used words like incorrigible?"

"*Because* you used words like incorrigible. And creepo."

He was crazy about her. The perfect specimen of a man, the man who was obsessed with music, who had made her dinner from her limited ingredients in her pantry, was crazy about her. She studied him, staring him right in the eyes this time. It was so clear. Why had it taken a few stolen kisses and everything in between to realize it?

He was hers. He was the one she was supposed to be with. She loved Neville, but she was swept away by how much she loved Owen. Her heart couldn't be given to Neville at the altar because another man had pilfered it.

"I'm crazy about you too," she whispered, a steamy quality edging into her voice. They stared at each other for a long breath, two people pledging their hearts to each other with an official quality that had not yet been broached. He reached across the table, squeezed her hand, reading her mind without a word passing between her lips.

***

Amelia stood at the tiny kitchen sink, rinsing their plates. Owen's arms were wrapped around her, his lips planting hesitant, sweet trails on her neck. She couldn't think clearly, could barely move, she wanted him so badly. As she finished rinsing the last dish and was turning to face him, the apartment door swung open. She froze. Her heart stopped, passion suddenly disappearing, icy fear replacing it.

Neville. He was home early.

Neville appeared in the kitchen as Owen and Amelia separated. Neville had a smile on his face, flowers in his hand. His face transformed, though, when he saw them together. His eyes flickered from Amelia to Owen, from Owen to Amelia, and the question flew out. "What's this?"

Amelia froze. It was her time to fess up, to tell him what was happening. She was falling for Owen, had planned on telling Neville everything the next day. It was unexpected he returned early, but it didn't make a difference. She would tell him she was sorry, she couldn't marry him. She would end it, start her life, whatever it looked like, with Owen.

The words stuck in her throat. Owen patted her shoulder in encouragement, but looking into Neville's eyes, she froze. She saw the pain, the questions lingering. She didn't know how to do it, hadn't predicted feeling this terrible.

"Amelia? What is this?" Neville edged closer, seething in his own hell.

She paused, a pain stabbing at her chest because she knew what she had to say. She had to tell him what she should have told him after that first kiss. "Neville, I'm so sorry. I meant to tell you sooner." She spit out the clichéd words because that was what women always said in that situation, right?

The pain on Neville's face, the shock, was undeniable. Her heart panged. She hated this so much. She'd never wanted to hurt him like this. How had she let this happen? How did she let herself get caught up between two men?

Neville seemed to wait for further explanation, frozen, holding the bouquet at his side. For some reason, the sight of the drooping flowers made her feel worse. She just looked at Neville, tears forming in her eyes. "Please, let me explain."

"Save it." He threw the flowers at her feet with a strength he had never exerted before.

"Neville, I'm sorry, please, listen," she begged, but it was too late. Neville was gone.

She stood looking at Owen glassy-eyed, not sure what to say or where to even begin. She crumpled into Owen, feeling a wave of relief and sadness at the same exact moment.

Owen and Amelia spent the night much differently than one might expect. Although they fell asleep in each other's arms, there was no intimacy, no proposals, and no professions of undying love. There was just a guy and a girl holding on to each other, wondering how life got so messy, and wondering where they went from there.

***

The next morning, Amelia, feeling like she was run over by a bus or like she drank a vat of whiskey, dragged herself out of bed and shoved on her yoga pants and T-shirt. Sneaking out without waking Owen, who was fully clothed and asleep in her bed, she headed to walk Henry. It seemed fitting she would have her most difficult client today after one of the most difficult nights of her life.

Her mind was numb on the drive over, a blank canvas. After pulling into the driveway and letting herself in the house, she leashed up the dog and shoved him out the door. She stood in the rain, of course—poetic justice, perhaps?—her mind finally processing everything that had happened. She had done the right thing, she knew. Her heart belonged to Owen, and as much as it hurt Neville now, it was better that he knew the truth. And she knew someday, she would probably be thankful. Grandma Charlotte was right; she didn't belong in Neville's world of practical, rational, logical thinking, of five forks at dinner, of "songwriting is just a hobby." She fit in Owen's world like a glove, even though she wasn't even sure what that would look like. Stability wasn't everything, and safety was sometimes boring, at least to her.

She stood, waiting for Henry to get up, waiting for him to get going, wondering where, in fact, her life was going. She knew she had done the right thing, so why did her life feel like such a haggard mess? Why did she feel like a disappointment? Why did she feel so sad?

As much as she wanted her love life to be cut and dried, one or the other, she knew it wasn't so simple. She fit with Owen, was crazy about him, but she *had* loved Neville. Neville wasn't simply an easy solution to her unstable life, wasn't just a man to settle down with. She *had* loved him, had been wrapped up by him. True, it was a different love than what she felt for Owen, maybe even inferior to the love she felt for Owen. But it had, she knew, been love all the same. Water cascading down her face, she realized something very grown-up, something she hadn't really considered before.

Love wasn't an either/or sort of feeling. It wasn't clean-cut. It was, quite literally, a mess. It was choosing between priorities, it was choosing a vision for your life. It was sometimes about figuring out what mattered most and who fit the vision. It wasn't only about passion and sex; it was about dreams and visions for the future.

She loved two men. But she loved Owen in a different way, a way she knew could fulfill her for the rest of her life, a way that fit the vision of her life's path.

That didn't make losing Neville any less painful, though. She hated how she'd hurt Neville, hated the fact she'd broken his heart. She hated that she hadn't let him down easy, that she'd betrayed him with not one but two kisses. She felt awful about the woman she was, guilt exploding in her heart.

With the pursuit of a life with Owen, she'd sacrificed the life that went along with Neville. However, she'd also sacrificed Neville's heart to the pain of rejection and betrayal. It hadn't been fair to him. She would always regret that.

She pulled her cell phone out of her pocket. No missed calls. No texts.

What did she expect?

She pulled up her contacts list and saw Neville's name, the familiar number she'd texted and called so many times. The number she used to anxiously wait to see pop up on her phone. She wondered if she should call him, talk to him, and explain again how sorry she was.

But what was the use?

A million apologies could never fix the heart she'd cracked in half with her lies. She'd done that to Neville. She couldn't go back.

As she was pondering life's odd sense of timing and complexities, she lurched forward with ungodly force, literally hurtling into the space in front of her. *Of all days,* she thought as she stumbled and tripped, getting tied up in Henry's leash as he saw the one thing that could get him moving, the one thing that gave him the momentum to drag her across the neighborhood—a damn squirrel.

As Amelia stumbled along, trying to slow the stubborn mastiff down, she thought to herself how easy it was to become tangled in life and love's ridiculous web of chaos.

Chapter Twenty-Six

Charlotte
July

Charlotte's face fell and her stomach flip-flopped. The feelings of terror, sorrow, and complete anguish she felt when Charlie was pronounced dead permeated through her again, this time with an intensity that threatened to bowl her over. She lowered herself into her seat, too stunned to speak.

"Mom?" Annie asked, reaching toward her to put her hand on her mother's shoulder. "Mom, I'm so sorry. Are you okay? Talk to me. See, Amelia, this is why I didn't think we should say anything."

"Mom, you had to tell her, you just had to."

Charlotte heard them in the background, heard their bickering that had become commonplace since Amelia broken up with Neville. Even though she heard them, though, she heard nothing at all.

How could this have happened? How could Annie let this happen?

"Mom, honest, we've looked everywhere. We've had signs up for two weeks now. We haven't given up just yet, but you know, Butternut *was* old."

Charlotte glared at her daughter, rage firing in her pupils. "He's old, so you think he doesn't matter, huh? Is that what you say about me too?"

"Mother. *Of course not.*"

Charlotte sighed, burying her head in her hands. "I'm sorry, Annie. I know you didn't mean for this to happen."

"It's okay. It's just, well, I've heard from Macy they had a cat that did this. When he got old and was ready to pass on, he left the family, going off to die alone. Maybe that's what Butternut did," she offered gently. Amelia was on the other side of Charlotte, stroking her back.

Tears flowed openly now, grief overtaking her. "I just can't believe this. Of all the cats. He was the one, the one who meant the most. Your father found him, a tiny, two-week-old kitten. And now?"

"I know, Grandma, it's hard. Look, we'll keep looking, we will. But maybe it was Butternut's time. Maybe Grandpap needed him more than us, you know?" Annie gave Amelia a pleading look, probably nervous at the mention of Charlie. But this idea actually soothed Charlotte. She nodded gently.

"Maybe you're right, honey. It's time to let go. I do wish you had told me sooner."

"We didn't want to worry you. We were hoping to find him," Annie whispered. "I'm sorry."

Charlotte wiped away the tears, still sad, but knowing her daughter had done her best. "Well, I guess we should make arrangements."

"Arrangements for what?" Annie asked. Amelia also looked confused.

"Why, the funeral of course. Just because we don't have a body doesn't mean we can't celebrate Butternut's life." Amelia and Annie waited, as if they were anticipating a laugh, but Charlotte was serious. Butternut had been as big a part of her family as anyone else. He deserved respect.

"Mom, um, I know you loved him and all," Annie broached carefully.

"Oh, stop. I know you think it's crazy. But I don't care. I need this, Annie. I need to say good-bye. And since he's lost, well, this will give me closure. You were planning on having a picnic on the Fourth of July anyway, right? Let's just set aside some time during that to have a service." She was being perfectly reasonable. She wasn't asking Annie to plan something separate or go to any trouble. Just a small service, maybe a flower and a stone to commemorate the cat who had meant so much to her, her soul cat.

"Okay, Grandma, sure, we can do that." That was her granddaughter, always looking out for her.

"And invite Owen, of course, dear. Has he popped the question yet?" Charlotte hadn't hidden her excitement when Amelia had told her the news about Neville being kicked to the curb.

"Grandma, it's not like that with us. We're just enjoying being together right now. No rush." Despite her attempt at acting demure, Charlotte could see the hint of a grin on Amelia's face. The name itself stirred her.

"Okay, okay, as long as you're happy. Now why don't you two scoot? You've got some details to arrange for Saturday, and I've got my dance class." She swiped her tears away, pulling herself back together. Life was filled with sadness and enveloping sorrow. You just had to find a way to push it aside, to dance into a better tomorrow. So that was what she would do.

Annie rolled her eyes. "Well, okay then. I'll pick you up Saturday. And Mom, one more thing." Annie hesitated.

"Oh, no. I know what's coming. You're inviting Catherine to this shindig on Saturday, aren't you?" Charlotte recoiled.

"She *is* Joe's mom."

Charlotte huffed. "Fine, I don't care. Invite her. We'll be one big happy family. As long as I get shotgun." She headed to her room to change into her exercise gear.

"Okay, great. And please don't start any dance class smackdowns today, okay? I've got the service to plan, and I would hate to have something pull me away from that."

"Got it, dear. No worries."

And with that, Charlotte was off to her sweatpants and Latin hips.

***

Dressed in her favorite jeans and a red blouse, Charlotte meandered through the lobby of Wildflower carrying her best photo of Butternut. She felt a little teary already at the thought of saying good-bye to the cat who had meant so much, but she also knew she had to. She had said good-bye to so many things in the past year, but with those good-byes had come some good things. She had found a new place, new friends, new love. She had learned sometimes endings in life truly did bring new beginnings. She would never have another cat like Butternut, but maybe that was okay.

Leonard was already on the entranceway sofa, waiting for her.

"You look beautiful," he exclaimed when he saw her.

"Oh please." She shook her head. "Annie should be here any minute." She took a seat by Leonard, resting her arm on his arm.

"Is this Butternut?" Leonard gently took the photograph from Charlotte. Charlotte simply nodded.

"Pretty cat." Charlotte playfully hit his hand away, taking back her picture.

"You liar. You don't even like cats."

"I never said that." Charlotte just gave him the look.

As Leonard leaned in to kiss her cheek, as she was reveling in the bliss of the moment, of the companionship, a subtle voice-clearing attempt interrupted them.

She didn't even have to look up. She just muttered, "Hello, Catherine." Charlotte stared straight ahead. She might be okay with Catherine coming to the picnic under the circumstances and all, but she didn't have to like it.

"Charlotte. Leonard." Catherine feigned politeness. Charlotte finally looked up to take in the queen's outfit. Catherine did not disappoint. She had on a stars-and-stripes silk blouse with an elegant wrap that probably cost a fortune. Charlotte secretly hoped she sweat all over it since it was 85 degrees. Who wore a wrap at this time of year? She wore jeans, but not just any jeans—skintight skinny jeans. Charlotte believed Amelia called them jeggings. She finished the look with some Jimmy Choo shoes and, of course, oodles of diamonds.

"You do realize this is a picnic we're going to, right? As in a barbecue. Outside," Charlotte chided.

Catherine rolled her eyes and sighed, pushing her Michael Kors bag up higher on her shoulder. "There's nothing wrong with having some class, even at a barbecue. Besides, Joe said something about a service? Did someone die?"

Charlotte eyed Catherine. "Yes. Butternut."

"What? Who is Butternut? Is that a last name?"

"He was my cat," Charlotte articulated. Catherine let out an incredulous laugh.

"You mean to tell me I got glammed up for a service... for a cat? Are you kidding me?"

Charlotte felt anger burning in her chest. Leonard sensed it, too, because he quickly put an arm around Charlotte. "Let it go," he whispered.

Before anything could escalate, before Charlotte

could show Catherine what "just a cat" would get you in her world, they all heard a honking horn. Annie was beeping outside. The three sauntered outside, Catherine leading the charge. To Charlotte's chagrin, Catherine bolted for the front seat.

"Shotgun," she yelled, climbing into the car.

Yes, it was going to be quite the Fourth of July. Charlotte couldn't help but hope a stray firework would land directly on a particular lady wearing stars and stripes.

***

"Okay, everyone, before we get to the food, we're going to have our celebration for Butternut," Amelia announced, hanging on Owen's arm. Despite Charlotte's sadness, she couldn't help but notice what a great couple they made.

Joe, Annie, Amelia, Owen, Charlotte, and Leonard wandered to the makeshift memorial Amelia had put together. The dear girl had gathered photographs chronicling Butternut's life and made a picture out of them. They sat on an easel under Annie's gorgeous hemlock tree, some flowers scattered on the ground. Charlotte was touched.

Catherine, lagging behind the group, asked, "Can I at least get a glass of wine before this cat thing happens?"

Charlotte and Joe glared at her, but Annie, wanting to keep the peace, obliged.

"Okay, so I thought we'd all maybe say a few words about our memories of Butternut?" Amelia inquired. No one, not even Charlotte, really knew how to proceed with a cat funeral. Regular funerals were hard enough. Did one pray? They didn't even have a body to pray over or a grave to mark.

Oh, well. It was the thought.

"I'll start," Amelia offered. "I remember this one beautiful moment I had with Butternut. I had the chickenpox, and they left a few scars on my arms. When I went back to school, everyone was making fun of me. I called Grandma Charlotte just sobbing about it. She invited me over. When I got there, tears still flowing, Butternut ran right up to me and started licking my leg. Grandma, you said he could sense I needed him. You were right."

"Really? The cat had magical senses? Ew, gross, if it had licked my leg, I would've booted the thing into kingdom come," Catherine blurted.

"If you can't have some respect, then you best leave," Charlotte touted.

"No one's leaving," Annie retorted, trying to save the situation and giving Joe an exasperated look. "Let's save the fireworks for later, ladies."

"Okay, let's take a moment for a musical piece?" Amelia interjected, turning to Owen in desperation. Charlotte nodded as Owen reached for a guitar.

The patched-together group, somehow morphing into more than friends and less than a family, stood in silence, staring at the pictures of the cat they were celebrating, as Owen strummed "Amazing Grace."

Charlotte, for the first time that day, let the tears trickle down her face. It was more than just a cat. It was a friend. It was a link to Charlie.

Good-bye was, in fact, hard.

As the others stood, heads bowed, Charlotte glanced across the yard, her eye landing on a bird in the tree by Annie's neighbor's house. It was a beautiful red bird. Butternut had loved birds, always meowing at them through the windows. If she used her imagination, she could almost picture him, scratching, meowing fiercely at the window to get to the feathery creature.

But then, as Owen hit the chorus, she froze. She wasn't imagining it. *Butternut was there! He was in the window!* Her baby wasn't dead; he was scratching from inside the neighbor's second-story window, meowing at her. She would know him anywhere. He was really alive. That crazy neighbor of Annie's had kidnapped him! Well, more accurately, he had catnapped him!

How dare he.

Charlotte shoved through the circle, pushing her way toward the neighbor's house. Stomping her feet with a new sense of purpose, she stormed across the lawn as Owen stopped strumming.

"Charlotte?" Leonard called, as the group murmured in confusion. Charlotte heard questioning tones, but she didn't care. She had one thing on her mind, a mission that wouldn't be forestalled.

"Butternut, I'm coming, baby," Charlotte exclaimed as she moved toward the house. She was getting her cat back, come hell or high water. She was getting back Butternut, and the creepy neighbor would feel the wrath of a crazy cat lady.

Then she stopped, felt herself falling to the ground. A pain so sharp, so intense, stabbed into her. Had she been shot? Had the crazy neighbor seen her coming and got out his pistol? She grabbed her chest in pain, feeling for blood, expecting to feel a hole. As she crumpled to the ground, however, she caught a glimpse of her sweet cat jumping down from the window. She couldn't get any more words out, couldn't breathe.

Everything went black.

Chapter Twenty-Seven

Annie

"Annie, here," Joe said, interrupting her pacing to hand her a cup of mediocre coffee. She just shook her head, grateful for the gesture but too nervous to worry about caffeine. Amelia also stood close by, wearing her own rut in the waiting room floor, a worried look plastered on her beautiful face. Even Catherine looked concerned, serious. No one spoke, no one really looked at each other. Everyone was in their own world where the only thing that mattered was Charlotte.

Annie despised hospitals and their septic, sanitary smell. She hated the sad sights, the horrifying sounds, and the feelings of entrapment. Here, one's choices and desires had little impact. Everything, it felt, was out of your hands, at the mercy of the doctors and a higher power. Everything was about waiting, pacing, hoping against all odds things would be okay.

There had been some pretty scary moments after the upsetting sight of Charlotte falling to the ground. There had been the stretcher, the worried looks on the faces of the EMTs, the panic of the ER doctors when Charlotte had arrived. There had been the other ER patients, mostly victims of fireworks gone wrong, and tears from family members told bad news.

So far, there had been no news, nothing to hang on to, good or bad. There was just waiting. Endless, mindless waiting. Like a convict pushing time to move faster, Annie willed the clock to speed ahead, for a doctor to come and tell them what was going on. Then again, she was terrified of the answer.

Joe wrapped her in his arms from behind, again interrupting her pacing.

"Let's sit for a while." He pulled her gently toward a chair. She was so glad for him, glad someone could tell her what to do and how to act. She leaned into him, still afraid, but feeling momentously better. He calmed her, he made her feel safe. He was the only thing keeping her from going out of her mind.

Approaching footsteps interrupted Annie's thoughts. "Are you Charlotte's daughter?" the doctor asked, eyeing her up. She leaped to her feet in a millisecond.

"Yes, hi, what can you tell me?" She encroached on the doctor's personal space but didn't care. She needed answers. The others crowded around.

"Charlotte had a minor heart attack. Now, the good news is, she's conscious. She's not completely lucid because of the meds she's on, but she's going to be okay. You got her here fast enough I expect a full recovery.

However, given her previous medical history, I am concerned. We are going to have to watch her closely. I want to run some more tests. We may be looking at some surgery."

At first, Annie was flooded with relief. Mom would be okay. But then she heard surgery. "What, like a bypass? Is it safe at her age?"

"It can be done, with risks, of course. I want to run some tests to assess the damage and the risk of another heart attack. We'll make the decision later. Right now, I want to focus on keeping her calm and recovering."

"Can we see her?"

"Yes, but two at a time, please."

Leonard and Annie ran unabashedly toward the hall, the doctor shouting directions. Neither looked back.

***

"Mom," Annie practically yelled, reaching in to gently hug her mom. Despite the IVs and the situation, Charlotte looked amazingly calm.

"Hey honey," she whispered, her voice cracking.

"Mom, I'm so glad you're okay." She perched herself on the hospital bed, daintily avoiding the wires and IVs. She kissed her mom's forehead.

"You gave us quite a scare," Leonard said on the other side, also leaning in to stroke Charlotte's hair.

"You're not getting rid of me so easily." She winked, reaching for both her daughter and Leonard's hands. "I'm gonna be fine."

They stood for a moment, taking in their luck. Annie

realized how much she still needed her mom. She felt guilty, thinking about how much more time she should have been spending with Charlotte. This was a wake-up call.

"Now listen," Charlotte began.

"Mom, you need to take it easy. You need to rest. You had a heart attack."

Charlotte just shook her head. "You can fight me, or you can listen. I need to tell you something." Leonard and Annie looked questioningly at each other but let her continue.

"Butternut's alive." Again, Annie and Leonard exchanged a look over Charlotte. Annie would chalk this up to pain meds.

"Okay, Mom, let's just talk about it later, okay?"

"Do not look at me like I'm crazy," she said, eyeing both of them. "I mean it. Butternut's alive. I saw him."

This was getting even more worrisome. Hallucinations were probably a normal side effect of the drugs in her IV, right? She would have to talk to the doctor. Right away.

"I'm not hallucinating," Charlotte said, as if she had read Annie's mind. "I saw him. That's where I was going when I had my heart attack. He was in your neighbor's window. He stole him."

There was a moment of silence as Annie tried to assess how to proceed.

"Okay, Mom, I know you're upset and I know you just had a heart attack, so I don't want to upset you. But

Mr. Liddle didn't steal Butternut. Why would he do that?"

"Because he's beautiful, of course. God, he's probably worth a lot of money."

"Okay, honey, listen, I'll go talk to them about it. Don't you worry," Leonard said. Leonard and Annie looked at each other again, making a tacit agreement this would be the best route to go.

"Do not placate me. You better mean it. He has my cat. You need to get him back." The heart monitor sped up as her voice began to rise. A nurse rushed in.

"Ms. Noel, you need to calm down. Doctor's orders. Now everyone out," the middle-aged nurse directed. Annie felt a little annoyed this woman was telling her what to do, but deep down, she knew she was right. Charlotte needed to rest.

"Okay, we'll take care of it, Mom. Promise." Annie leaned in for another kiss. Leonard also reassured her with words and a kiss.

Once they left Charlotte's room and were out of earshot, Annie turned to Leonard. "Pain meds, right?"

He didn't have to ask what she was talking about because he was obviously thinking the same thing. He looked at her, shrugged, and said, "Pain meds. In a few days, she'll snap back to reality."

Boy, did Annie hope so.

***

Over the course of the next week, Annie figured out two things for sure. First, her mom hated being in the hospital. After a few days of tests and gloppy cafeteria food, Charlotte was basically trying to escape from the hospital every chance she got. She begged to be let go, promised to do whatever it took. She just wanted to return to Wildflower.

Annie had been there on Tuesday when the doctor had told Charlotte the bad news—she would need bypass surgery to unclog her arteries.

"Doctor, I appreciate your concern, but I'm sure I'll be fine. Nothing a stricter diet can't fix, right?" Charlotte had pleaded, looking from the doctor to Annie.

"I'm sorry, Ms. Noel. This is necessary. We have to do this surgery so we don't risk another incident. Now, we're going to let you rest for a few days. Surgery is scheduled for Saturday."

Annie had grabbed her mom's hand, reassuring her all would be okay, but deep down, she wasn't so confident.

The second thing Annie learned since Charlotte's accident was how truly amazing Joe actually was. She had known that, been discovering that over the past months. She had seen the tenderness in his heart, felt the compassion of his soul. But over the past few days, she'd seen irrefutable proof Joe was certainly a keeper.

Between keeping up with things at home, at Wildflower, and at the hospital, Annie found herself wearing down. There were never enough hours in the day. Guilt panged in her every time she had to leave the hospital, feeling like she should be spending every second she could with Charlotte. Luckily, she wasn't alone. Amelia, Owen, and Leonard were spending every possible minute with Charlotte too. But Annie couldn't shake the feeling she should spend as much time as possible with her mother before the operation on Saturday. One just never knew what could happen. She quickly pushed the idea aside.

During all the trials of the week, Joe had been by her side. When he wasn't handing her coffee or holding her hand through the hospital visits and doctor's updates, he was helping ease her load. He stopped by her house and fed the cats, he went and checked on Charlotte's apartment, sorting mail and helping to arrange bills. He even covered for Annie at an event she was supposed to be working with Macy, donning a catering hat to help pitch in for the Mitchells' fiftieth wedding anniversary. Through it all, despite her fears and stress, she couldn't help but think how lucky she was to have found him.

Her heart was swelling with love for Joe, a love no longer deniable. Yes, she was still terrified and apprehensive about opening her heart fully, about accepting the risk of a full-blown relationship. Thinking about it, though, she realized she didn't have a choice. Sure, it was a risk to be with Joe, but it was the only option she had. The past few months had been a difficult sea of changes, threatening to drown her. Joe had been the rock she clung to in the rage of the storm, the rock that had helped her surface as a new, stronger woman. He reminded her she was worthy of love, she still had love to give, and life after Dave was possible. He made her feel safe, made her excited about life again. Loving him could lead to peril; there was always risk in love. But it was a risk she would have to take.

For now, though, their relationship consisted of tepid, watery coffees in the hospital lobby and talks about Charlotte's condition. When Saturday morning rolled around and Annie found herself standing in Charlotte's room pre-surgery, she was so thankful to have Joe holding her hand. As she started to tear up at her good-bye to Charlotte, he squeezed her hand, reassuring her without a single word.

"Mom, I love you, we'll be right here when you get out." She kissed Charlotte's cheek. Amelia, too, added to the sentiment and gave her grandmother a kiss, followed by Leonard.

"Will all of you stop acting like I'm dying? You're not getting rid of me yet." Charlotte winked, smiling despite her obvious apprehension.

As the nurses came in to wheel Charlotte to surgery, she abruptly yelled, *"Wait!"* The nurses froze, and the family looked at Charlotte to see what was wrong.

"Annie?" Annie approached the bed.

"What is it, Mom?"

"Did you get Butternut back yet? You've been avoiding my question all week. Don't think I didn't notice."

"Mom, we'll talk about this later." She had, in fact, been avoiding the question all week, figuring Charlotte didn't need any stress. When Charlotte asked her if she had confronted the neighbor, she had always been mercifully interrupted by a nurse or something else hospital related. The other days, she said she would be storming over to the neighbor's house that very night, hoping Charlotte would forget by the next day.

"Annie, listen. If something does happen to me, this is the only time we have to talk about it. Now, I know you think I'm crazy, but I'm not. Butternut is over there. Please, please go get him back."

Annie sighed, giving Charlotte a half smile. "Okay, Mom. I promise I'll investigate today." She gave her mom's hand one last squeeze before leaving.

As Charlotte rolled away, Amelia approached her mom. "Butternut? What is she talking about, Mom?"

Annie told Amelia the details.

"What if she did see him? Maybe we should check into it." Amelia swiped away tears.

"Honey, your grandma was having a heart attack. I don't think she was thinking clearly. Once she gets better and off all of these strong meds, she'll realize it just doesn't make sense." Annie felt bad for lying to her mother but knew it was the right thing to do.

"I guess you're right."

They spent the next several hours pacing the hospital floor yet again, waiting for the news every family wanted to hear, hoping unlike Butternut, Charlotte would, in fact, come back to them.

Chapter Twenty-Eight

Annie

Bubbles piling up around her neck and soft music playing in the background, Annie sank deeper into the claw-foot tub, warm water cocooning her in a sea of warmth. She had felt guilty for taking this hour to mindlessly soak, but Joe had convinced her she needed to recharge. Taking his advice, she left Amelia and Owen at the hospital with Charlotte, Joe giving her a ride back to her house. She'd convinced him, begged him, to go back to his house and also get some rest. He'd been so supportive, spending the entire time by her side.

"I'll be fine," she'd promised. "Go home, take a shower, and get some rest. I'm going to drive back to the hospital after I take a bath. I'll call you when I get there."

He had been hesitant, but ultimately agreed to heed his own advice and take a break.

Now, soaking in the luxurious scent of lavender, she realized how tired she truly was. It had been a long day, and the stillness of the house was just what she needed.

She deserved some time to herself, so she succumbed to the indulgence, even if it was a simple bath.

Charlotte had come out of surgery just fine that morning. She'd made it to the recovery room without major complications, managing to crack jokes to the nurses and hit on another Adam Levine look-alike in recovery—she told Amelia all about the encounter, to everyone's chagrin. She was in good spirits, seeming refreshed despite the major surgery.

But then the doctor had shared the news with her. Charlotte had asked when she would be released, able to go back to Wildflower.

"Ms. Noel, this was a major surgery, especially at your age. We're going to need to take it easy and get someone to keep a constant eye on you. You'll be here for another week, and then we will be arranging for you to head to Golden Hill for at least a month until you're in the clear."

Charlotte had looked at Annie, pure confusion on her face. "Golden Hill? Annie, isn't that a nursing home?"

The doctor butted in, answering for Annie. "Ms. Noel, yes, it is a nursing home facility, but you will be there only as a rehabilitation patient."

Charlotte looked stunned. "Annie, I can't go to a nursing home. I want to go back to Wildflower."

Annie's heart had sunk. "Mom, I know. But listen, it's temporary, just until you're all better, okay? It'll be fine. We'll all visit you, and you'll be home before you know it."

Leonard leaned in to give her a kiss. "I'll be there every day. And besides, I'm sure you'll liven the place up. Who knows, maybe you'll even find another Catherine to wage war with." Charlotte slapped his arm, grinning in spite of herself.

Thank goodness for Leonard, Annie had thought. He made Charlotte see things rationally, mellowed her, fit her perfectly.

So Charlotte conceded to the arrangement, but Annie knew she was still upset deep down. Annie couldn't help but worry about her mother, worry about how this would affect her. She wasn't just concerned about Charlotte's physical state but her mental state as well. This would be a rough month for all of them.

As the water chilled, Annie pulled the drain on the tub, slowly rising from the depths of the water to face the chill of reality. The real world was a tough place to be, stress a ceaseless constant. But, she realized, Joe made it all better. He was the bright spot, her biggest motivator. She knew she could get through because he would be by her side.

Annie slowly dried off, stepping into some jeans and a T-shirt. She headed to the kitchen, deciding to make herself a cup of hot tea and head to the deck for a few more minutes of serenity. After her Keurig spit out the fiery liquid, she ambled onto her back deck, basking in the setting sun's final rays. It was a beautiful night, and she was thankful she had these few moments to herself.

Glancing around the yard, her eyes landed on the

spot where Charlotte's heart attack had happened. That had been a terrifying few moments. Annie had thought she'd lost her mom. She'd thought she had, in the blink of an eye, become an orphan.

As she shuddered from the prospect, her eyes caught something else. At first, she thought she had lost it, lack of sleep combining with her anxiety over her mom's health. But no, as she glanced away and looked back, she knew she wasn't hallucinating.

There, in the second-story window of her neighbor's house, was a cat, scratching and scratching.

It wasn't just any cat. It was the familiar white-and-orange cat, who had not long ago slept on her couch, scratched her furniture. It was the cat who'd left his hair on every pair of Annie's black pants, who mercilessly kneaded her legs during television at night.

It was none other than Butternut.

And he was in the neighbor's house, just like Charlotte had suggested.

***

In a panic, Annie fumbled with the buttons on her phone. She selected Joe from her contacts, her natural go-to in an emergency.

He didn't answer.

She tried again.

Still no answer. He must have taken her advice and jumped in the shower or taken a nap.

Debating whether she should just deal with the problem herself, she decided this couldn't wait. She needed help immediately, so she selected another number and waited for her to pick up.

"Mom? Are you okay?" Amelia frantically asked, as she answered her phone.

"No. Yes. I don't know. Is Owen there?"

"Yeah... why?"

"Put him on the phone, please." Her words flew out of her mouth at the speed of light, tumbling together into what was probably an incoherent string of sounds. Amelia probably thought she'd been drinking.

"Okay...."

It was a painstakingly long time until Owen came on the other line.

"Annie?"

"Owen, can you come over? I'm having a bit of an emergency."

"What's wrong?"

"Charlotte was right. The neighbor, the creepy one who looks like he eats baby kittens for breakfast, well, he has Butternut. I saw him in the window." She didn't mince words. There wasn't time.

"Are you serious?"

"Very. And I don't know what to do. I have to get him back, but Mr. Liddle gives me the absolute creeps. I don't want to go over alone, especially if he stole the cat. Who knows where his mind is?"

"Be right there." Owen abruptly hung up.

Annie sat down at the kitchen table, her foot tapping away her nerves. What was happening to her life? When would things ever be normal?

Not anytime soon, she thought. *We're about to go snatch a cat named Butternut back from a creepy cat-stealing psycho.*

At least my life is never dull, she thought as she sipped on her lukewarm coffee.

***

"Mom, are you 100 percent sure?" Amelia asked as soon as she stormed through the door with Owen.

"Yes, Amelia. I'm positive. Grandma isn't crazy. Mr. Liddle has Butternut."

"But how could that have happened? Did he break into your house to steal your cat?"

"Well, to be honest, the guy is a weirdo, so I wouldn't put it past him. But no, I think he must've snatched him from the backyard."

"Why was Butternut in the backyard?" Charlotte had never let her cats go outside.

Annie sheepishly shrugged. "He'd been meowing at the door lately. I felt bad for him being cooped up all day, so I've been letting him out during the afternoon. He always comes right back, but when he didn't the other week, that's when I got worried."

"Mom, you told me it was an accident he got out."

Annie simply shrugged. "Well, does it matter? All that matters now is how the heck we're going to get this cat back."

"She's right. Listen, I'll go over there and talk to him," Owen said.

"Owen, wait, Mom's right. He's pretty creepy. Like, he talks to his plants, never comes out until nighttime, creepy."

"Yes, he's very weird. He's only lived over there for a year or two now, but the guy gives me the absolute willies. Yuck. He's so odd," Annie said, feeling a little bit bad about her judgment. Then again, he had their freaking cat, so she couldn't muster up too much pity.

"What's the worst that could happen? Is he going to lock me in his basement? I think it'll be fine," Owen assured. Before anyone could think twice, he was out the door.

Annie and Amelia crowded by the front window so they could get a partial view of Owen at Mr. Liddle's front door.

"This is crazy." They stood silently watching the drama unfold.

"Isn't my life always crazy?"

Five long minutes later, Owen came stomping back over.

"He won't open the door. I know he's in there, I heard him rustling about, but he refuses to answer."

"Now what?" Amelia sighed.

Owen marched toward the back of Annie's house and headed onto the deck. He looked up to the window in question. As Amelia and Annie joined him, they saw Butternut still scratching.

"Oh, my God, look at the poor thing."

Owen stood, eyeing the cat in the window, a

perplexingly deep look on his face.

"Annie, do you have a ladder?" Owen asked, still staring.

"What?"

"A ladder?"

"Owen, what are you thinking?" Amelia asked.

"Well, that window looks pretty old. I think I could break the seal and crack it open enough to get the cat out."

"You're going to break into Mr. Liddle's house and steal Butternut back? That's your plan?" Amelia asked incredulously. "Are you kidding?"

"Well, it's not really stealing. He stole Butternut to begin with, and I won't let the psycho keep your Grandma's cat a second longer."

"Owen, this is a bad idea. What if you get caught? What if Mr. Liddle hears you and shoots you or something?" Annie said, adding to Amelia's concern.

"Really? Guys, I've seen this dude once or twice. He is creepy and seems to have sociopathic tendencies, but I don't think he's a mass murderer. Seriously. It'll be fine."

"Wait a second," Amelia said. "Why don't we call the cops?"

Owen sighed. "Really? You're going to call the cops about a cat theft? Do you really think they're going to take it seriously?"

Amelia and Annie looked at each other, grimacing.

Finally, Annie spoke. "The ladder's in the garage."

"Mom, he can't do this," Amelia shouted.

Owen ignored her and headed to the garage. Amelia looked at Annie, who shrugged. With that, she took off after him.

Ten minutes later, the deed was in motion as Annie stood on her deck, wondering if she should get 911 on standby.

"What's going on?" a voice demanded from behind her. Annie clutched her chest, feeling like the family was going to suffer its second heart attack.

She turned around to see Joe rushing toward her in a panic. He must've seen her phone calls and been worried.

"You wouldn't believe me if I told you," Annie said as Joe gauged the sight of Amelia and Owen with a ladder by Mr. Liddle's house, and Butternut scratching away.

***

"Guys, be a little bit quiet about it, won't you?" Annie hissed across the yard. In spite of the precarious situation, she laughed a bit. Those three would never be bank robbers or burglars, that was for sure. Between Owen dropping the ladder in a loud clink, Amelia nagging at him that this was the absolute worst idea in history, and Joe directing both of them to hurry up, Mr. Liddle most definitely heard them coming. Annie was nervous, but she had to stay focused. She was the lookout.

Annie looked up to see Butternut was still at the window. She didn't sense any other activity from the house.

"Hold the ladder," Owen ordered Amelia and Joe as

he propped it against the house. They did just that as he began climbing. He was nimble and fast, Annie couldn't help but notice. He made the operation look easy.

When he reached the window, he started jimmying it. It didn't budge. All of the noise scared the cat away from the window, and Owen started wobbling. He kept trying, putting his muscle into the window, even shoulder blocking it a few times. It still didn't budge.

"Shit. I can't get it," he hissed, peering down the ladder at Amelia and Joe.

"Can you just break it?" Amelia asked.

"Oh yeah, that seems like a great idea." He smiled to ease the sarcasm in his voice.

"And jimmying the window is a better one?"

"Do you want me to give it a try?" Joe asked. Owen just continued working, focused on the problem at hand.

Operation Swipe the Cat was falling apart as Annie watched.

"Guys, get back here before he sees you. We're going to have to figure something else out."

But Owen was stubborn. He probably felt like his manhood was on the line.

"No, I'll get it. Just wait," he assured, again trying to heave up the old, rickety window.

"It's no use, come down," Amelia squabbled. The two were like a married couple already.

"Amelia, wait." He grunted with his effort, muscles rippling.

Annie was so focused on the ladder situation

she forgot about her one job—lookout. When she remembered, she cast her eyes downward, and her heart stopped. She felt like there would be two of them in the hospital bed soon.

"Can I help you?" a scratchy voice coughed as they all froze, now gripped by panic.

Mr. Liddle, dressed in tight sweatpants, a button-up shirt, and a sweater vest, was breathing heavily, eyeing them up.

In his arms, he was stroking a large white-and-orange cat.

"Shit," Annie proclaimed, this time not bothering to whisper.

****

As Owen scrambled down the ladder, Annie rushed across the lawn, approaching Mr. Liddle to run interference. She instantly got chills, and not in a good way.

"Mr. Liddle, how are you? Listen, we tried to knock on your door, but you didn't answer. You see, Owen here noticed a bees nest by your second-story window. He was worried because I'm deathly allergic, so he was trying to knock it down."

Mr. Liddle continued wheezing, petting the bawling Butternut. What the hell was she going to do?

Mr. Liddle nodded, a grin verging on sadistic on his face. "Why thank you, Owen. You're a good boy." His creepy eyes didn't focus on anything in particular. Owen was at the bottom of the ladder.

"Yeah, no problem."

"Do you want to pet my kitty?" Mr. Liddle asked, still creepily.

The four of them looked at each other, trying to figure out how to broach the subject without getting tied up in Mr. Liddle's basement. Joe protectively stood by Annie's side, glaring at Mr. Liddle. Annie put a hand on Joe's arm to signal she had this under control, but Amelia rushed forward.

"Listen, Mr. Liddle, let's be real here. That's not your cat," Amelia blurted.

Annie looked at her in horror, mouthing, "What are you doing?" Amelia shook her off.

"That's my grandma's cat."

Mr. Liddle looked horrified. "No, this is my Mr. Whiskers."

Wow, this was getting freakier by the second.

"No, it's not," Amelia shouted now, anger seething.

"Amelia," Annie reassured, extending a hand to her shoulder.

"Mom, come on. This is ridiculous. He knows it's not his cat."

"Young lady, this cat was in my yard. He was a stray, so I took him in. And now he's mine." Mr. Liddle turned defensively to better protect Butternut.

Amelia was ready for a smackdown, but Annie stepped in front.

"Mr. Liddle, I'm very sorry for the confusion. This is my fault, really. You see, I've been watching my mother's cat for her, and I left Butternut outside. I understand you probably thought he was a stray, but he's not. He's my mom's, and she loves him very much." Annie looked into his unfocused eyes.

Mr. Liddle seemed to consider this for a while. "Well, I can't give him up."

Suddenly, Owen pounced, grabbing Mr. Liddle's arm and whirling him around. "Look here, that's not your cat. Now give him to me." It was a side of Owen Annie had never seen. Joe rushed to help.

"Forget it," Mr. Liddle exclaimed, kicking Owen in the shin. Owen dropped in pain.

Joe stepped forward, ready to pounce on Mr. Liddle, anger building on his face.

"Okay, okay, okay. Let's all settle down," Annie demanded, pulling Joe back. Owen rested for a minute before getting back up, sheer embarrassment flooding his face. He tried to act tough, which only made the situation even more ridiculous.

Annie softly said, "Mr. Liddle, what would it take for me to get Butternut back?"

Mr. Liddle looked confused, and then asked, "Wait? The cat's name is Butternut?"

Annie closed her eyes. This was impossible. "Yes. Now, I'm sure we can come to some sort of an agreement, right?"

Mr. Liddle thought for a few minutes. "Well, I think maybe we could strike a deal."

"Okay, name it."

"Well, first, I would like to be reimbursed for his vet

bill. I took him for shots last week."

"How much do I owe you? We would be glad to."

"Seven hundred dollars."

"Are you fucking kidding me?" Amelia shrieked. "You stole my grandma's cat, and now you want us to pay seven hundred dollars?"

Annie gave Amelia a death glared that said *shut up*. Amelia shook her head. "Okay, you've got it."

"And one more thing," he added.

"What's that?"

"How about a date?"

"You asshole," Joe said, an anger rising in him that Annie hadn't seen before. This was getting ugly. Annie stepped between Joe and Mr. Liddle, hands outstretched to keep Joe from pummeling Mr. Liddle into the ground.

Annie felt vomit rising in her throat. "Mr. Liddle, I would be honored to go on a date with you, but I'm in a relationship."

Mr. Liddle sighed. The group took a collective breath, wondering what would happen next.

"Okay, but promise me if you break up, you'll keep me in mind." He winked. Amelia visibly gagged. Joe wringed his hands.

"You've got it." Annie fake smiled through her words, her smile easily rivaling that of a Miss America contestant. Behind the smile, though, bile was rising in her throat. She would certainly be having horrific nightmares tonight.

"I'm gonna miss you, Mr. Whiskers," Mr. Liddle

proclaimed, kissing Butternut on the head. The cat also looked like he may want to vomit.

Annie went inside to get her checkbook. Seven hundred dollars was ridiculous, and she now officially knew Mr. Liddle was more than socially awkward. He had lived next door for two years now and never interacted with them. She had a feeling though, maybe he knew more about her than she thought. Maybe she would buy a Doberman. Or two. And some extremely thick, efficient blinds.

She handed Mr. Liddle the check, which he sniffed. But, to her surprise, he handed Butternut over without complaint, turned, and went inside his house.

Owen, Annie, Joe, and Amelia eyed each other up.

"What the hell just happened?" Owen asked.

"I have no idea," Annie said.

"I feel like you should call the cops. And get a security system," Amelia said, visibly shaking off the gross vibes.

"Or just let me take care of it." Joe's hands were balled into fists.

Annie didn't argue. "For now, let's get Butternut inside. I have somewhere I want to take him."

Once safely locked inside Annie's home—she would never leave the door unlocked again—they fed Butternut, got him some water, and whisked him away to Groversport Memorial.

Annie didn't care if there was a no-cat policy or not. She knew this was exactly what her mother needed right now. Plus, she had paid seven hundred dollars to get a damn cat back, so she sure as hell was going to make it worth her money.

Chapter Twenty-Nine

"My baby," Charlotte exulted when the cat wranglers brought in Butternut. It made Amelia smile to see her grandma so happy. It was worth seven hundred dollars and a run-in with Mr. Creepo, as she was now calling him.

Butternut curled up beside Charlotte on the hospital bed. The four had been met with quite a few evil stares from nurses on the way in, but Gloria, Charlotte's main nurse, had smiled and helped them sneak him into the room.

"This will be so good for her," Gloria had reassured. It was truly the case.

Owen put his arm around Amelia, and she sank against him. Things had been crazy the past few weeks. Work was hectic; Smoothie Q was in its busiest season, and pet owners going on vacation meant dog-sitting services were needed more than ever. Amelia was spending every possible second at the hospital, though, worrying about Grandma Charlotte and trying to help her mom. There had been little time for romance and dates with Owen.

But the beautiful thing was—it was okay. With Owen, there wasn't the need for fancy pretenses or schedules. Unlike Neville, he was fine with going with the flow, with random takeout dinners and snuggling on the couch. He was okay if they were hanging out at 6:00 a.m. or midnight. Despite the current chaos of their lives, he was okay with every second he got to see Amelia. She felt closer to Owen than she ever had to Neville, despite their dateless situation.

That wasn't to say there wasn't romance. With his apartment being so close, there were plenty of late nights with Owen and plenty of sleepless mornings too. It felt good to pursue the relationship casually. If she were being honest, though, it just felt good to be with Owen.

He understood her, got her, and made her love her life. He never put her down for working the jobs she did. He never made her feel like she wasn't goal-oriented enough or impressive enough. He was crazy about her, chipped black nail polish and all. He loved that she wasn't really a high-heels kind of girl. He appreciated her wacky sense of sarcasm. He got the relationship she had with her grandma and mom.

He just got her. Every wild, mismatched piece of her.

After taking in Charlotte's visit with Butternut, Amelia turned to Owen.

"I better get going. I have an early shift tomorrow at the bookstore," she said. He nodded, telling Charlotte good-bye and giving Butternut a scratch. Annie stayed behind to round up the cat and to catch up with Grandma Charlotte.

Heading to the elevator hand in hand, Owen looked down at her, smiling.

"What?"

He shook his head. "Nothing. It's just, God, life is exciting with you." He winked.

"You call stealing an already stolen cat and fighting with a psycho exciting? You need a life," she teased.

He laughed. "You might be right. But seriously, what other girl could offer me such mad, crazy entertainment?" He purposefully bumped into her shoulder with his.

They walked into the elevator, and he squeezed her hand, prompting her to look up at him.

"What now?" She grinned, feeling fluttery in her chest. Even in a hospital elevator, he made her smile.

"I love you, Amelia." Seriousness infused his voice, flooded his eyes.

She contemplated him for a long moment, wanting to savor it, even if it did smell like antiseptic in the elevator.

"I love you too."

Their kiss in the elevator was long and sensuous, the kiss of two lovers encroaching on new territory, more serious territory. They had known all along there was a pull, a passion between them. But now, they knew this passion and attraction was deepening, building into something more long-term. Pulling back from the kiss, Amelia looked up to see they were almost at the bottom floor. Owen glanced up as well.

"Damn," he mumbled, hands smoothing her hair as he kissed her forehead. He grinned mischievously as he pulled back to look down into her face. "You know, they do make an Emergency Stop button for a reason."

"Oh, yeah? Why's that?"

"For this." He cornered her by the elevator buttons. He pushed the Stop button as he took her lips in his mouth, flooding her with passion again.

She pulled back for a second, just long enough to ask, "What if an alarm goes off?"

He looked into her eyes, his hand rustling his hair. "It'll just be all the more exciting," he whispered, leaning back into her with vengeance.

She knew he was right.

***

Leaving the bookstore at noon the next day, Amelia could still feel a cheesy smirk on her face. It hadn't left since those ten minutes in the elevator. Luckily, no alarm had gone off. And other than a few knowing looks when they reached the lobby floor and some ruffled hair, they hadn't been caught.

Who was she? She had gone from a fine-dining, pink-wearing girl with Neville to… what? A girl who did it in an elevator? A girl who ate pizza on the couch instead of caviar, who stole cats from second-story windows?

Her smirk widened.

This was just what she was looking for.

Life with Owen, she knew, would never be dull, would never be a show. It would be messy and chaotic. Alarms would probably go off from time to time, but there would be no false pretenses, no faking her way through. It would be unconventional, untraditional, and anything but average. She would be whatever she wanted to be, and that would be good enough for him.

You couldn't find a love stronger than that, she was sure.

Going back to her apartment, she opened the door to a surprise. Owen sat on her living room floor on what appeared to be a picnic blanket. Spread before him were hoagies from her favorite deli down the street and some chocolate chip cookies from Anne's Bakery, another of her favorites. Owen looked up with a boyish grin. He stood and approached her.

"What's all this?"

"Our picnic lunch. I mean, wow, last night was amazing, but I felt pretty bad. I mean, a guy should at least take a girl to dinner before doing it in an elevator with her."

She shoved him. "You're weird. But one more question? If it's a picnic, why are we inside?"

"Well, I felt like you would most likely be so swept away by this romantic gesture that you would probably want to jump me afterward. I didn't think it would be appropriate to behave that way in public. Again."

"You are truly—"

"Incorrigible?" he interrupted, leaning in to kiss her.

"Are you ever going to let it go?"

He pretended to think about it. "Nope."

"Good," she replied, kissing him before pulling away. "I'm starving. Let's eat."

They spent the next hour eating sandwiches, talking about work, and staring into each other's eyes like lovesick teenagers. But Owen had been right. Something about the picnic blanket, the conversation, and most of all, the gorgeous body of the man sitting across from her made her hungry for more than lunch.

When lunch moved from the picnic blanket to the bedroom, neither complained. They simply succumbed to passion, basking in the beauty of their newly confirmed love.

294

Chapter Thirty

Amelia

A soft light warming her face, Amelia groggily rolled over. The sight before her was something she could definitely get used to—Owen. Still sleeping, a soft wheeze in his every breath verging on a snore, the covers pushed low enough for her to get a perfect view of his rock-hard abs in all their glory. She would never get tired of it.

Rolling into him, she kissed a trail from his perfect pecs up to his lips. He breathed in, squinting, awareness slowly bringing a soft smile to his face.

"Morning," he groggily whispered into her hair, rolling over to wrap an arm around her.

"Morning," she whispered into his lips, smiling despite the fact she wasn't ever a morning person. Of course, that was before Owen became an accessory in her bed.

"How'd you sleep?"

"Well, I think you know the answer to the question."

It had been a long night. A good night, but a long one.

He stroked her hair, basking in the sight of her. She felt a little bit self-conscious.

"I think I should take a shower. My hair is a gross mess." She pulled his fingers away.

"You look fine," he replied, and she believed him.

For a moment they lay there, taking each other in, reveling in the place they now found themselves. And then she made a decision, a big one, one she hadn't anticipated.

"I want to show you something."

"Oh, yeah?"

"Just wait." She rolled away, reaching into a drawer in the nightstand. Hesitantly, she handed him a piece of crinkled notebook paper.

"What's this?"

She took a breath. "I haven't shown them to anyone." She handed them to him, turning to look at the ceiling as he read, feeling like her heart was going to burst from fear. This was big. She'd never shown anyone her writing, never felt good enough to stand up to judgment. But with Owen, she felt like she could bare a part of her soul hidden from everyone else. She felt like she could share with him, trust him with a hidden part of who she was. He made her want to reveal her true self, her true passion.

He did something surprising. Without asking, without hesitating, with morning sunshine floating in, he started singing. He started singing her song.

In a voice smoky with sleep, he gave her chills, made her hear her words differently, made her see the potential.

I thought I was lost, gone forever more,
But you found me, you know me at the core,
My heart is yours, even though it's scarred,
You've shown me love isn't that hard.

Here in your arms, I don't have to hide.
Your soul sings to me, a known lullaby.
I've found who I am, I know where I belong.
Here in your arms, I've found my song.

He gave it a rock edge she hadn't expected. When he sang it, it came to life. It didn't sound cheesy or unworthy. It sounded real.

He stopped, pausing to look at her. "This is amazing."

She looked at him and saw truth in his eyes. "Really?"

"Yeah. Seriously. This is good. But I just have a question. Is this about us?"

She smiled now. "Of course it is," she teased. "Who else would it be about?"

"Can I sing it in my show next week?"

Amelia reacted automatically, "Owen, you don't have to."

"Stop it. I want to. It's amazing. I need to snag this before a celeb does."

"Owen, it's really not ready."

"Yeah, but with us working together, it could be. Come on, say yes," he pleaded, nudging her with his nose. "This could be what we both need to get our careers going."

She smiled. A career doing what she loved. Could that really happen? If anyone could make it happen, if it were possible, it would be Owen.

She breathed out through her teeth, giving way to her anxiety. "What if you get booed off stage?"

"Then I'll give them my awesome smile and flash my abs."

She shook her head. "I love you. I don't know why, but I do."

"I love you too," he answered, kissing her again. "Can I ask you something else?"

"What is this, an interrogation?"

"I know you broke up with Neville not very long ago. But I just— I want to know. Do you see us getting married? Do you want to marry me?"

She froze, not expecting such a heavy question to come from seemingly playful banter. "Are you..."

He grinned. "Amelia, listen. I'm gonna lay it all out there. I love you. Before you, I saw my life as an endless string of rock songs. But now, I know I want more. I want you. All of you. Forever. And if it means to keep you, we have to get married tomorrow, I will. But if it means you don't want to get married, you want to keep seeing where this thing is going, that's fine too. I want you, all of you, any way I can get you."

298

She pierced him with her gaze. That was what happiness felt like. That was what love felt like.

"I love you too. I want to be with you too. But, I mean, I'm fine without the ring and all of the official stuff. At least for now. I said yes to Neville because with a man like him, marriage was a requirement. It was a formality. But I've never been crazy about the idea, to tell you the truth. It's not that I don't believe in marriage or what it stands for. But I don't think we need a ring and vows to be with each other," she said. He was silent, so she added, "I mean, unless you want to get married. Because I will. I love you. I want to be with you. Forever."

He cut her off with a kiss. It was a few minutes before they pulled away from each other, lips reluctantly parting.

"Amelia, I don't need you in a white dress in a church to be with you forever, to be committed to you. I just, I don't know, I don't think the whole tying the knot thing is our thing, at least not right now. I see us living it up, seeing where life goes, together. Let's just be."

"Sounds perfect to me. Let's live in sin for a while and see how it goes."

"You're incorrigible."

In that moment, she knew with unwavering clarity he was forever hers.

Chapter Thirty-One

Charlotte

"Charlotte, if you don't stop pushing buttons…," Leonard snarled, situating himself in the chair beside her bed so he could reach the laptop.

"Well, sorry Mr. Hotshot Tech Guy, but I'm not used to these contraptions," Charlotte snapped back, grabbing the laptop off her lap and pushing it out of Leonard's reach.

They both looked up at a giggle. It was the nurse on shift, Janice.

"You two are like a married couple already, honestly," she teased, walking over to help.

With the push of a few buttons, Charlotte smiled to see everyone back on the screen.

"Now don't touch anything. And try not to turn it up too much. Administration would kill me if they knew I helped you with this." She winked.

On the screen, Charlotte smiled to see Amelia, Annie, Marla, Bridget, and Joe huddled around a screen of their own. It was dark and looked pretty crowded, but the five squeezed around the camera.

"Hi, Grandma. Did you figure it out? We lost you for a few minutes," Amelia shouted into the screen.

Leonard leaned over so he was in line with the camera lens on the laptop. "Your grandma can't keep her hands off the thing. She pushed a button, even though I told her not to."

"Oh, stop it. It's fine now, see?" Charlotte said to Leonard, forgetting about the screen.

"Well, don't touch anything. The show's going to start any minute."

Charlotte wished desperately she could be there, sharing in the moment with Owen and Amelia. She had pleaded and begged with the doctor, trying to convince him it would be like music therapy. When that didn't work, she had begged Amelia, Owen, Leonard, and even Marla to help her escape, just for the evening.

But no one agreed, all afraid for her health and what the crowded, loud location would do to her.

She was feeling much better, but if she were being honest, she wasn't 100 percent. But what did you expect when an eight-one-year-old had major surgery? She longed for her days at Wildflower, days when she wasn't confined to a bed. Days she could have attended this big concert, this big moment.

Tomorrow she would be transferred to the nursing home, temporarily of course. She was uncomfortable with the whole idea but knew she didn't have a choice.

Annie was so busy with her new career, she couldn't possibly ask her daughter to let her stay with her until she healed. Besides, she needed constant monitoring. She knew she would get through. She wasn't going to let it beat her. She would do everything she could to get better faster and to get back to her friends, her home.

A little less than a year ago, she had thought Wildflower would never feel like home, would never soothe her soul. Now things were so different. She had Bridget and Marla there. And she had Leonard.

Leonard had been a godsend the past few weeks, practically living at the hospital with her. He was by her side for every moment, promising to never leave. It had been the first big test in their relationship, and they were getting through it closer than ever. She couldn't wait to make it official.

Tomorrow would be a hard transfer. But today, well, today was a beautiful moment for Amelia, Owen, and her family.

Amelia had been the one, of course, to arrange for Charlotte to be Skyped in—whatever the heck that meant. All Charlotte knew was at 7:00 p.m., she would be able to see Owen on the stage for his new gig. And, most importantly, she would be able to hear Amelia's song performed live.

Amelia was a bundle of nerves; Charlotte could tell from her posture on the screen, from the look on her face. This was a big moment for her granddaughter. Up until this point, songwriting had been a hidden hobby, a pipe dream. Now, it was coming true. The sky would be the limit. Amelia was pursuing her deepest dreams, and it was all thanks to Owen.

Annie, too, was getting a second chance. Seeing Annie on the screen, turned toward Joe, Charlotte knew the romance blossoming was strengthening every day. Despite Joe's family members, Charlotte was happy. Annie deserved the new excitement, the new chance at life. With the job and Joe, she was on her way to happiness too.

"I think it's starting," Leonard said, pulling her out of her thoughts. "Look, the crowd's quieting down."

And what a crowd it was. Without being there, Charlotte could see the bar was packed. Amelia turned her iPad so Charlotte had a full view of the stage. Owen paraded out and took the microphone.

"How's everyone doing?" The crowd let out a cheer.

"So tonight's very special. Our band's going to be playing a new, original song tonight. It's called 'Second Chance,' and it's by Ms. Amelia Amsley. Let's give this lovely, talented lady a hand," he said, and the crowd obeyed. Charlotte knew Amelia was blushing. "I hope you like it."

The band started playing. As Charlotte listened to the lyrics her granddaughter had penned, her heart swelled with pride. She didn't take her eyes off the screen, listening to every word. True, rock wasn't really her preferred genre, but she wouldn't have cared if it were being played by an Amazonian tribe. Her granddaughter's song was being played live. It was really happening.

When the song was over, Amelia came back on the screen. "Grandma, what did you think?" she asked, all smiles as the crowd continued cheering.

"I loved it, baby. I'm so happy for you," Charlotte said, unable to stop smiling. Leonard gave her a thumbs-up.

As Amelia said good-bye and Charlotte and Leonard closed the computer, they were both still grinning.

"That was awesome, huh?" Charlotte leaned back against her hospital pillow.

"It sure was. I'm so happy for those two."

"Me too. To be young and in love again, huh?"

Leonard smirked. "Or to be old and in love, too, right?"

She laughed. "Yes, I suppose you're right. Young lovebirds, old lovebirds, it doesn't matter, does it?"

He looked at her seriously now. "Charlotte, I think over the past few months I've realized it doesn't matter at all. In life, we're always trying to look ahead, to figure out what's next. When I came to Wildflower, I thought it was the closing of my life's chapters. I thought there was nothing left to see. And then you came along, and I've realized every single stage of life is beautiful and wonderful in its own way. I think life isn't about age. It's about finding things that make you happy, that fulfill you, at every single stage of your life."

She smiled at him, patting his hand. "Look at you, Mr. Sentimental now. I agree with you. This is beautiful.

Sure, we might not be at rock concerts like the young ones, not really. But we've got a great thing going, and I wouldn't trade it for anything."

"Charlotte, I've been thinking. What are we waiting for? Let's get this wedding going. I know we said we weren't in a rush, but why wait? I want to make the most of this part of our lives. Let's plan this wedding. Let's get married soon."

She glanced at Leonard, and the years swirled around her. Memories of Charlie, of her sadness of moving out of their home, of the new life she was building cascaded through her mind. Through it all, the heartbreaks and losses, through the new starts and new moments, one thing remained steady.

Her love for Leonard.

He had her heart now, all of it. She could never forget who she was or the life she had lived, and she didn't want to. It was a part of her. It was what had brought her to this moment. But she also knew what Leonard was saying. You had to make the most of every moment, of every opportunity. Leonard made her so happy. Why not get married soon? Why not mark the new stage of life with a joyous occasion?

So she turned to Leonard and, for the second time, she simply said, "Yes."

Epilogue

Charlotte
OCTOBER

"Places, everyone," Cassie sang in her chirpy voice, but Charlotte didn't mind. Not today. She was standing inside the side entrance to the building, waiting for her cue.

"You ready?" Owen asked, offering her his arm. She readjusted the bright yellow bouquet in her hands and nodded. Owen gave her a reassuring smile, and they were off.

Walking into the warm October air, Charlotte was taken aback by how beautiful everything looked. Annie and Macy had outdone themselves. The courtyard had been transformed into a whimsical, romantic ceremony locale, complete with fall flowers, an archway decorated in gauzy lace, and a beautiful white runway.

Annie had been hesitant about planning the wedding for the date Charlotte had picked.

"Mom, that's Halloween weekend. Don't you want

to pick another weekend?"

"It's kind of fitting. We're all bags of bones here anyway, so why not go with it?" Charlotte stated, a mischievous look in her eye.

Annie had rolled her eyes, but swore she would only go ahead with it if she didn't have to have pumpkins and costumes. Charlotte had begrudgingly agreed; she had thought it would be fun to get married in a pirate costume or something.

As the music played and Owen eased them down the aisle, Charlotte beamed in her simple buttercup dress. Amelia had wanted Charlotte to go on *Say Yes to the Dress* and choose a flashy, sparkly dress, but Charlotte had wanted something a bit simpler. After all, she didn't feel white was quite appropriate at her age. Whom was she trying to fool?

At the end of the aisle, Charlotte's eyes landed on Leonard. He stood stoically, his cane an appropriate accessory to his crisp gray tux. He smiled and winked at her, and she knew it was all going to be okay.

Around them were the residents of Wildflower, all seventy of them. She smiled at her new family, at the community she had been hesitant about. She smiled as she saw Bridget and Marla, seated near the front. She glanced to the front to see Amelia and Annie in their soft blue dresses, standing as bridesmaids. She even grinned to herself when she saw Catherine near the front of the aisle, dressed, of course, in a scandalously tight white dress. Too bad she would be disappointed she wasn't ruining the "don't wear white to a wedding" rule. Charlotte was so happy to be back among friends, back to the place that had sneakily stolen her heart. Her time at the nursing home had only solidified the fact Wildflower was far from the Tumbleweed Meadows she had originally thought it was. Wildflower was a place full of life, of friendship, a place she was so glad to be back at.

It had been a long road to get to that point, a point Charlotte had never expected. She had come to Wildflower a broken, lost woman who had given up on life. She had been prepared to let the rest of her life sift on by. She thought her days would be filled with endless reruns on television and maybe a few books.

Now, as Owen passed her off to the man who would soon be her husband, she grinned at the thought. Little did she know that day a year ago when she toured the place with Cassie's annoying voice she would be walking into a completely new life. She had found new friends, new hobbies, and she had found Leonard.

Charlotte had always thought love after seventy was preposterous. She remembered giggling at friends who were attending weddings for their grandmothers, thinking the whole idea was ludicrous. Who got married at that age? What in the heck was the point?

Now, things were so different. Her heart had been awakened for a second time in her life. She had found a new, deep connection, one that made her feel alive again. A connection that made her okay with walking down the aisle, made her want to make her new relationship official in every way.

It wasn't the same as a first love. But that was okay.

No, second loves aren't the same, Charlotte thought as she laced her hand in Leonard's. *Second loves are a completely different breed of love altogether.*

***

The rest of the day floated away in a magical cloud; everything was perfect. From the heartfelt "I dos" to the first kiss—without any slapping, to Charlotte's surprise and relief—Charlotte felt more love around her than she had ever hoped to experience.

Owen's band, of course, was the entertainment at the reception. Charlotte smiled as she saw Amelia steal him away, leaving the band alone on stage during a song, which became instrumental, of course. The two of them were absolutely made for each other.

There probably wouldn't be another wedding any time soon for them, though. They had vowed to not tie themselves down with official ceremonies. The two were getting ready to go on a tour across the country, Amelia writing new songs for the band that was quickly climbing to a small sense of fame. The two were excited to see where the whole thing took them, and Charlotte knew they would fare well. They were so supportive of each other and exuded happiness. She couldn't wait to see where life took them, although she would miss them for the next few months. Amelia had promised to give her a more thorough tutorial on how to Skype before leaving, but Charlotte wasn't so sure how that was going to go.

By midway through the reception, Annie had calmed down enough to take off her work hat and just have fun. She, too, was doing well, still exploring life with Joe. They were actually headed out the following week as well, going to visit Joe's nieces and nephews in Massachusetts for a week. Their relationship status was also strengthening, and Charlotte wouldn't be surprised if Annie came back with a ring.

That, of course, would make Joe official family, meaning Catherine would also become family. Charlotte wasn't thrilled with the idea. As she slow danced with Leonard to a ballad, she peeped over to see Catherine flirting with the newest Wildflower resident, Chester. Maybe the woman just needed a man; Charlotte would try to see to it the woman caught the bouquet. Even though Catherine was infuriating, Charlotte had finally admitted to herself she also made life a bit more interesting. She could foresee more antics and dramas, but maybe that was okay. It kept them young, kept them on their toes. In a strange way, even Catherine had become an essential fixture in Charlotte's new life.

"I love you," Leonard whispered in her ear, snapping her out of her trance.

"I love you, too." She smiled, looking into his eyes.

She saw so much there. She saw so many more moments, so many more memories. She saw them enjoying however many more years they had, hopefully decades, watching the relationships of Amelia and Annie grow. She smiled, realizing how lucky she was to have such a beautiful life, a beautiful love. She was so happy Amelia and Annie had also found new love.

It took one year, a slap in the face, and a bowling game for Charlotte to fall in love again.

It took one year, a messy divorce, an unfortunate dropping of the f-bomb, and a man in a flannel for Annie to fall in love again.

It took one year, an Adam Levine look-alike, a stuffy dinner, and some takeout pizza for Amelia to fall in love again.

Love isn't always the answer, Charlotte thought as she swayed with Leonard under a starry sky, but then again, sometimes it was. Sometimes love changed everything. Sometimes love came when you least expected it. Sometimes you gave up on life, gave up on finding out who you were supposed to be.

And then, when you'd forgotten what it felt like, when you'd dismissed the ideal entirely... then, well... then came love.

Acknowledgements

First and foremost, I want to thank my amazing friends and family who have supported me on this writing adventure. My parents Lori and Ken have always been my biggest fans and supporters. From the time I could talk, they worked feverishly to instill a value of education and reading in me. They taught me to love books, to express myself in writing, and to believe in the power of learning. I owe all of my successes in life to them. Without their encouragement and love, I would have never accomplished any of my goals. You are my best friends, my role models, and my heroes.

I would also like to thank my husband Chad, the love of my life. Since the first time we met at the art table in seventh grade, I knew you would be a special presence in my life. We grew up together, maneuvering all of life's milestones and heartaches along the way. Thank you for always telling me to believe in myself and to dream big. Thank you for dealing with me during the writing process and when my confidence in my work falters. Thank you for always helping me to keep things in perspective. Thank you for making me laugh every single day.

Thanks to all of my other family members and friends who go above and beyond to support my writing. Grandma Bonnie, thank you for always coming to my book events and for sharing my news on Facebook. Your support means so much. Thank you to Christie James, Hannah Hauser, Jamie Lynch, Kristin Mathias, Alicia Schmouder, Lynette Luke, and Kelly Rubritz for always being at my book events, reading my works, and supporting me. Thank you to everyone in my school district for your kind words and support, especially Dr. Letcher. Thank you to all of my coworkers, friends, acquaintances, and fans who have supported my writing endeavors.

Thank you to all of the teachers who have guided me on my writing path. Sue Gunsallus, you taught me to value literature of all types and showed me what readers want in writing. Without you in my life, my passion for literature and writing would not have been ignited as fervently as it was. Thank you to all of my Mount Aloysius professors as well. You helped me grow as a writer, and I will be forever grateful to all of you. Finally, thank you to Diane Vella for seeing my passion for writing at an early age and inspiring me to go for my dreams.

Thank you to all of the wonderful students who have impacted my life over the past few years. As a teacher, my job is to spread knowledge and teach content.

However, I am the one who has truly learned so much from all of you. You teach me new perspectives on literature and life itself. You show me what it means to dream big and to believe dreams can come true. I have been blessed to know all of you, especially those from Writer's Workshop at the junior high. It is my hope that my writing career has shown all of you aspiring writers that publishing is truly possible.

Thank you to the amazing team at Hot Tree Publishing for helping me to see *Then Comes Love* published. I am so blessed to work with such a dedicated, skilled group of people. Thank you Becky, Olivia, and the rest of the team for your dedication to helping me make my book the best version possible.

Finally, thanks to Henry, my couch-cuddling, cupcake-loving mastiff for being the best companion a writer can have.

About the Author

A high school English teacher, an author, and a fan of anything pink and/or glittery, Lindsay's the English teacher cliché; she loves cats, reading, Shakespeare, and Poe.

She currently lives in her hometown with her husband, Chad (her junior high sweetheart); their cats, Arya, Amelia, Alice, and Bob; and their Mastiff, Henry.

Lindsay's goal with her writing is to show the power of love and the beauty of life while also instilling a true sense of realism in her work. Some reviewers have noted that her books are not the "typical romance." With her novels coming from a place of honesty, Lindsay examines the difficult questions, looks at the tough emotions, and paints the pictures that are sometimes difficult to look at. She wants her fiction to resonate with readers as realistic, poetic, and powerful. Lindsay wants women readers to be able to say, "I see myself in that novel." She wants to speak to the modern woman's experience while also bringing a twist of something new and exciting. Her aim is for readers to say, "That could happen," or "I feel like the characters are real." That's how she knows she's done her job. Lindsay's hope is that by becoming a published author, she can inspire some of her students and other aspiring writers to pursue their own passions. She wants them to see that any dream can be attained and publishing a novel isn't out of the realm of possibility.

Discover more about Lindsay:
Facebook: Facebook.com/LindsayAnnDetwiler
Twitter: Twitter.com/LindsayDetwiler
Website: www.LindsayDetwiler.com

About the Publisher

Hot Tree Publishing opened its doors in 2015 with an aspiration to bring quality fiction to the world of readers. With the initial focus on romance and a wide spread of romance sub-genres, we envision opening up to alternative genres in the near future.

Firmly seated in the industry as a leading editing provider to independent authors and small publishing houses, Hot Tree Publishing is the sister company to Hot Tree Editing, founded in 2012. Having established in-house editing and promotions, plus having a well-respected market presence, Hot Tree Publishing endeavors to be a leader in bringing quality stories to the world of readers.

Interested in discovering more amazing reads brought to you by Hot Tree Publishing or perhaps you're interested in submitting a manuscript and joining the HTPubs family? Either way, head over to the website for information:

www.HotTreePublishing.com

www.ingramcontent.com/pod-product-compliance
Lightning Source LLC
Chambersburg PA
CBHW051246210726

48287CB00002B/363